RED VELVET

BLACKWOOD CELLARS SERIES #2

CARLA LUNA

MOON MANOR PRESS

First paperback edition: September 2021

Cover Design: *Bailey McGinn*
Editing: *Free Bird Editing*
Proofreading: *One Love Editing*
ISBN: 978-1-7368661-3-9 (paperback)
ISBN: 978-1-7368661-2-2 (ebook)

Published by Moon Manor Press
carlalunabooks.com

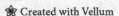 Created with Vellum

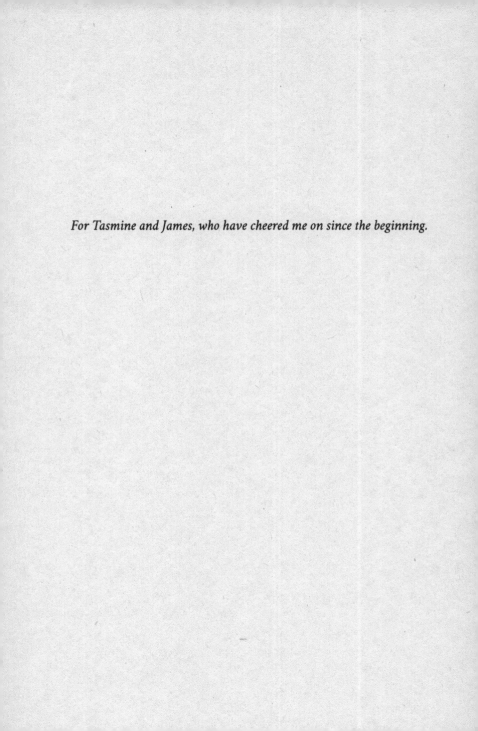

For Tasmine and James, who have cheered me on since the beginning.

CHAPTER 1

Few things pleased April Beckett more than taking a pan of sweets out of the oven. Even when she was at her lowest, the smell of baked goods always brightened her mood. She set the cupcake tins on two bamboo trivets, removed her oven mitts, and brought out her phone. After ensuring the cupcakes were angled correctly, she took a photo and posted it with a caption: *Red velvet beauties, waiting to be frosted. #bakersgonnabake #cupcakesofinstagram*

As she was setting the bowls and measuring cups in the sink, her phone pinged.

It had to be Brody.

Sure enough, Brody Blackwood, her good friend, movie buddy, and former crush, had commented on her post: *PLEASE say these are for Treatday Thursday.*

Of all her coworkers at Blackwood Cellars, no one appreciated her baking more than he did. She replied: *Of course! Bringing them in for Delilah's Bday.*

In response, he sent a series of smiley face emojis.

His unabashed affection for her baking skills filled her with a warm glow. Though she'd been seeing Chris for five months, she still harbored a tiny crush on Brody. How could she not? He'd been one of the first people to befriend her when she'd relocated from Santa Barbara to the Temecula Valley—an hour north of San Diego—to work for his family's company. And he was brilliant, funny, and totally hot for a self-proclaimed computer nerd.

She filled the sink with soapy water and shoved in the rest of her utensils. Once the dishes were done, she'd whip up the cream cheese frosting.

At the sound of a key turning in the lock, she froze.

Shit.

If Chris was making an impromptu booty call, she was ill prepared. Her faded sweats and messy hair were fine for a quiet evening to herself, but not for a night with her smoking-hot friend with benefits. Worse yet, her couch was cluttered with a wide assortment of tops, jeans, and dresses, as she narrowed down the choices for their weeklong trip to Wisconsin. Since he kept his apartment in immaculate condition, the disorder was bound to irritate him.

The door opened and Chris peered inside, holding a bike helmet under his arm. His forehead was damp with sweat, but it did nothing to diminish his good looks. Six foot two of lean muscle, thick black hair, and cheekbones that could cut glass. Factor in the skintight bike shirt and shorts he wore, and he was a sight to behold.

"Hey, April..." The words died on his lips as he took in the piles of clothing on the couch.

"Chris. I wasn't expecting you." Her hand flew to her head, where her topknot had unraveled to the point of no return. "How about I go freshen up? Why don't you have a seat on the..." Clearly, the couch wasn't an option. She pointed to the faded green armchair, where her spoiled Siberian cat had settled in for the night. "Take the chair. Just give Princess Peach a shove."

He wrinkled his nose. "You know how I feel about cat hair on my clothes. And I won't be long." He sauntered over to the breakfast bar and frowned at the cupcakes. "Baking again? Butter and refined sugar are terrible for your waistline."

April cringed. Though she was on the curvy side, none of her previous boyfriends had ever criticized her figure. But Chris claimed he did it out of compassion. After one too many lectures about her cholesterol levels, she'd vowed to seek out healthier baking choices. Yet here she was, breaking her word.

"They're not for me," she said. "I'm taking them to work."

"I thought you weren't doing Treatday Thursday anymore."

She undid her apron and hung it on a peg. "It's Delilah's birthday tomorrow. Red velvet cupcakes are her favorite."

"Why not bring in fresh veggies? Or a fruit tray?"

Because that's Healthy Hanna's job. If April was the devil on every dieter's shoulder, then Hanna from HR was the angel, with her array of heart-healthy snacks, like kale chips and radish hummus.

Chris turned his attention to the couch. "You donating a bunch of stuff to Goodwill? About time."

Did he think her clothes looked that bad? Granted, some of her outfits were out of style, but they weren't unwearable. "I was trying to pare down the options for my brother's wedding. We're going to be there for six days, and the weather might be iffy since fall in Wisconsin isn't dependable."

"But you're not leaving for another week."

Did he just say "you're"? She gave a shaky laugh. "You mean *we're* not leaving for another week."

He leaned against the breakfast bar and let out his breath. "Yeah. About that...?"

No. Please don't back out now.

"You promised." She hated how whiny she sounded, but he'd agreed six weeks ago. If anything, she'd been pleasantly surprised at how easily he capitulated. "After I went with you to the Oakland Triathlon, you said you'd do this for me."

"I never should have agreed to it. Attending a destination wedding? With your entire family? That implies we're getting serious."

"But—"

"You know how I feel about commitment. Right now, it's not an option."

That aspect of their relationship didn't bother her because she wasn't in love with him. Not the way she assumed love was supposed to feel—a deep emotional connection that bound you to the other person, body and soul. But Chris was gorgeous, athletic, and driven. Much hotter than anyone she'd ever dated. Guys like him could have their pick of women. Yet, somehow, he'd chosen *her*.

She twisted her hands together. "I didn't ask for anything long-term. Just a date for Ollie's wedding. Six nights together in a cozy cottage on Lake Michigan. Think how much fun we'll have."

"April..."

"Plus, my family's really competitive, so you'll fit right in."

Whenever they asked about him, she rarely missed a chance to mention his athletic prowess. By bringing him to the wedding, she'd finally show them she'd landed someone worthy of their approval.

When he didn't respond, she held her breath, hoping he might reconsider. As the seconds ticked by, the loud thump of her heart echoed in her ears.

"I like hanging out," he said. "You're always up for a good time. But..."

She tried to keep her voice from breaking. "But I'm only worthy of a booty call?"

He groaned. "That's not what I meant. I'd be up for a normal vacation, like a weekend in the mountains. But weddings have this weird impact on women."

"What are you talking about?"

"I mean, one minute you're happy being single; the next,

you're watching the bride walk down the aisle and wishing you were her."

"That's not going to happen," she said.

In all her twenty-four years, she'd never contemplated marriage—not to Chris or anyone else. She had yet to experience the powerful, all-consuming pull of attraction that led to a lifelong commitment. Right now, all she wanted was for Chris to make an effort. Some gesture that showed he cared.

"Sorry, babe," he said, "I can't do it."

Despite the warmth of the kitchen, ice-cold dread seeped into her veins. She grasped to find something—*anything*—to make him change his mind. "What about your plane ticket? Do you want to waste all that money?"

Though he wasn't hurting financially, he'd complained about the cost and the lengthy layover. But she hadn't been able to find any deals or direct flights from San Diego to Green Bay, Wisconsin.

He shrugged. "I got a changeable fare, so I can save the credit for another trip. No big deal."

Not to him, obviously.

He glanced at his Garmin sport watch. "I should go. I still have ten miles left on my training, and then I need to work in a session in the weight room. How about you call me when you get back? We can hook up then."

She stared at him, too stunned to answer. Canceling now was a dick move. She swallowed past the lump in her throat, willing herself not to cry.

If she were strong enough, she would have called him on his selfish behavior months ago. He'd canceled on her before, most notably when she'd planned a beachside getaway, and he'd backed out at the last minute. Not only had she lost two hundred dollars on the deposit, but he'd never offered to help pay for it.

But before Chris, her bed had been empty for months. Even

the crumbs of his affection were better than slowly morphing into a lonely cat lady.

"Sure," she muttered.

He leaned closer and stroked her cheek. "That's my girl. I'll make it up to you in the bedroom." With a wink, he headed for the door. "Have fun at the wedding, but try not to overindulge. Go easy on the sweets."

What the hell?

What was Delilah always telling her? To sit up straight, look people in the eye, and speak her mind. April had let her family walk all over her for years. She needed to stand up for herself, even if the prospect made her stomach churn.

She clenched her fists, digging her nails deep into her palms. "No."

Chris did a double take. "No, what?"

"No, I can eat whatever I want at the wedding. And no, you can't make it up to me in the bedroom. Because if you bail this late in the game, then we're done."

"Why are you being so difficult? Can't we enjoy what we have and leave it at that?"

No. After being available for Chris whenever he needed her, after cheering him on at *all* his races, she'd asked him for *one thing*. Granted, it was a big ask, but he'd given her his word. And by breaking it so casually, he'd shown her exactly how little she meant to him.

She shook her head. "I'm done, Chris."

He gave a huff of disbelief. "You're dumping *me*? Are you serious?"

Her insides twisted into a knot. Maybe this was a terrible mistake. If she acted like she was joking, she could still salvage things.

But what was she trying to salvage? A few quickies a week, with a guy who disparaged her weight and fashion choices? The occasional weekend away, spent watching him compete? Even if the sex was decent, it didn't make up for the criticism or the hours of self-doubt that plagued her every time he joked about her "muffin top."

"This trip means a lot to me," she said. "And you promised you'd go. If you can't be there for me, then I don't want to be with you anymore."

He rolled his eyes. "You're making this into a bigger deal than it needs to be. But if that's what you want, then it's your loss."

With that, he was gone, slamming the door behind him.

For a brief, blissful moment, the fire inside April burned bright. Screw Chris. She was through with all his calorie counting and all his *rules*. Like no sleeping over. After they were done, he always dressed and headed for the door. No matter how many times she asked him to stay, he claimed spending the night would derail his morning run.

For once in her life, she hadn't given in like a meek little mouse. She snatched a cupcake off the cooling rack and ate half of it in one bite. Even without the frosting, it was delicious.

See what you're missing, Chris?

Then reality sunk in. Her brother's wedding was in less than a week, and she didn't have a date.

Showing up without a date shouldn't matter. She'd been single when her two older sisters had gotten married. And for every Thanksgiving, Christmas, and family vacation for the past four years. Except, this time, she'd bragged about her plus-one. If she didn't bring Chris, her sisters would assume she'd made him up. Just like Sam Jameson, the guy she'd invented five years ago to get them off her case. A lie no one had ever forgotten.

She couldn't face another minute without backup. With trembling hands, she sent Brody a text.

If you're free tonight, I need you. Code Red.

CHAPTER 2

Brody Blackwood arrived at April's apartment within thirty minutes of her text. He rang the doorbell, juggling a bag of takeout Chinese food in one hand and a six-pack of Tsingtao beer in the other.

When April opened the door, her frazzled appearance made his heart ache in sympathy. Wisps of chestnut-brown hair had escaped from her messy bun, her Godzilla t-shirt was dusted with flour, and her large, hazel eyes were red and swollen.

He set down the food and enfolded her in a hug. She clung to him tightly, pressing her body against his, and he was distracted by how nice she felt. Soft and warm and sexier than usual.

Which was ridiculous. She was one of his closest friends. He was only reacting to the softness of her curves because he hadn't gotten laid in three months. He released her and stepped back. "What did the bastard do this time?"

She wiped her eyes. "What makes you think this is about Chris?"

"Of course it's about Chris." Grabbing the food and the beer, he followed her inside. After setting the bag of takeout on the table, he got out the cartons. The savory aroma of lo mein made his mouth water.

"Did you get deep-fried wontons?" she asked. "Please tell me you got wontons."

"With two orders of sauce. I also got kung pao chicken and lo mein with shrimp." He'd chosen her favorites, knowing she'd be more likely to eat them if she wasn't trying to please Chris.

She took a deep breath. "Thanks. I've missed this so much. I'll get us some plates."

He trailed behind her, stopping at the sight of the freshly baked cupcakes. He reached for one. "These look fantastic."

She grabbed a wooden spoon and waved it at him. "You need to wait until tomorrow. I still have to frost them."

"Fine. I'm having two."

She grinned. "I figured they'd go well with a big cup of coffee. Or three, in your case."

His caffeine consumption was legendary among the Blackwood Cellars staff. And nothing beat a cup of French roast paired with one of April's treats. The girl was a genius in the kitchen. On his last birthday, she'd brought in a raspberry chocolate swirl cheesecake that sent him into a food coma.

Princess Peach leapt off her chair and approached him, meowing and bunting him with affection. He scratched her soft white fur but stopped her from jumping on the table. Once April set out plates and cutlery, they dished out the food. Over bites of lo mein, interrupted by the occasional groan of pleasure over the wontons, she filled him in on the situation.

He wasn't surprised. He'd pegged Chris as a dick from day one. But he'd been in no position to cast judgment, seeing as how his last girlfriend, Taylor, had been a shallow piece of work.

"Ditching Chris was the right move," he said. "I wish I could have seen his reaction."

She laughed. "He was shocked, all right. That one minute of victory was incredible. But..."

"But what? I know he was decent arm candy, but he treated you like shit."

Her voice trembled. "No, he didn't."

He sighed. "How many times did he promise to show and then cancel at the last minute, because he had to fit in another training session? And what about those comments about your weight? One of his nicknames for you was the Pillsbury Doughgirl. That's shitty."

When she bit her lip and looked away, he was hit with a rush of guilt. He didn't want to hurt her. But he also didn't want her thinking Chris's behavior was acceptable. "Sorry. I'm not trying to make things worse."

"I know. And you're right—Chris didn't respect me. I realize I'm better off without him, but that doesn't solve the problem. He was my plus-one for the wedding. I told my entire family about him."

"Tell them you broke it off. If they ask why, you can say you caught him cheating." Even as he said it, he winced, remembering the callous way Taylor had ended their relationship. She'd told him she'd fallen for someone else. And she'd done it via text.

"Excuses won't cut it. If I don't bring Chris, they'll think I made him up. It doesn't help that he never let me post any photos of us on Instagram." She groaned. "My sisters will be ruthless."

Brody batted away Princess Peach, who was hungrily eying the kung pao chicken. "Seems harsh."

"It's my own fault. It's like the fable 'The Boy Who Cried Wolf.'"

"And you're the boy in this scenario?"

She dipped another wonton into the sweet and sour sauce. "Exactly. I don't want to get into the details, but several years ago I invented a fake boyfriend and posted pictures of us online. It blew up in a spectacular fashion, and my sisters have never let me forget it."

He could only imagine. From the few tidbits April had shared about her two older sisters, he got the impression they were highly critical. Now she'd be stuck at their mercy for an entire week. He wished there were a way to help her out in return for all the support she'd given him after his breakup. Without her friendship on those nights when he called her with a "Code Red," he wouldn't have survived the past three months.

"Hang on," he said. "Your family has *never* seen a photo of Chris before?"

She scowled. "You know how he was about social media. He refused to post anything because he claimed his psycho ex would to track him down and make his life hell."

A fake excuse if ever there was one. "Sounds dubious. Did you ever consider he might be married? Didn't you say he never spent the night?"

"Maybe that's why he couldn't leave town for six days." Tears welled up in her eyes. "I feel so stupid. What if he has a secret family?"

Brody hated him even more now. But they were getting off topic. "Back to the photo thing. Are you telling me your family has no idea what Chris looks like?"

"Only what I've told them. They haven't come to visit since last year, and I wasn't dating him then. So, without any photos, I don't have a shred of proof."

He pushed his plate aside. Another helping and he'd be forced to unbuckle his jeans. Though he and April were comfortable around each other, he needed to show some self-restraint. "What if you brought someone else as your date and pretended he was Chris?"

"What? Like a paid escort?"

He laughed. "What are you talking about?"

"Like the movie, *The Wedding Date.* It's a rom-com where this girl hires a guy to pretend he's her date at her sister's wedding. I don't remember much about it, except they had sex on a boat, and it was incredible." She gave a dramatic sigh. "But she paid the guy three thousand dollars."

"You don't need it. How about I volunteer as tribute?" For that, he got a chuckle. They'd binge-watched all *The Hunger Games* movies a month ago, during a hot, miserable weekend when he'd been desperate to get Taylor off his mind.

She gave a cute little snort. "You don't have to battle it out in the arena for me."

In the back of his brain, alarm bells started going off. *Danger. Red Alert. Do Not Pass Go.* But he ignored them and plowed on ahead. "I'm serious. Why don't I take Chris's place? I've never been to Wisconsin, but I'd like to go."

"To *Wisconsin?*"

"You know how much I love cheese. And the wedding's in Door County, right?" When she nodded, his enthusiasm grew. "That area has some great independent wineries. If I visited them as recon for Blackwood Cellars, I could write off most of my expenses."

She stared at him, her hazel eyes wide. "You'd do that for me?"

Was he making a huge mistake? The last time he attended a wedding, he made a total ass of himself. He still hadn't fully recovered from the debacle.

But this was April. The one friend who'd been there after Taylor left him. Not only had she let him crash on her couch, but she'd also baked him two pans of brownies. One to eat and another to take back to his apartment.

"I think I could pull it off," he said. "Your family's never met me, so I could easily pretend to be Chris for six days."

April set her chopsticks down. "You sure? You were a wreck when you got back from your brother's wedding in Maui."

The memory still stung, like a cut that refused to heal. Taylor had been his plus-one for Marc's wedding, but she'd dumped him, via text, two hours before her plane was due to arrive on the island. He'd been so distraught he'd gotten wasted at the rehearsal dinner, made an inappropriate speech, and passed out at the table.

It wasn't his finest moment.

Nothing could equal the agony he'd experienced when he recovered and realized what he'd done. Though Marc and the rest of his family had since forgiven him, he still had moments when he lay awake in misery, replaying the entire hellscape.

"You told me you were done with weddings *forever*," April said.

"I still don't like weddings. And I don't plan to get married any time soon—if ever. But going to Door County with you might be good for me. Right? It could snap me out of my funk. I haven't exactly been...outgoing since I got back from Maui."

That was putting it mildly. Over the last three months, he'd felt so ashamed of his behavior at Marc's wedding he'd curtailed most of his social interactions. Instead, he spent his nights holed up in his apartment, either gaming online or binge-watching epic series like *Game of Thrones*. Other than his friendship with April, he'd retreated deep into himself.

She bit her lip. "You haven't been to happy hour with us since July. You've missed every karaoke night. And you didn't go to Pamila's engagement party last weekend, even though she works in our department. Now you want to spend an entire week at a *wedding*? While pretending to be someone else?"

When she put it that way, the whole enterprise sounded likely to trigger his anxiety. But unlike Maui, this wasn't a romantic trip. He had no expectations other than spending a fun week in Wisconsin with one of his closest friends. There was no chance of heartbreak.

"I hate that I've missed out on everything," he said. "If I went with you and forced myself to act social, I might get back on track. You'd be doing *me* a favor."

She looked down at Princess Peach, who had settled on the ground by Brody's feet, probably hoping to catch a few stray morsels of food. "What about Peachie? You were supposed to check on her while I was gone."

"Could Delilah do it? She likes cats, right? And you're bringing in cupcakes for her birthday, so she might be more receptive."

"Good point. I'll ask her." She grinned. "I can't believe I'm agreeing to this ridiculous scheme, but I'm going to say yes."

He let out his breath in relief. He might be jumping off the deep end, but it could be the push he needed to break out of his shell. Besides, he'd have April at his side, to offer support and encouragement. Maybe by the time they returned from Wisconsin, he'd feel like his old self again.

And if he didn't? Then he might have to consider the recent offer he'd gotten from his father, who ran the Blackwood Cellars office in Napa. A plum management position, overseeing a major systems upgrade. Before his painful breakup with Taylor, he wouldn't have dreamed of moving back to his hometown in the Napa Valley. Though he had an amicable relationship with his parents, the eight-hour drive between Temecula and Napa gave him some much-needed distance. But he might have more luck getting over Taylor if he wasn't surrounded by all the memories they'd made in Temecula.

He still wasn't sure if he wanted to leave. Or if he'd be happy in a management role. But he could put off the decision until after the trip.

"I'll let the office know I'll be gone for a week," he said. "It shouldn't be a problem."

"You can take off with so little warning? I had to request the vacation time three months ago."

He rarely mentioned the privileges he received as a Blackwood, but in this case, they worked in his favor. "Trust me, you can get away with a lot when your family owns the company."

She gave him a hopeful look. "Think we can pull it off?"

For the first time in months, he felt a spark of enthusiasm. As a kid he'd always loved movies like *Catch Me If You Can* where characters tried to pull off a tricky con. Now he was joining their ranks.

"Nothing to do but try." He held up his beer. "To Door County."

She clinked her bottle against his. "To Door County."

CHAPTER 3

*A*pril finished her novel and let out a sigh of contentment. Few things beat a steamy romance with a well-earned happy ending. She turned to Brody to see if he'd mastered the sudoku puzzle from the in-flight magazine, but he was conked out, his head resting against the airplane window. She resisted the urge to smooth his messy hair. He had great hair—thick, ash brown, and frequently disheveled. The kind of hair she could imagine tangling her fingers in if they were in bed together. Not that they would *ever* find themselves in that situation.

Brody didn't feel that way about her. He was here as her ally. Her support. End of story.

Setting her paperback aside, she closed her eyes, hoping to sneak in a quick nap. She'd almost dozed off when the flight attendant came by with her soda.

"Do you want me to set this down?" the woman asked.

April rubbed her eyes. "Thanks. I could use the caffeine. I flew out of San Diego at six this morning."

The attendant set the Diet Coke on April's tray table but hesitated before handing over the other cup. "Will your friend want his drink?"

"Sure." April took the cup of Dr. Pepper and placed it on Brody's tray. The sweet, caffeinated soda was his go-to when he wasn't drinking coffee. "How long until we land?"

"Half hour or so." The woman gestured to April's shirt. "Packers fan? Are you excited for the big game on Sunday?"

"Huh?" As far as April was concerned, she could have been speaking a different language.

"You're wearing green and gold—Green Bay Packers colors." When April gave her a blank look, the woman raised her eyebrows. "The football team. You *are* flying into Green Bay."

"Right. I don't follow football much. I'm going to a family wedding in Door County."

"You'll love it. Door County's perfect this time of year. The autumn leaves are spectacular."

After she left, April assessed her outfit. Packers colors? Not even. Though she was wearing a dark green sweater, her scarf was *black* and gold, decorated with shimmering stars. Brody had given it to her last Christmas, after he'd seen her admiring it in a boutique window in Old Town Temecula. He was always being thoughtful that way.

As she glanced over at him again, she wished—not for the first time—that he hadn't fallen for Taylor. If not, she never would have gotten involved with Chris.

She had first met Brody two years ago, when her graphic design skills landed her a job as a digital marketing assistant at Blackwood Cellars, a multimillion-dollar wine empire located in the Temecula Valley. Like her, Brody worked with digital content, except he was on the development end. Not only was he a coding whiz, but his family owned the company. He might show up at work in jeans, but he'd eventually come into a small fortune as one of the Blackwood heirs.

April had caught his attention when she contributed to the office tradition known as Treatday Thursday. She whipped up a batch of homemade cinnamon rolls and left them in the break room. After devouring three of them, Brody sought her out and thanked her profusely.

Two weeks later, they bonded over a shared affinity for Marvel movies, and she immediately developed a huge crush on him. Every time they hung out, she hoped he'd take things to the next level, but he always chased after skinny, blond, long-legged beauties. She, on the other hand, was a short, curvy brunette who was packing a few extra pounds.

When Brody started dating Taylor, April thought she'd lost him for good, as their nights of movie marathons and Chinese takeout came to a halt. She hit an all-time low when Taylor took her aside, in confidence, at Brody's St. Patrick's Day party and gave her some painful advice. "I get that you've been crushing on Brody *forever*," she said, "but you need to move on. He doesn't think of you that way."

Though Taylor's words had devastated April, they'd also spurred her into action. A month later, she'd gotten involved with Chris after meeting him at a charity 5K run organized by Blackwood Cellars. He might have been judgmental and commitment phobic, but being with him was better than being alone.

Or so she'd thought. But now that he was out of her life, she was surprised by how little she missed him.

But even if Chris was history, April didn't want her old feelings for Brody to come racing back. Not when he'd never reciprocate them. Better to enjoy his friendship than risk a painful heartbreak.

Brody sat up and adjusted his glasses. April liked them, because they gave him an ironic hipster look and amplified his stormy gray eyes. "Hey," he murmured. "We almost there yet?"

"Just about. Once we land in Green Bay, we need to pick up the rental car. The drive to the resort should take about an hour or so, depending on traffic."

He took a sip of his soda. "Let me pay for the car. I'll put it on the Blackwood Cellars account."

"Thanks. I appreciate it." She wasn't going to argue, not after she'd dropped almost a thousand dollars on the cottage rental at the resort.

As the pilot announced they were beginning their descent into Green Bay, April clipped her seat belt over her lap. "Don't forget, as soon as we get there, I need to start calling you Chris."

"Got it. Before we land, why don't you run me through some questions so I can make sure I'm up to speed on your family."

She couldn't help but smile. Brody hadn't been content to memorize a few facts. Instead, he'd asked her to send him a Google Doc with information on the Becketts so he could study it ahead of time. He'd also helped her clear all traces of him from her Instagram account. Not only had she unfollowed him, but she'd also archived all her photos where they appeared together. Too many of them showed him in peak nerd mode, like when he'd accompanied her to Comic Con or dressed as Harry Potter at the Blackwood Cellars Halloween party. Though her sisters thought Instagram was a waste of time, she wouldn't put it past them to snoop around in her feed.

"Okay, Professor Blackwood, here goes," she said. "Why is my brother getting married in Wisconsin?"

"Easy. The bride-to-be—Magdalena Flores—grew up in Green Bay. She met your brother Ollie in grad school at UW-Madison. Go Badgers."

"Badgers?"

"The UW mascot. Get with it, Beckett."

She rolled her eyes. "Oh, so now you're this big sports fan?"

He laughed. "Hardly. But I'm guessing Chris might know this stuff. Anyway, Ollie and Magdalena are currently living in Madison until Ollie finishes his doctorate in..." He paused. "Biomedical engineering, right?"

"Right. What about the rest of my family?"

"They all live in Santa Barbara, which is where you grew up. You're the youngest. Ollie's twenty-six. Adrianna—who goes by Dree or Drianna—is twenty-eight. Avery's thirty." He gave her a curious look. "Did your parents plan it so you'd all be *exactly* two years apart?"

"Of course they did. They're highly focused. Unlike me, they're total type A personalities." Yet another reason she'd never quite fit in.

The change in air pressure plugged her ears, making her wince. Grabbing her purse, she rifled through it until she found a pack of cinnamon gum. She took a stick for herself and handed one to Brody.

"Thanks." He popped the gum in his mouth. "Let's see...your dad has his own architectural company, and your mom's a partner in a big law firm. Avery followed in her footsteps, and she married Hunter four years ago."

"Another lawyer," April said. "Not criminal law either, which might be kind of juicy, but highly complex corporate law."

She'd endured one too many dinner conversations where Avery, Hunter, and her mother discussed their cases, in excruciating detail.

"So, Avery's big on law, and Drianna's an investment banker, right?" When April nodded, Brody continued. "It's safe to assume Drianna is your *least* favorite sibling, given that her nicknames include Drizella, Her Dreadfulness, and Draco. Two years ago, she married Ian, who's also in finance."

"And who's boring as hell. Don't get trapped alone with him because he only likes talking about two things: golf and mutual funds." She groaned. "That sounded really bitchy, didn't it?"

"Maybe, but I appreciate the warning. I learned the hard way never to ask my cousins about their golf games." He took off his glasses and cleaned them on his shirt. "I have to say, your family's really committed to this whole two years apart thing. Does that mean they expect you to walk down the aisle in two years?"

She sighed. "Don't think they haven't brought it up *numerous* times. When I went home for Christmas last year, Dree kept saying, 'Clock's ticking, shrimp'—like I have to follow a set schedule."

Since the weddings had taken place every two years, April was next up. But so far, she'd never brought anyone home to meet her family. The one time she'd invented a fake boyfriend, her lie had been debunked in a humiliating fashion. Just the thought of it made her cringe in embarrassment. Yet another reason she was grateful Brody had stepped in to support her.

Considering what a huge undertaking the week would be, she was slightly concerned about his mental well-being. Though he'd been nothing but enthusiastic so far, he had yet to face her sisters. There was a good chance he might crack under the pressure.

As the plane came to a bumpy landing, Brody placed his hand on her arm, as if to stop her from falling forward. Since she was wearing a seat belt, the gesture was hardly necessary. But it was sweet.

"Thanks for going along with Operation Fake-Chris," she said. "It's such a relief to have a date for this wedding. Maybe I'm being too sensitive, but I'm tired of everyone teasing me because I don't have a boyfriend. And making fun of my life in general."

Though she loved her family, she was relieved they lived three hours away. Spending an extended amount of time with them always triggered her anxiety.

"What do they make fun of?" Brody asked.

"I'm not athletic. I love kids' movies. And I don't have a real job."

"Excuse me? Your job is completely legit. And your design skills are amazing."

His praise brought a warm flush to her cheeks. "Thanks. But I don't pull in a huge paycheck like Avery and Drianna do. They think all I do is play around on the internet, post a few pictures of wine bottles, and call it a day. They keep asking when I'm going to get serious."

The passengers around them sprung to their feet, but April stayed put. Since they were stuck at the back of the plane, they wouldn't be getting out anytime soon.

Brody regarded her intently. "I thought you liked your job."

Was it her imagination, or did he sound hurt? She placed her hand on his arm. "I love working for Blackwood Cellars. I'm not sure what my endgame is, in terms of a career, but right now, I'm happy where I am."

Working for one of the biggest wineries in the world was a great gig. She'd lucked out when she'd secured the job, only two months after graduating from UCLA with a degree in graphic design. A degree her family considered "barely marketable."

Given that she was completely self-sufficient at age twenty-four, with a good job and her own apartment, she wished her family would treat her like a fully functioning adult. Instead, they acted like she was one financial catastrophe away from moving back home to Santa Barbara.

All her life, she'd been the baby, and she wanted her parents to see her differently. Maybe if they weren't so focused on her love life, she could convince them her work life was going just fine, thank you.

The row in front of them stood up, so she did the same. She opened the overhead compartment, brought out her carry-on, and retrieved Brody's laptop case. She handed it to him. "Must be nice working for your family's company. At least your parents respect what you do."

He shouldered the case and grabbed his backpack from under the seat. "They do, but they're not convinced I'm completely stable. I really screwed up at Marc's wedding. Compared to him, I'm kind of a mess. My older brother always has his shit together."

Since Marc worked in the Napa office, April had only met him a few times. Unlike Brody, he dressed like a professional and exuded confidence. A nice guy, to be sure, but he didn't share Brody's quirky sense of humor. "Marc's okay. But he's nothing like you. You're…"

Brody raised his eyebrows. "What?"

Smart, cute, and a lot of fun. And you're seriously hot.

Heat rose in her cheeks again. She had to stop thinking of him this way. "You're…fun. Smart. And you're not a mess."

"Thanks. I'd like to believe it. I keep telling myself my dad's offer was because he wants me to step into a management role, not because he feels like he needs to keep an eye on me."

April stopped short as a rush of unease coursed through her. "What offer?"

"Keep moving. We're backing up traffic."

She went on ahead, stewing in silence until they exited the plane. When they got to the gate, she pulled him aside so as not to obstruct the flow of passengers. "Is this offer in Napa?" When he nodded, she couldn't control the waver in her voice. "Why didn't you tell me?"

"Sorry. I was going to mention it last week, but after Chris bailed, I didn't want to make things worse."

Considering he was her friend and not her lover, she didn't have the right to make any demands. But she couldn't imagine life in Temecula without him. "Do you want to leave?"

"Up until last month, I would have said no. But lately, my dad and Marc have been pushing me hard. They think I'd be better off if I moved back to Napa. And they want me to take on more responsibility at Blackwood Cellars."

"But you've never been about that management life."

"Yeah." He gave her a quick grin. "Networking is the worst. Same with wearing a suit and tie. But I promised them I'd consider it. In the meantime, I'm not going to stress. I just want to enjoy our time in Wisconsin."

"Right." She let out a shaky breath. "You have enough to deal with, trying to pretend you're Chris."

For now, she had to let it go. The last thing he needed was more pressure.

As they made their way to the baggage claim, she mulled over their conversation. Changing family perceptions was a huge challenge. But unlike Brody, she had no intention of striving for a more demanding career just to meet her parents' expectations. She needed to make them understand that even if she wasn't a lawyer, an architect, or a financial genius, her plans and dreams were just as meaningful as those of her siblings. She was a mature adult capable of charting her own course.

But that couldn't happen if all they did was focus on Chris's absence and debate whether she'd made him up. Bringing a fake date might not be the height of maturity, but it was the best solution.

As long as they didn't get caught.

CHAPTER 4

hough Operation Fake-Chris had been Brody's idea, he wondered if it was a mistake. Three months ago, he'd nearly derailed his older brother's wedding with his drunken stupidity. He considered himself lucky no one had stayed angry with him. But they *pitied* him. Which was infinitely worse. Since then, his self-esteem had taken a major hit. If not for April, his social activity over the last few months would have been limited to online gaming with a few buddies. And now he was committing to *six days* of wedding-related activities?

Maybe he should have taken a few baby steps first. Like joining April and his other coworkers for happy hour or karaoke night. Instead, he was going balls-out.

He was also doubting his ability to pull off a con of this magnitude. If he screwed up and revealed his identity, April would suffer. She might be better off admitting she'd dumped Chris and invited Brody to take his place.

But he didn't have the heart to suggest it. He'd already hurt her when he confessed that he was thinking of leaving Temecula. If he reneged on his commitment to act like Chris, he'd be letting her down even more.

Now, driving up the Door County Peninsula, past farms and orchards, he was glad he'd decided to stay the course. Even if April had been dismayed by his news about Napa, she'd recovered quickly. For the last half hour, she'd entertained him with funny anecdotes about her family, pausing occasionally to photograph the scenery. Three times, he had to pull over so she could properly frame the shot. Not that he blamed her. October in Wisconsin was truly Instagram-worthy. He'd never seen such incredible fall foliage, the leaves painted in bright shades of crimson, gold, and orange.

"It's so beautiful here," April said as she photographed a sign advertising pick-your-own pumpkins. "I feel like I'm in a Hallmark movie."

"Aren't those set at Christmas?"

"Shows what you know. They have seasonal movies, too."

"If you say so." He'd only seen two Hallmark movies and could barely remember them. Possibly because he and April had been sloshed on rum-laden eggnog at the time.

"Look." She pointed to another sign, which featured a wizened old lady wearing a kerchief and holding up a carton of cherries. "Molly's Country Market. That sounds so fun. Can we stop there? Please?"

Her enthusiasm was impossible to resist. "Sure. Any reason?"

"We can stock up the cottage with snacks and buy gifts to take home. I read on the Door County website that these country markets usually carry local jams and salsas."

"You had me at the word 'snacks.'" He pulled into the lot, next to a grassy lawn covered with pumpkins of various sizes, lined up in rows. Beside them stood a full-size scarecrow sporting a pumpkin head and a faded straw hat.

Inside the market, the sheer amount of cherry products overwhelmed him. Not merely dried cherries and cherry jam, but cherry salsa, cherry mustard, cherry syrup, cherry vinegar, and fresh-baked cherry pie. The store also contained the usual tourist tchotchkes, as well as numerous items with the Green Bay Packers logo. These Wisconsinites loved their Packers.

April grabbed a dish towel embellished with cherries and a matching set of oven mitts. She gestured to the pile of shopping baskets at the front of the store. "Can you snag one for me?"

"Here." He handed it to her after tossing in a package of chocolate-covered dried cherries. "What's the deal with the cherries?"

"The peninsula's full of cherry orchards, and in July, you can pick your own." She gave him a smug look. "I did my homework, Blackwood."

"Obviously." He grabbed a jar of cherry-honey mustard dip and a package of pretzels. "How about these for a late-night snack?"

"Perfect." She headed toward the refrigerated section of the store. "We have to get fresh cheese curds. That's another big Wisconsin thing. My brother tried them during his first week of grad school, and he said they squeaked when he bit into them."

"They sound dubious." Though Brody was a fan of all things cheese-related, he couldn't imagine what squeaky cheese might taste like.

"He said they were good. If you microwave them for twenty seconds, they get all melty and delicious."

The thought made Brody's stomach growl. "You've convinced me." He picked out a block of caraway cheddar. "I'm assuming our cottage has a mini fridge?"

"Yes. And a coffee maker. I checked ahead because I know how much you need your coffee in the morning." She grinned at him.

"I'm not the only one. I seem to recall a certain *someone* freaking out when the Nespresso in the break room died."

She bowed her head in mock solemnity. "RIP, Nespresso. Thank you for your service."

When they went to purchase their goodies, Brody brought out

his credit card, but April insisted on paying. "My treat. It's so nice to travel with someone who loves snacks as much as I do." She gave him a sweet smile. "You don't know what a relief it is to know you're not judging me."

His chest tightened. Damn, Chris was an asshole. He placed his hand over his heart. "April Beckett, I will *never* judge your food choices. Even if I think your love of jam borders on the obsessive." Case in point, she'd put four jars of jam in her basket.

"Don't mock my jam. The week after we get back, I'm trying a new recipe for crusty French bread and bringing it in for Treatday Thursday. Think how good it'll be with this cherry-rhubarb jam."

His stomach growled again. The last time she'd brought in homemade bread, it had been wrapped in a dish towel, still warm from the oven. He'd had to limit himself to three pieces. "I stand corrected. Bring on the jam."

"That's better."

ONCE THEY PASSED the town of Baileys Harbor, signs for the North Bay Resort appeared. As part of his pre-trip research, Brody had looked it up on TripAdvisor and was pleased at all the favorable reviews. Set along the shores of Lake Michigan, the resort boasted a huge, timber-framed lodge with three floors of rooms and a fine dining restaurant. In addition to the main lodge, the sprawling grounds held dozens of private cottages and ten miles of nature trails.

They drove along a narrow country road lined with tall evergreens until they reached the entrance to the resort. As they exited the car, Brody inhaled the strong scent of pine trees, which brought to mind his family's lodge up in the mountains at Big Bear Lake. If this place was anything like Big Bear, he'd enjoy it.

At check-in, the desk clerk gave them a map and explained the layout. Most of the private cottages could only be reached by foot, which meant guests had to leave their cars in the central parking lot next to the main lodge. April and Brody unloaded their suitcases from his rental car and wheeled them through the lot. They passed a large, octagonal pool, now empty due to the cool fall weather. At the edge of the pool area, a wooden signpost held markers pointing to the various cottages. To their right, Lake Michigan glistened in the sunlight, the gentle waves lapping against a sandy beach.

Brody examined the signpost. "Cottage Four is up the hill and to the left."

"Hang on." April checked her phone. "My sister Avery texted. She and Drianna are coming to meet us."

"Should we take our stuff to the cottage first?"

Before April could answer, two women rode across the parking lot on cruiser bikes. Both were tall, slender, and blond, bearing no resemblance to April.

The taller of the two hopped off her bike. Her sandy-blond hair was pulled back in a tight ponytail, and a smattering of freckles dusted her nose. On her shirt was a stylized logo for the "Tough Mudder Half," which sounded like a half-marathon involving a hellscape of obstacle courses. She gave Brody a once-over, her icy blue eyes taking in every detail.

"So. You *are* real. I'm Avery."

Facing one of April's fearsome older sisters was more intimidating than he'd imagined. "Hi. I'm…Chris…" Shit, he was blanking on Chris's last name. "It's nice to meet you."

"I'm Drianna," said the other woman. Her hair was close-cropped, accenting her angular features. Like Avery, she wore an equally impressive shirt, boasting a Spartan 10K Beast, whatever the hell that was. She took a twenty-dollar bill out of her jeans pocket and handed it to Avery. "Fair's fair. You win."

April gaped. "You were betting on me?"

"On Chris," Drianna said. "I was convinced he was fictional. Avery thought we should give you the benefit of the doubt."

"I figured you learned your lesson after the Sam Jameson affair," Avery said.

Drianna turned to Brody with a sly smile. "Did April tell you about that?"

Had Sam Jameson been the name of her fake boyfriend? "No, but it's fine."

Drianna shrieked with laughter. A loud, horsey laugh, which grated like nails on a chalkboard. "This story *has* to be shared."

April clenched her hands. "It's not like you haven't shared it with everyone else in our extended family numerous times."

No wonder she hadn't wanted to show up without a date. Brody tried to come up with an excuse to leave—to spare her the humiliation—but he couldn't think of anything. Besides, if Drianna didn't get the story out of her system now, she'd probably bring it up later.

Drianna leaned in closer, her breath smelling of mint gum. "Back when April was still in college, we teased her because she never went out much. Didn't party. Didn't date. Just hung out with this geeky bunch of losers who liked to play video games and D & D. Then, one day, she tells us she has a boyfriend—this hot guy named Sam Jameson. From the pictures she sent us, he looked seriously ripped."

"We wanted to meet him," Avery said. "But she never brought him home, because—supposedly—he was on the college soccer team and played a lot of weekend games."

April's cheeks reddened. Wanting to console her, Brody took her hand.

"A few months after April started dating Sam, my friend showed me a book on her e-reader," Drianna said. "One of those smutty romances with a hot, half-naked guy on the cover. It was Sam! I did a deep dive and found him in a bunch of stock photos."

Avery chimed in. "At first we thought April was dating a cover model. But we found out the guy lived in New York. His name was Leo Thompson, not Sam Jameson. We called April out when she was home for Christmas that year, and she fessed up to all of it."

April sighed. "What can I say? I'm a whiz at Photoshop. And I was drinking Jameson whiskey with my roommate when I came up with the idea."

"How old were you?" Brody asked.

"Nineteen, I think? During my sophomore year." She glared at Drianna. "But the way everyone talks about it, you'd think it happened last year."

Five years was a long time to tease someone about a goofy college mistake. Brody had done his share of dumb things in college—most people did—but no one in his family had spent years rubbing his nose in it.

Drianna jabbed her finger in Brody's direction. "You sounded too good to be true, so we figured you were another Sam."

"Nope. I'm real." He squeezed her hand. "Should we go check out that cottage, honey?"

Drianna grabbed his arm, her grip surprisingly strong. She wasn't someone he'd want to face in a dark alley. "Not so fast, *Chris*. I looked you up online and found nothing. Why are you off the grid?"

He flinched under her steely gaze. Though he'd prepared his answer ahead of time, the force of her stare made him balk, like a criminal trapped in a police interrogation room.

April scowled at her sister. "I already told you the reason."

"Yeah, but I want to hear it from him," Drianna said.

Damn. Was she being protective or just nosy?

Either way, if April needed him to step up his game, he wouldn't let her down. He lowered his voice, as though sharing a secret. "Back when I was in college, I was dating this girl in the Comp Sci department. She seemed okay at first but got really clingy. If I went out with my other friends, she'd text me all night to 'check in on me.' Sometimes she showed up at my apartment when I had people over. After a while, it got to be too much, so I broke things off. I tried to do it gently, but…" He paused for dramatic effect.

"But what?" Avery asked.

"She became obsessed and left nasty comments on my Instagram. When I blocked her, she cloned my Facebook account and sent out racist posts, pretending to be me."

Drianna narrowed her eyes. "Sounds pretty sophisticated."

He nodded solemnly. "You wouldn't believe how much damage a determined hacker can do. That's why I shut down all my accounts."

The pause that followed almost torpedoed his confidence. If he couldn't pull off a simple explanation, what hope did he have of maintaining this charade? But Avery gave him a sympathetic nod. "That's rough."

April cleared her throat. "Are we done now? I'd like to check out our cottage."

"Dinner's at the Bay Breeze restaurant inside the main lodge. We'll be going over the details for tomorrow's race." Avery grinned. "Chris will love it."

There's a race?

Pretending to be Chris was going to be harder than he thought.

CHAPTER 5

The trail to the cottage ran alongside Lake Michigan, then meandered to the left, under a grove of evergreens. Fallen leaves and dried pine needles crunched under their feet as they walked in silence. After agonizing over the Sam Jameson story for all of five minutes, April couldn't keep quiet any longer. "You think I'm an idiot, don't you? My sisters made me look stupid."

Brody blinked as though coming out of a trance. "Do they always treat you that way?"

"It's how they are. And I'm the baby of the family, so…"

She was making things worse, so she pivoted toward the bigger issue that loomed ahead of them. "I should have emphasized how insanely competitive my family is. We can't just have fun at a wedding. We have to compete in the Beckett 10K Challenge and the family softball game. Sorry I didn't warn you sooner."

His brow creased. "A 10K race? When is it?"

She winced. "Tomorrow morning? Sorry. I was hoping my family wouldn't insist on it. You did bring running gear, right?"

"Sure. It was on your list of things to pack so that I'd look like

Chris." He placed his hand on her shoulder. "Stop apologizing. I can handle a race."

His touch sent butterflies spiraling through her. "Really? I mean, I know you're in good shape, but…"

He smirked. "Have you been checking me out?"

Her cheeks burned in mortification. She didn't want to reveal how often she'd daydreamed about him, or how aware she'd been of his physical regimen. "No. But…you know…"

"What?" His grin was infuriating.

She looked down and kicked a stray pinecone out of her path. "When you were with Taylor, you started going to the gym a lot. Biking. Running. Stuff like that."

Even if he wasn't as obsessed with the cult of fitness as Chris was, Brody was in great shape. He biked thirty or forty miles on the weekend and often hit the gym after work.

He gave her a gentle nudge. "Don't worry. I won't blow my cover. I've done a 10K before. Remember the charity run Blackwood Cellars did for the food pantry? I crushed it."

Not exactly. First of all, the race had been a 5K. Second, she'd been at the finish line, helping time the runners, and Brody hadn't broken any records. He'd arrived in the middle of the pack. In contrast, Chris had been the top finisher in his age group —something she'd bragged about to her family.

"The thing is…my sisters are fast. They compete in a lot of races. Same with my mom." She almost suggested he fake an injury—something light, like a twisted ankle—but stopped herself. She didn't want to insult him by questioning his athletic ability.

"I'll tell them I ran a marathon last weekend, and I'm still recovering." He laughed. "Not that I'd ever consider anything that hard-core."

A decent excuse, but April's sisters might smell a rat if they beat him with little effort.

When she saw their cottage, all thoughts of the 10K vanished.

Nestled among the trees, it resembled the tiniest of tiny houses, with a front porch overlooking the water. She could easily imagine relaxing with Brody on the Adirondack chairs, sipping wine and watching the sunset. As she unlocked the door, she almost squealed in delight. Though the cottage only contained one room, it was twice the size of a typical hotel room. On one side, a huge, panoramic window offered a stunning view of the lake. A cozy stone fireplace provided the perfect setting for chilly fall nights. Tucked into one corner was a small table with two chairs and a coffee station holding a Keurig and a set of bright red mugs.

It was absolutely perfect, except for one thing.

The only place to sleep was a king-size bed, covered with a navy quilt and a pile of blue and gray pillow shams. Granted, the bed was huge, but it was singular.

Shit. Why hadn't she considered the one-bed situation?

Because you assumed you'd be cozying up to Chris every night.

She couldn't even ask Brody to sleep on the couch, because no such couch existed. Instead, two overstuffed armchairs faced the window.

"Nice place," Brody said.

Hadn't he noticed the bed? Wasn't he bothered by it? It was all she could think about. "You like it?"

"It's great. Nice to have a little privacy. Especially since your sisters seem kind of nosy."

Why wasn't he saying anything about the bed? As she stared at the navy blue monstrosity, her heart rate accelerated.

She set down her suitcase. "The bed's pretty big. King-size. So...are you okay if we share it? I don't snore. And it won't bother me if you're there or anything...so..."

Stop talking. Now.

He was barely paying attention. "Sure. Whatever works."

"Great." She wiped her forehead. Here she was, making a big deal out of the bed when he couldn't care less.

Duh. Because he's not into you.

Why should that change because he was pretending to be her boyfriend? She had to stop herself before she made things weird.

He checked his watch. "If it's okay with you, I might go for a run on one of the trails. We have time before dinner, don't we?"

"We do, but wouldn't you rather sit on the porch and have a drink?" A pre-dinner run sounded like something Chris would do. As much as she wanted Brody to pull off the fake-Chris scenario, she didn't want him to *be* Chris.

He rubbed the back of his neck. "I should probably get a few miles in. All I've been doing lately is biking and lifting weights. I don't want to embarrass myself."

Oh, God. He's never going to convince anyone he's Chris.

All she could do was offer him a weak smile. "Good plan. Do you mind if I pass?"

"Aren't you doing the race?"

"With my asthma? I wouldn't last a mile. I'll be timing it, like I always do." The one time she'd tried to compete in a family race, she'd fallen flat on her face and humiliated herself.

When Brody went into the bathroom to change, she set their purchases from the country market in the mini fridge. In addition to all their snacks, they'd bought a bottle of locally made pinot noir to tide them over until they visited the area wineries. Though she hadn't planned on drinking alone, she decided to open the wine in the hopes it would help her relax. After the encounter with her sisters, her anxiety was ramping up to sky-high levels.

Was she asking too much of Brody? He'd looked unnerved when Drianna questioned him, and that was just the beginning. After today, five more days of activity awaited him, most involving her entire family. Her nosy, demanding, *competitive* family.

He emerged, wearing fleece joggers, sneakers, and a tight compression shirt that showed off his upper body. She couldn't help but stare. In the office, he always wore loose, casual t-shirts. Seeing him like this did strange things to her heartbeat. Now she wanted to know what he'd look like with his shirt off.

Down, girl.

"Everything okay?" he asked.

She shook her head, clearing her mind of wicked thoughts. "Yep. Have a good run."

He took off, shutting the door behind him. She was glad for a few minutes alone, just to process everything running through her head. Drianna's hostile interrogation. The one-bed situation. And the Napa bombshell.

Even if Brody never developed romantic feelings for her, she didn't want him to leave. Though he wasn't her only friend in Temecula, she leaned on him more than anyone else. Other than the painful months he'd spent with Taylor, he'd always been there for her, whether she needed a movie buddy or a shoulder to cry on. They could keep up their friendship long-distance, but it wouldn't be the same.

When the door opened, April tensed up. Was Brody admitting defeat already? If so, they'd never pull off this ruse.

"Hellooo," a friendly voice trilled.

"Ginger!" April beamed at the sight of her favorite cousin.

Ginger Beckett was dynamite in a small package—petite, high-energy, and lots of fun. Today she was clad in a riot of bright colors—a turquoise tunic, lime-green leggings, and rainbow-striped cardigan. Her pixie cut was dyed a bright orange.

April ran over and enfolded her in a hug. "You look great. Nice hair."

"You like? I call it my Pumpkin Spice look. Mom flipped out because she doesn't think it'll look good in the wedding photos, but—come on—it's not like *I'm* the bride." She glanced around the cottage. "Cute place. I'm over at the lodge, sharing a room with my folks. I was going to fly in on Thursday, but they wanted me here for the whole week so we could *bond*. Since they paid my way, I couldn't exactly say no."

April shuddered. She couldn't imagine sharing a hotel room with her parents for an entire week. "That's a lot of togetherness."

"Agreed. I told them they'd have more privacy if they put me in a separate room, but they didn't want me to be *lonely*." She let out a huffy breath. "Like I'm some sad little five-year-old desperate for friends."

April held up the wine bottle. "Want a drink?"

"Yes, please. I tried convincing my dad to stop for booze on the drive up from the airport but had no luck."

April motioned her over to one of the comfy chairs facing the window. After fetching a couple of glasses, she poured them each some wine and sat down beside her. The first sip of the mellow pinot was like a balm to her frayed nerves. "I needed that."

"Really? I thought you'd be in your glory—finally bringing home a date to flaunt in front of Her Dreadfulness."

April giggled. "Stop. Drianna's not *that* bad."

"She's the worst. What did she think of Chris? Did he pass the test?"

"She asked a lot of questions. It's going to be tough."

"Why? Because he's such a 'man of mystery'? Honestly, his aversion to social media is weird. And no photos? It's like he's a vampire. Or married." Ginger frowned. "He's not, is he?"

"What, a vampire?"

"No. Married, you dork."

Though she knew they were alone, April lowered her voice. If she didn't confide in someone, she'd burst. "To be honest...he's not Chris."

"What? Is he a paid escort like that guy in *The Wedding Date*?" Ginger grinned. "And does he come with benefits? Remember that scene where they have sex on the boat? Smoking hot." She fanned herself.

"No. He's my friend. Brody. The guy who works at Blackwood Cellars."

"The guy you were crushing on for a full year? The hot tech guy? This is great." Ginger downed her wine and refilled the glass. "What happened to no-carbs Chris?"

April took the bottle and topped up her drink. "I dumped him six days ago." She explained the chain of events to her cousin.

"Damn. Brody's gotta be into you. This is a huge favor."

She wished it were true. There had been times when she'd wondered if he regarded her as more than a friend. Like last New Year's Eve when they'd both been single. They spent the evening at her place, drinking champagne and watching *The Princess Bride*. Brody's teasing grew so flirtatious she thought he was poised to make a move. But minutes before the stroke of midnight, his fourth glass of champagne sent him bolting into the bathroom to throw up. In the morning, they were both so hungover they could barely carry on a conversation.

Since then, Brody had kept her firmly in the friend zone.

She shook her head. "He's had plenty of chances to take things further, and he's never tried once."

"This is the twenty-first century. Why haven't *you* taken the initiative?"

"I've thought about it. A lot. But I don't want to lose his friendship. And he's still getting over his ex. This is the first time in months he's done anything social."

"Still, this is a sweet setup. Case in point—there's only one bed."

"It's like the giant elephant in the room. I was freaked out, but he didn't seem to mind."

"Because he wants to get with you."

"No, he doesn't." April checked to ensure Brody wasn't approaching the cottage. "You know how I'm sure? Because Taylor enlightened me, back in the spring."

"Taylor?"

"His ex. The one who broke his heart by dumping him the day before his brother's wedding." She tightened her grip on her wineglass. "When she and Brody started dating, she got all pissy because he still hung out with me. But it was totally platonic."

Ginger raised her eyebrows. "Was it, though?"

"Sure. All we were doing together was watching Marvel movies and playing *Final Fantasy*. Stuff she didn't even like. But she asked Brody to give them up, because she didn't feel comfortable with him spending time with me."

"What a pain." Ginger set down her glass. "Like, it's totally possible to have friends of the opposite sex."

"It gets worse." April drank another slug of wine to brace herself. "A few weeks later, Taylor told me I needed to 'get over' Brody. Apparently, she'd asked him if he was into me, and he told her he'd *never* feel that way about me. Because, obviously, I wasn't his type."

Tears welled up in her eyes, but she wiped them away. She'd already shed enough tears. Hell, she'd spent most of that weekend wallowing in self-pity. She'd never fooled herself into thinking Brody was secretly lusting after her. But "obviously not his type"? That could only mean one thing. She wasn't beautiful or sexy enough for him to consider as a romantic partner.

"Sounds like Taylor was jealous of your friendship," Ginger said. "For all you know, she could have been lying."

April gave a sad little shrug. "Maybe. But it was enough to steer me right into Chris's arms, which wasn't the brightest move on my part."

"At least the sex with him was great. Right?"

She couldn't help but laugh. "Well, actually...the sex with Chris wasn't *that* great. I mean, it was better than being alone, but...he wasn't all that generous in bed."

She'd experienced far too many nights, lying beside him after he finished, feeling thoroughly unsatisfied. But since he expected praise, she acted like he was a world-class stud.

"And you put up with that for five months?" Ginger gave a loud snort. "You're better off without him. If things don't work out with Brody, then after you get home, we need to launch Operation Great Sex and find you someone fabulous. In bed and out. Okay?"

"Okay." At the moment, April had enough to deal with, sharing a bed with Brody while trying to keep her feelings in check.

But at some point, she needed to move on.

CHAPTER 6

The first mile was sheer hell.

Brody hadn't exactly been truthful with April. Though he was in decent shape, he hadn't run in months. Most nights, he went to the gym after work, lifted weights, and hit the bag. Weekends were for long bike rides. But he'd stopped running, mainly because it was something he and Taylor had done together.

After a mile, he slowed down, caught his breath, and tried to focus. He didn't care if he beat Avery or Drianna, but he didn't want to humiliate himself. Or embarrass April, who was counting on him to act like Chris.

He started up again, breathing in the refreshing fall air, enjoying the colorful foliage, and adjusting to the steady rhythm of his feet hitting the trail. If anything, the run helped him unwind. Despite what he'd told April, their current situation was stressing him out. Not just because he was pretending to be Chris, but because the cottage only had one bed.

Though he'd reacted calmly about the king bed, he hadn't expected it. He'd foolishly assumed the cottage would have two queens. Now he had to face the prospect of sharing a bed with April for six nights.

Both of them were single. In a cozy, romantic setting. At a wedding.

It was a perfect storm.

All of a sudden, he couldn't stop thinking about her. The adorable way she laughed. The way her smile always lifted his spirits. And—when he'd first seen the bed—the way she might look, lying beside him, without a stitch of clothing.

Which was a completely unrealistic fantasy. In the two years he'd known April, she'd never shown an interest in anything but friendship. She loved hanging out in sweats, watching action movies, and shooting the shit. When he was with her, he could relax and be himself, exposing his geekiest passions, like his secret love for '80s anime or his dream of designing video games. They shared a level of comfort he'd never experienced with any of his girlfriends. Given how much he relied on her, the last thing he wanted to do was push things too far, have her reject his overtures, and ruin things between them.

Besides, the last time he'd fallen for someone, he'd gotten his nuts served to him on a platter. A guy could only take so much.

By the end of the second mile, he hit his stride, but he turned around. If he put in too many miles, he'd never survive the upcoming race.

As he approached the cottage, he removed his shirt and used it to mop the sweat from his forehead. He stopped short when he got inside. April and another woman—a petite redhead—lounged on the armchairs facing the picture window.

The redhead, or orange-head, if his eyes didn't betray him, winked at him. "Hey, Chris. I'm April's cousin, Ginger. She told me you're training for another triathlon."

"Umm...yeah. Hi." He felt like he should be flexing or something. Stupid Chris.

Ginger gave him a cocky grin. "As it happens, I'm thinking of doing a triathlon next spring. Any tips for me?"

He probably should have read up on triathlons. They involved biking and running, but he couldn't remember the third thing. Archery? Or was that a pentathlon?

April nudged Ginger. "Stop teasing him." She gave Brody an apologetic smile. "Sorry. Ginger has no intention of running a triathlon."

Ginger raised her wineglass. "Damn straight, I don't."

"Also, I told her the truth. Because I need an ally, in case of emergency."

"Okay. Good to know." Brody stepped back a few paces, aware of how much he was sweating. Ginger was staring at him so intently he wished he'd kept his shirt on. "I'm going to jump in the shower."

"Sounds good," April said. "We'll head down to the lodge for dinner once you're ready."

He grabbed his clothes and escaped into the bathroom. As he was closing the door, Ginger said softly, "You didn't lie. He's not my type, but I can appreciate how hot he is."

He let out a deep breath as the lock clicked shut. Did April think he was hot? He couldn't hold a candle to Chris, who was so lean and muscular he was like a walking protein shake commercial. As Brody undressed, an image popped into his mind. April. Naked. Running her hands up and down his bare chest, pressing herself against him.

Enough. He didn't have time for erotic fantasies, not when he needed to be on point as Chris. To distract himself from visions of showering with April, he went over the Chris facts that she'd included in her Google Doc.

As the brand analytics manager for the Avensole Winery, Chris's expertise was in marketing and data crunching, rather than website and app development, but at least he worked in the wine industry. He'd run in ten triathlons, six marathons, and one

Iron Man, which meant he knew a lot about competitive racing—an area where Brody's knowledge was woefully lacking. Why hadn't he thought to research it ahead of time?

When he came out of the shower, April had swapped out her leggings for a tight pair of jeans. They covered her butt in a way that kick-started his imagination again.

Focus, damn it.

He pulled out his phone. "Give me a sec. I have to check a few things before we leave. What's a decent time for finishing a marathon?" He tried bringing up his browser, but the Wi-Fi in the cottage was painfully slow.

"The average time for a normal guy is about four hours, give or take. If you're a good runner, it's more like three and change. You need to finish in just under three hours to qualify for the Boston Marathon."

He looked up from his phone. "How do you know that?"

She gave a huge eye roll. "Chris talked about it all the time. When he ran the Camarillo Marathon, he was bummed because he missed the Boston cutoff by five minutes."

"Okay. What about triathlons?"

"Easy. Usually they involve swimming, biking, and running. When Chris did the Oakland Triathlon in August, he had to swim a mile, bike twenty-five miles, and finish with a 10K run. But the Iron Man Triathlon is much harder because you have to run a whole marathon *and* swim over two miles."

Shit. Brody might have been in good shape, but he couldn't pull off something like that.

April placed her hand on his arm. "It's not like you have to compete in a triathlon this weekend. All you have to do is brag about your accomplishments."

Right. He'd met Chris enough times to know how the guy operated. He just needed to sound semi-knowledgeable and slightly arrogant. "I'm good. Let's go. Where to?"

"The restaurant's at the main lodge, so we can walk."

"Perfect. Remember, we're a couple now, so we have to act romantic. If you need to objectify me, feel free."

"You wish. But I'll play along, *darling*."

He smirked. "I prefer Honey Pie."

"How about Sweet Cheeks?" She gave his butt a playful smack.

He was tempted to retaliate but restrained himself. If he thought about her butt too much, he might end up with a hard-on, and that wouldn't be a good look. "Or maybe Stud Muffin? Since I love your baking."

She gave him a gentle shove. "No baking love, remember? You don't eat anything made with butter, refined sugar, or white flour."

He shuddered. During the six months he'd dated Taylor, she'd asked him to follow her strict eating regimen, which meant limited carbs and no sweets. He'd done it for her, but he'd sorely missed April's baked goods.

They walked along the trail through the woods, their feet kicking up dried leaves. When they spotted a white-tailed deer in the distance, April stopped and drew in her breath, keeping still until it faded from view. Without thinking, he took her hand, and she held on tight. Was it part of the act? A way to show solidarity? Either way, he liked it.

They entered the main lodge and passed through the lobby, toward the entrance of the Bay Breeze. The front of the restaurant contained a noisy bar, packed with customers. For a Monday night, the place was surprisingly busy. In the background, wall-mounted TVs broadcast a football game. Brody usually avoided places like this. Nothing worse than trying to hold his own during football season. The only sport he followed was college basketball because he liked calculating his bracket for March Madness.

The main restaurant set his mind at ease. No blaring TVs or loud music. Instead, the spacious dining room had a rustic feel, with oak paneling, a wood-beamed ceiling, and a huge fieldstone fireplace. Along the wall were mounted fish and framed photos in black and white, depicting the North Bay Resort in its early days. April waved at her family, who were seated at a table near the fireplace.

Brody took a deep breath.

Showtime.

CHAPTER 7

$\mathcal{B}$rody was about to introduce himself to the Becketts when a surge of fear gripped him. His throat closed up, and he swallowed uncomfortably. The last time he'd been at this kind of family gathering was his brother's wedding in Maui.

Remember, you're Chris. Smug, arrogant douchebag. He'd never be intimidated by anyone.

Avery pointed to the purple Fitbit around her wrist. "About time. You two are ten minutes late."

April squeezed Brody's hand and gave him a dewy-eyed smile. "Sorry. We got distracted. Didn't we, honey?"

Her words provided the encouragement he needed. "It's easy to get distracted when I'm with you, sweetheart." He kissed the top of her head, inhaling the scent of rosemary and mint. In response, she leaned into him, filling him with the sudden urge to take her in his arms and kiss her properly.

But he had to stay focused. He gave the group a broad smile. "Nice to meet you. I'm Chris Rockwell."

The woman who stood to greet him resembled Avery and Drianna. Like them, she was tall, blond, and slender, with a hint of a tan. "I'm so pleased you could join us for the wedding. I'm Jill Beckett—April's mom."

In contrast, April's dad and her brother, Oliver, or Ollie as he was known, shared April's chestnut-brown hair and hazel eyes. But when they stood to shake hands, their height was evident. April seemed to be the only family member who'd gotten stuck with the short gene.

As Brody sat down beside April, he scanned the table, looking for Avery and Drianna's husbands, who he assumed would be joining them. April must have expected the same thing because she spoke up first. "Aren't Hunter and Ian coming to dinner?"

"I doubt it," Avery said. "They spent the afternoon golfing, and they wanted to grab a drink on the way back. Hunter texted an hour ago and told us not to wait."

Drianna scowled. "Ian barely spent fifteen minutes here before he took off. Typical."

"Come on, Dree," Avery said. "It's vacation. The boys deserve a little fun."

Drianna turned away, her expression dark. Before the silence could build to higher levels of awkwardness, Ollie jumped in and introduced his fiancée, Magdalena, who was petite, with light brown skin, long, curly black hair, and a wide, generous smile.

"Hi," she said. "You can call me Mags. Thanks for flying all the way out here. And for six days! Most of my family won't get here until Friday. We're from Green Bay, so Door County's nothing new to us."

"Our family goes hard at weddings," Ollie said.

"Yep," Avery agreed. "Go big or go home. Our last two weddings included five days of events."

Mags laughed. "I still think that's wild. I've never heard of a family with a tradition of running a 10K before a wedding."

Neither had Brody. For what it was worth, he thought five days of events seemed excessive.

"No need to worry about tonight's dinner menu," Mrs.

Beckett said. "We ordered a few bottles of wine and some family-style dishes to share. Unless you have food restrictions?"

"I thought April mentioned you being on the Paleo diet?" Drianna said to Brody.

He almost laughed at the idea until he remembered he was supposed to be Chris. "I'm taking a week off for the wedding. I didn't want to inconvenience anyone."

Not something the *real* Chris would have done. Instead, he would have chastised them for their unhealthy food choices.

"Good thing," Mags said. "Because Wisconsin's known for beer, brats, and cheese—all things that weren't around in the Paleolithic era."

In the center of the table was a giant platter, filled with an assortment of finger foods—celery and carrot sticks, cut-up radishes, cornichon pickles, crackers, cheese cubes, three kinds of dip, and cinnamon rolls. Which seemed odd. Who served cinnamon rolls as an appetizer?

Mags laughed at Brody's quizzical expression. "You're wondering about the relish tray, am I right? It's a Wisconsin thing. Found in traditional supper clubs." She reached for the platter and passed to him. "Help yourself."

He grabbed a couple of olives and some pickles but passed on the cinnamon rolls since they looked dry. Ever since he'd tried April's homemade cinnamon rolls, he wouldn't settle for anything less.

Mrs. Beckett passed a bottle of red wine around the table. Brody examined it when it reached him. "Badger Hollow Winery. That's a local place, right?"

Mags nodded. "It's in Baileys Harbor, ten minutes south of us. You passed it on the drive up here."

April took a few crackers and a spoonful of dip off the relish tray. "We could check it out tomorrow, if you want," she said to Brody.

"Why? So you can take photos and post them on Instagram?"

Drianna's voice held a nasty edge. "I didn't realize this was a *work* weekend."

April let out her breath. "For your information, Dree, I do more than post pictures online."

"Oh yeah, I forgot. You tweet about them. And create cute captions. Must be nice."

What was her problem? Brody was tempted to fire off an angry retort, but he held his tongue, hoping April would defend herself.

"It *is* nice," April snapped. "And it's a real job."

"It's fine for now," Mrs. Beckett said. "But you'll want something more challenging after you've been there for a few years. At least it's better than working in the service industry. My paralegal's daughter graduated with a degree in graphic design, same as you, but couldn't find work anywhere. Now she's a barista at some little coffeehouse."

Drianna reached for the relish tray and added celery sticks to her plate. "You're lucky you have a job, shrimp."

At the way April tensed up, Brody suspected she didn't appreciate the nickname. But now he understood what she'd meant earlier when she said her family didn't respect her job. Which infuriated him. Not only was she a remarkably talented designer, she also worked for a company that owned ten percent of the global wine market.

"I still think you're wasting your talent," her dad said. "If you came to work for my firm as an assistant, you could see if architecture's something you'd be interested in."

April frowned. "Dad, you bring this up every time I come home. If I wanted to be an architect, I'd have to go back to school and get a master's degree. That's three years of classes. Then I'd have to pass a huge licensing exam."

"But you'd end up with a guaranteed job at my firm," Mr. Beckett said. "You could take over when I retire."

"I dunno, Dad," Ollie said. "Architecture's a long haul. And it's a ton of work."

Avery waved her fork at him. "Says the guy who's getting a PhD. You've been in school forever."

"Because I love research," he said. "That's my jam. But it's not for everyone."

Brody appreciated Ollie's take. He seemed like the only member of the family who understood April.

Drianna scoffed. "Why are we wasting time discussing this? April doesn't have the drive to be an architect. Her head's in the clouds."

Brody let out his breath in annoyance. But before he could interject, April squeezed his thigh under the table, shocking him into silence. When he glanced her way, she gave a small shake of her head. Like she didn't want him to make waves.

But he couldn't sit there and watch April's family shit all over her. Not if he had anything to say about it.

APRIL NEEDED Brody to keep quiet. He might resent her family's attitude, but she'd grown used to it. At every big gathering, she'd had to endure the same stupid conversations in which they nagged her about her job, her future, and her lack of a boyfriend. At least now she didn't have to deal with the boyfriend issue. The rest wasn't worth debating. Eventually, they'd move onto another topic.

"I wish I had a job where I could play on social media all day," Drianna said. "Things at work have been stressful as hell. There's this one guy—"

"The one who's gunning for your failure?" Avery snapped. "Stop being so paranoid. No one's out to get you fired."

Drianna narrowed her eyes. "How would you know? You don't work in my office."

"But I've heard enough of your conspiracy theories. We all have."

April focused her attention on Drianna. Her sister had always been tightly wound, but tonight, she seemed more agitated than usual. "What's going on at work?" she asked.

"Don't encourage her," Avery said. "Otherwise, we'll spend the next hour listening to her rant about Gary the Gaslighter, the guy she claims is trying to sabotage her."

Their mom shook her head. "He can't be that bad, Drianna. Maybe if you tried approaching him as a colleague rather than rival, you wouldn't keep butting heads with him."

"Seriously, Mom, are you standing up for him?" Drianna said.

"I'm saying you make things harder for yourself than they need to be." She gave Drianna a conciliatory smile and turned to Brody. "Chris, tell us a little about your job. You're also in the wine industry, right?"

April was afraid Brody might wilt under pressure, but he glibly eased into his Chris persona, describing his job almost word-for-word from the Google Doc she'd sent him.

"It sounds like you have a lot of responsibility at Avensole," Avery said.

Drianna nodded. "Agreed. But doesn't it bother you that your girlfriend has such a cushy job while you work your ass off?

"I like it when April has more time for me," Brody said. "That way she can come watch all my races. I love having a one-woman cheering squad."

April beamed at him in response. "And I love cheering you on, sweetie."

He gave her a smile so adoring she wished it were more than just an act, especially since the *real* Chris had never spoken of her with such appreciation.

Brody turned his gaze back to Drianna. "I'm glad April asked me to come with her to Wisconsin. Her last project was so demanding I hardly ever saw her."

"What project?" Drianna asked.

April was about to tell her sister to ease up on the interrogation, but Brody spoke first. "I'll show you. Can you hand me one of those wine bottles?"

As Avery passed him a half-empty bottle, he took out his phone. She wagged her finger at him. "No phones at the dinner table, Chris. That's a Beckett rule."

Brody ignored her and photographed the wine label with his phone. "Nice. This particular wine—Wild Wood Red—has a four-star rating on Vivino. It's a hearty blend of mixed red varietals that goes well with pasta and red meat. Hints of cherry, spice, and peppery oak. The equivalent Blackwood Cellars wine would be their Riverbank Red, which is priced two dollars less and has a slightly higher score. Definitely a better deal."

"Is that the Vivino app?" Ollie asked. "I've heard about it."

"Not quite," Brody said. "It makes use of Vivino's label-recognition algorithm, but it was designed for Blackwood Cellars."

When he paused, April realized he was waiting for her to speak up. A wave of anxiety crested over her, but she wanted to show her family that her job involved more responsibility than posting images on social media.

"When we created the app, we partnered up with Vivino to use their data and their algorithms, but we designed it with our wine club in mind," she explained. "Anyone can use the app, but the wine club members get a lot of perks. We're still in the process of adding more features."

The shocked look on Drianna's face was priceless. Especially when Brody added, "Pretty impressive, huh? April created it."

She was about to contradict him, but he placed his hand on her thigh. Even if he was only warning her to play along, his touch sent her heart soaring. She tossed back the rest of her wine, then held out her glass so he could refill it.

"April, you created an app?" Ollie said. "That's incredible."

She flashed him an appreciative smile. Whenever these conversations came up, her brother was usually in her corner. He was the only one who understood she wasn't lazy, she just didn't share the same intense drive as the rest of the family.

"I thought you only worked on the design," Avery said. "Like, the images and stuff."

"She's being modest," Brody said. "The design, the layout, the logo—that was all her. And she spent hours beta testing it. Trust me, I know because she was up so late, working on it."

All of that was true, except Brody and his team, led by a computer science whiz they'd nicknamed Jimmy the Kid, had been responsible for the coding and the back-end programming. Though April had taken the lead on the design team, she'd only been given the job because no one else in their department had wanted to put in the extra hours. But she'd risen to the challenge, busting her ass to meet their deadlines. The app had been her favorite project at Blackwood Cellars, in part because she and Brody had spent so many hours working on it together.

Drianna scowled. "Sounds like bullshit to me. April, you said that Brody guy did all the computer stuff."

Brody let out a sigh. "Typical Brody Blackwood, claiming all the credit."

"I know, right?" April said. "Isn't that just like a male in the workplace?"

"That's what I was talking about earlier," Drianna said. "I'm dealing with a ton of toxic shit at work."

"Maybe it's your attitude that's making it toxic," Avery said.

April was surprised at her oldest sister's tone. Though Avery often tried to one-up Drianna, she always had her back. Had things changed between them? Or had Drianna's complaints worn everyone down? Not for the first time, April was grateful she limited her visits back home.

Before she could ask Drianna more about her job, their mom redirected the conversation again, this time by asking Magdalena about her favorite places to visit in Door County. While the rest of the table was focused on Mags, April leaned over until her lips were inches from Brody's ear. "You holding up okay?"

In response, he grinned and gave her thigh a reassuring squeeze. Any qualms he'd had about playing Chris seemed to have vanished. She reached down to place her hand over his. When he twined his fingers with hers, she let out an involuntary shiver.

If she wasn't careful, her crush on him was going to come back, even stronger than ever.

CHAPTER 8

By the time dinner ended, April was so full she could barely move. In addition to the relish tray, the Becketts had ordered family-style servings of four main courses —prime rib, pan-fried walleye, roasted chicken with garlic mashed potatoes, and fettuccine Alfredo. Since Chris wasn't around to reprimand her, April indulged in a little of everything, including dessert.

Feeling slightly tipsy from the wine she'd consumed at dinner, she leaned on Brody as they made their way back to the cottage. "Thanks for standing up for me. You didn't have to lie about the app."

"I didn't lie. That scoundrel, Brody Blackwood, always takes the credit for everything."

"He's such a typical *man*. Good thing you're not like that."

"I'm far more sensitive. A truly enlightened male."

She snorted with laughter. No one would ever call Chris enlightened.

Her laughter dried up when they entered the cottage. She'd been so caught up in the meal she'd put the one-bed situation out of her mind. "Um...if you want to use the bathroom first, you can go ahead."

"I'll get my stuff." He grabbed a handful of clothes from his suitcase and dashed into the bathroom.

With him gone, the room was too quiet. She wished the cottage came with a TV. Right now, an episode of *The Office* or a late-night talk show would lighten the mood. She walked over to the floor-to-ceiling windows and pulled the drapes shut so the morning light wouldn't wake them. When Brody emerged, he'd changed into a SkyNet t-shirt and a baggy pair of gym shorts. *Thank God*. She couldn't have handled it if he'd decided to sleep in nothing but his boxers.

She dashed into the bathroom, trying to ignore the butterflies rising in her stomach. At least she'd ditched the lacy negligee she'd planned on bringing. Instead, her ensemble consisted of an oversized sleep shirt and a pair of plaid pajama bottoms. The kind of clothes that exuded no sexuality whatsoever.

Get through tonight. After that, it won't feel so weird.

Brody was sitting up in bed, scrolling through his phone, with the covers pulled up to his waist. He appeared calm. Like it was perfectly normal for him to be sharing a bed with her. She slipped into her side and took a deep breath. Should they be setting up ground rules? What if one of them crossed over too far? What if she accidentally groped him in the middle of the night? What if he groped *her*?

Stop it.

He set his phone on the nightstand. Propping himself on one elbow, he leaned in closer. "Are you okay? You look flushed."

A few more inches and he'd be in her space. Practically on top of her.

At the thought of Brody lying on top of her, her body almost ignited. Was twenty-four too young to be having hot flashes?

She took a long drink from the water bottle on her nightstand. Anything to cool her fevered imagination. "I'm fine. I shouldn't have had that third glass of wine. It's not like I'm drunk, but I usually stop at two glasses. You know? And three, well, that's a lot, so..."

Stop talking. Now.

"Is this about the bed?" he asked. "Don't sweat it. If you want, we can put a pillow between us so you're not tempted to try anything."

"So *I'm* not tempted?"

He grinned. "Kidding. This is no big deal, right? I've spent the night at your apartment before."

But only when you've had too much to drink. And you've always slept on the couch.

The last time he crashed at her place was right after he returned from his brother's wedding in Maui, three and a half months ago. He'd shown up at her apartment, exhausted, hungover, and in desperate need of support. Though she let him stay, she wasn't tempted by his nearness since he spent most of the night wallowing in misery.

This was different. They were both single. And they were pretending to be lovers.

She offered him a faint smile. "It's fine. I'm being weird."

"This is probably a letdown, huh? If I was Chris, we'd be having sex by now." He lay down and crossed his arms behind his head, looking up at the ceiling.

She turned off the bedside lamp and propped one of the pillow shams between them. "If you were Chris, I wouldn't have had three glasses of wine at dinner. Or the peanut butter pie for dessert. So, it's not all bad."

It was nice to eat without judgment. The rest of her family were on the slender side, but they'd all indulged at dinner. Even if her sisters were running fanatics, they enjoyed a good meal as much as she did.

Brody was silent for so long April wondered if he'd drifted off to asleep. When he finally spoke, his voice was tentative. "Can I ask you something?"

"Sure."

"Promise you won't be offended?"

She stiffened. Anytime a man phrased a question that way, chances were good he was going to act offensively. But since it was Brody, she'd give him the benefit of the doubt. "Depends on what you're asking."

"Why'd you put up with Chris? You never used to worry about what you looked like or whether you were fit enough. But once you started dating him, that all changed. You stopped baking, even though you love it. Last week, when you brought in those red velvet cupcakes, was the first time in weeks you'd baked anything."

Hearing the words made April cringe. Had she been that weak? "I guess I was lonely."

"I get that, but still..."

Anger flared up inside her, sudden and unexpected. If he was going to question her decision to date Chris, she had every right to fight back.

"You know what, Brody? You might want to look in the mirror. One of the reasons I stopped bringing in treats was because *you* stopped eating them. Why? Because Taylor didn't do carbs, and she expected you to follow her lead. Not only that—we stopped going to the movies together. You were never online when I wanted to play *Final Fantasy*. You called it *childish*."

"I...I wasn't that bad."

Had he blanked it out? Or just been oblivious? She'd never confronted him over the issue because she wanted to spare his feelings. But not tonight.

"When Taylor said she didn't feel comfortable with you spending time with me, you gave in—just like that. No more movies. No more video games. Not even online. The only time we talked was at work. It hurt like hell."

When the minutes ticked by and Brody didn't respond, her rage ebbed away as quickly as it had sparked. How could she criticize him when he was spending an entire week with her, pretending to be her boyfriend? She was the worst.

"Sorry," she mumbled. "I was out of line."

He reached across the pillow sham, found her hand, and squeezed it. His touch surprised her, but she didn't pull away. "I'm the one who should apologize," he said. "I was a shitty friend. I was so obsessed with impressing Taylor that I stopped doing the stuff I loved."

She squeezed his hand in return. "I missed you."

"Is that why you started dating Chris?"

Now he was annoying her again, even if his guess was correct. She pulled her hand away. "Not everything is about you. Maybe I just wanted to get laid."

"Sorry."

She let out a deep sigh. "It's okay. You're sort of right. You'd dated other women before, but you never shut me out like that. I hated being home alone every night."

Without their movie marathons to look forward to, she'd spent too many nights curled up on the couch, reading historical romance novels and binge-watching *Outlander*. At least with Chris around, she'd been able to relegate her vibrator to the nightstand drawer.

Brody took her hand again, lacing his fingers with hers. "I'm sorry. I got too caught up with being the guy Taylor wanted. And I feel stupid about it now because it wasn't that I loved her as much as I loved the *idea* of her. That someone who was so gorgeous and successful would want to be with me. She was so far out of my league that landing her felt like a huge coup. Which is sexist and idiotic in so many ways."

"It is. But at least you admit it. And stop saying she was out of your league."

"Please. I was a total geek in high school. And for most of college."

"Who cares? You're not a geek now. You're brilliant, you're fun to be with, and you're really hot..."

Oh shit.

He gave a warm chuckle. That laugh was like a deadly weapon, sending flutters throughout her entire body.

"You *have* been checking me out," he said.

Good thing the light was off because her face was a fiery inferno. "I meant—"

"No backsies. You said it. I'm really hot. I'm taking that to the grave, Beckett."

"Fine. I said it. But you need to stop devaluing yourself. Don't let the Taylors of the world convince you otherwise."

"I could say the same about you." His voice was laced with tenderness. "You're smart, sweet, and incredibly talented. If Chris didn't appreciate you, then he was a complete tool."

No. Brody couldn't say things like that. Not when she was already fighting off her attraction to him. At this rate, she'd never be able to keep her feelings in check.

Her phone pinged, shocking her back to reality. She picked it up and saw a text from Ginger. *How's it going with fake-Chris? Having fun yet?*

April's blush increased in heat and intensity. She silenced her phone and set it facedown on the nightstand.

This had to stop. As nice as it was to exchange compliments with Brody, things were getting too personal. If she pursued him, and he wasn't interested, the next five nights would be unbearably awkward.

"Everything okay?" he asked.

"Yeah, that was...Avery. Reminding us about the 10K tomorrow morning. I guess we should get some sleep."

"Good plan. 'Night, April."

"'Night, Brody."

But despite the early morning ahead of them, she spent a long time lying awake.

She had to tread carefully. Even if she was grateful to have Brody at her side, she shouldn't assume he wanted anything more than friendship. Just because they were close now, didn't mean he'd changed. She wasn't his type.

She'd do well to keep that in mind.

CHAPTER 9

*B*rody squinted at the digital clock on the nightstand. 3:10 a.m. Not good. If he was going to compete in a 10K, he needed to be as well rested as possible. But sleep was proving difficult. Oddly enough, the race wasn't foremost in his mind. Instead, he kept agonizing over his conversation with April. Though he'd felt guilty about shutting her out when he was dating Taylor, he had no idea how badly he'd hurt her. He hated that he'd treated her so poorly, even if he'd done it unintentionally. Mixed in with his regret was the powerful and unexpected tug of physical attraction he felt toward her.

If at any time she'd pushed the pillow shams aside and met him halfway, he would have taken her in his arms, kissed her soundly, and let things play out from there. But she hadn't given any indication she shared his longings. So, he behaved like a gentleman.

Normally, when he couldn't sleep—and he'd had plenty of restless nights after Taylor had left him—he'd boot up his laptop and work on a coding issue. Powering through a few hours of tricky code usually redirected his anxiety-prone brain.

But he didn't want to turn on his laptop, for fear he'd wake

April. He stood and walked to the picture window, pushing aside the drapes until he caught a glimpse of the lake, gleaming under the moonlight. He was tempted to grab his sneakers and go outside. A walk in the night air might calm his troubled psyche.

"Brody?" April's soft voice startled him. "Are you okay?"

"Sorry." He pulled the drapes closed. "Couldn't sleep. I didn't mean to wake you."

"It's okay. I was having trouble sleeping, too." She sat up and turned on the bedside lamp. "If I made you feel bad before, I'm sorry."

He turned to face her. "What do you mean?"

"When I made those accusations. About the way you acted when you were dating Taylor. I was kind of harsh."

The vulnerability in her voice made his heart ache. He walked back to bed and crawled in next to her. In the low light, with her wavy hair tumbled around her shoulders, she looked even more enticing. What would happen if he leaned in closer and placed a gentle kiss on those lips? Would she respond with passion? Or pull away in shock?

On the chance she might react with discomfort, he restrained himself. "You were just being honest. Which I appreciate. Good friends should be honest with each other. It wasn't easy hearing those things, but I'm glad you called me on it."

"So, we're good?"

"We're totally good."

"Then what's keeping you up?" she asked. "Is it the race? Or something else?"

"I just have a lot on my mind. Like..." He couldn't admit he'd been fantasizing about her. After the intimate talk they'd had earlier, it would seem crass and opportunistic.

"Like the job in Napa?" she asked.

"Partly." Easier to focus on his possible promotion than his growing attraction to her. "I'm sorry I didn't tell you earlier, but I still don't know how I feel. It's a great opportunity, but..."

"But it might not be right for you?"

"Exactly. But I want to make my parents proud."

"They're not proud now?" April's voice was laced with indignation. "How is that possible? You created a killer app."

"*We* created a killer app, Beckett."

"Aww, thanks, Blackwood." She eased out of bed and ambled over to the mini fridge. "Since we're up, do you want some fudge?"

"Sure." Though he wasn't remotely hungry, he appreciated that her first impulse during a middle-of-the-night existential crisis was to procure snacks.

She returned with a small box containing a few pieces of cherry-chocolate fudge and held it out to him. He broke off a piece and popped it in his mouth. Sweet and delicious.

"We had a lot of fun working on the app," she said. "You think you're going to have that kind of fun in a management role?"

He gave a short laugh. "Doubtful. I hate long-ass meetings filled with business jargon. I hate networking. And I loathe giving presentations. Except the one we gave for the app, because you crushed it." He'd been so proud, watching her shine as she explained the customized features they'd created for their wine club members.

"Only because you were there with me. But if you hate all those things, then why would you consider management?"

A fair question. One he'd asked himself, numerous times, only to come up with the same embarrassing conclusion. Jealousy. "Because that's what my brother does. Don't get me wrong— Marc's an awesome guy. But living in his shadow isn't easy. My parents are so fucking proud of him. Dad just put him in charge of this new department to expand the company's reach even further."

"That's great. But that's his thing, not yours. Why compete with him?"

Why? Because Marc had always been the golden boy, the

perfect son, the one most likely to take the reins of Blackwood Cellars-Napa. Whereas Brody was the awkward computer nerd. His family might appreciate his contributions to the company, but half the time, they didn't even understand what he was doing.

Before he could try to articulate his complicated feelings, April spoke up again. "You once told me that you weren't even sure if Blackwood Cellars was your endgame. You said if you could do anything, you'd design video games."

Something he'd never told anyone else in his family, certainly not Marc or his parents. But April knew. And she respected it. "I'm not sure how realistic that is, though."

"Maybe not. But it might be worth a shot."

For a moment, he said nothing, meeting her gaze. She understood him better than anyone in his life. Why hadn't he ever appreciated her properly?

"For what it's worth, I can relate," she said. "You heard the way my family treated my job. Like it was inconsequential. My dad would be over the moon if I went into architecture. But I'd rather do something I love than mold myself just to please them." She let out a snort. "I'm such a hypocrite. Here I am saying this when I'm making you pretend you're Chris, so I can impress them."

"A fair point, but after hearing the Sam Jameson story, I get it."

She bit her lip, then gave him a shy smile. "For the record, you're totally rocking the fake-Chris persona. Except for one thing."

Damn, but she was tempting when she smiled like that. "What am I missing?"

"You're much nicer than him." She set the box of fudge on the nightstand. "Is there anything else I can do to help? I don't want you to go into the race all sleep-deprived."

Honestly? Sex would help. A lot.

Not that he'd suggest it. The last thing he wanted to do was scare her off.

"I think I'll be okay." He plumped his pillow and lay back down. "Good night."

She turned off the lamp. "'Night."

But when she reached across the bed and found his hand, he held on tight.

And wanted so much more.

CHAPTER 10

"Brody? Brody!"

"Huh? What?" Brody woke with a start, rolled over, and fell out of bed. He groaned as his body hit the floor.

April rushed to his side. "Are you all right?"

"I'm good." The only thing bruised was his dignity. As he stood up, his muscles screamed in protest. He was stiff and sore from yesterday's run, probably because he hadn't taken the time to stretch properly.

April was already dressed in a UCLA Bruins hoodie, yoga pants, and sneakers. "I let you sleep as long as I could, but the race is in half an hour. I thought you might want something to eat. Or a cup of coffee." She held out a red mug, embossed with the resort's logo.

As tempted as he was by the rich aroma of coffee, he shook his head. If he ate or drank anything, it might come back up during the run. "No, thanks. I'm gonna grab a quick shower."

"Aren't you going to be all sweaty after the race?"

"I need to warm up my muscles. I can shower again after." He rifled through his suitcase and found clean running gear, then stumbled to the bathroom.

Cranking the shower as hot as it could go, he sighed in relief as the scalding water coursed over him. Even if he was anxious about the 10K, he wasn't as worried about facing April's family. Not after the way he'd held his own at dinner. He'd not only performed his role without a single misstep, he'd enjoyed himself. By the end of the evening, he was feeling a little like the guy he used to be before the Maui debacle.

When he emerged from the bathroom, April was blasting "Eye of the Tiger" on her phone and jabbing the air like a boxer. "Okay, champ. Ready to kick ass? Avery texted and said everyone's there."

"Already?"

"They've been doing wind sprints in the parking lot for twenty minutes. Like I said, they go hard."

His earlier confidence vanished instantly. Who was he kidding, thinking he could compete in a 10K? He was going to come in last. If he finished at all.

As they left the cottage, April grabbed a clipboard and a stopwatch from her backpack. "The race starts at nine, but if you need a little more time, I can ask Avery to push it to nine fifteen."

"Is that a regulation stopwatch?"

"Yep. I have to record my family's official times. You never know when someone might have a PR." She grinned. "That's a personal record, for your information. Avery, Dree, and Ollie ran track and cross-country in high school."

Of course they did. He was so screwed.

Outside, the brisk morning air made him shiver. He rubbed his hands along his bare arms. Sunlight glistened over Lake Michigan, where a few hearty kayakers were already out on the water. Despite the gorgeous day, he couldn't shake his feeling of impending doom. It worsened as they approached the parking lot beside the lodge, where a row of orange cones delineated the starting line. April's entire family was there, warming up. Two tall, blond guys stretched next to Avery and Drianna.

Presumably they were Hunter and Ian—the two sisters' husbands.

April waved to her family, but Brody tugged on her arm before they got any closer. "Wait. Stop."

"Are you okay? What's wrong?"

His stomach twisted with guilt. He lowered his voice. "I'm going to lose. I thought I could get back into running, but yesterday was the first time I've run in three months. I'm stiff as hell and operating on minimal sleep."

"You're doing great. My family totally bought your act last night."

"Thanks. But they won't buy it today if I can't finish the race."

She bit her lip. "Let me think a minute."

April's dad and her brother sprinted back and forth across the parking lot, amped up and ready to race. Brody's stomach churned.

Kill me now.

Avery motioned to the group. "Bring it in, fam. I want us to start at nine on the dot."

April ignored her sister and kept her voice low. "Okay, Brody. I want you to lean on me and follow my lead."

"If you say so." What was he getting himself into?

As they got within hearing distance of April's family, she stopped and turned toward him. Speaking loudly enough that the others could hear, she cradled his face in her hands, her fingers soft on his skin. "Aww, honey, you don't look so good. You really overdid it last night."

Understood. He groaned in displeasure. "You're the one who insisted on finishing that bottle of wine. I shouldn't have listened to you."

"But it was worth it, wasn't it, sweetheart?" She leaned in until her face was inches from his. So close he could make out the flecks of green in her hazel eyes. And then she kissed him. A gentle kiss, her lips warm and soft on his, but the sensation sent a jolt of electricity right through him. Before he could kiss her back, she pulled away, then looked around, wide-eyed, as though suddenly aware her family was watching.

He stood there in shock, still reeling from her kiss.

Ollie laughed. "Get a room, you two."

April flushed. "We already did. Sorry. Chris isn't in great shape to run. This place is so romantic we went overboard last night and had too much to drink."

Avery leaned into a runner's stretch. "Hunter and I went to the bar after dinner. We didn't see you there."

"We...umm...bought some wine at one of the country markets on the drive here. For nightcap purposes. Anyway..." April dragged out the word, twisting her hands together. "It was a lot. We won't do *that* again."

"At least someone had fun last night," one of the husbands said. From the scowl Drianna gave him, Brody assumed it was her husband, Ian.

"Seriously, Ian?" she said, coming out of a hamstring stretch. "The night before a race isn't the time to party."

"Nor is any night, apparently," Ian muttered.

Whoa. Something going on there. No wonder Drianna was so grouchy.

"Should we postpone the race until Chris is better?" April asked.

What was she doing? Brody's stomach lurched again, until he saw her family's reaction. They weren't the type of competitors who would ever postpone anything.

"Sorry, honey," Mrs. Beckett said. "We have too much going on this week. And we're all fired up and ready to go."

April stroked Brody's cheek. "Do you want to race? Or would you rather sit this one out?"

He appreciated her giving him an excuse, but he had to try. The real Chris would never miss a race. "I'll run. I just won't be at my best."

She sighed. "Not like the Scripps Ranch 10K. You set a new PR there."

Drianna advanced toward him, like a tiger stalking its prey. "What was your time?"

He scrambled to come up with an answer, but April rescued him. "Thirty-eight minutes, twenty seconds. I was at the finish line, cheering him on."

"Nice work, dude," Ollie said. "Just over six-minute miles."

Brody gave a rueful shake of his head. "Thanks, but I wasn't hungover then. Or sleep-deprived."

April put up her hands in surrender. "My bad. It won't happen again."

Mr. Beckett came over to them and clapped Brody on the shoulder. Hard. "We're just glad you're here with us. Take it as slow as you need to."

Ollie laughed. "That's what she said." Which earned him a frown from his parents but made April giggle.

Damn, if April wasn't playing the oversexed girlfriend to the hilt. And enjoying it. Did it mean she secretly wished they'd gotten drunk and had wild, passionate sex? He'd give anything for a peek into her inner thoughts.

"T minus two minutes," Mrs. Beckett called out. "Chris, you sure you don't want to warm up a little?"

At this point, it wouldn't matter. He was going to tank. But thanks to April, he could blame it on the booze. And the sex. He couldn't forget about the sex.

"Chris?" April's voice shocked him back to reality. "You ready to start in two minutes?"

"Sure." Now was *not* the time to daydream about April.

"April, do you have everything you need?" her dad asked.

She held up the stopwatch. "Yep. And I'll be recording your times, like always." She glanced around the parking lot. "Where's Mags?"

"She's at the 5K mark," Ollie said. "She'll make sure everyone turns around when they're supposed to. She's not a distance runner, but she can whip anyone's butt on the soccer field. Her team went to State during her last two years of high school."

What was it with this family? The Blackwoods were in decent shape, especially his brother Marc, but none of them had ever competed in *anything* at the State level. Too bad drinking wasn't a competitive sport.

"Sixty seconds," Avery said. "Line up behind the cones. We're going to take Pine Drive leading out of the resort, until we get to West Cana Island Road. It's a county road, so we'll have to run single file, against traffic. Keep heading south until you reach the Bues Point Boat Ramp at Moonlight Bay, where Mags will be waiting, then you'll turn around and come back. Got it?"

Not at all.

And since Brody was sure to fall behind, he'd probably get lost.

CHAPTER 11

"On your mark, get set, go!" April hit the stopwatch and stepped back as her entire family, plus Hunter, Ian, and Brody, left the starting line. Within minutes, Brody fell behind, trailing Drianna's husband, Ian, who was more of a golfer than a runner.

April wished she could have spared Brody the indignity of racing against her family. At least her ruse had given him an excuse to do poorly. She hoped he wasn't annoyed she'd kissed him. Her impulsive act might have been a tad excessive, but she needed to convince her family they were lovers.

Plus, she'd enjoyed it. A lot.

Since she had a good half hour before the runners returned, she ambled back to her cottage to make another cup of coffee. Her first cup hadn't given her the caffeine boost she needed after such a restless night. She took it outside and drank it while sitting on the porch.

Overhead, the sky was a brilliant, cloudless blue. She closed her eyes and tilted her head, soaking up the sun and inhaling the crisp pinewoods smell. Once the race was over and Brody had recovered, they could take advantage of the gorgeous fall day.

After finishing her coffee, she headed back to the main parking lot, stopwatch at the ready. Drianna arrived first. When she saw she'd beaten the others, she raised her fist in the air. "Yes! Avery owes me twenty bucks." She slowed her stride, pacing the length of the parking lot as she cooled down. "Hate to say it, April, but your man wasn't looking too good out there."

"I figured," April said. "We totally overdid it."

"Did you?" Drianna walked over to her, getting up in her personal space. She wiped her forehead with the back of her hand. "I'm starting to smell a rat."

Shit. If Drianna discovered the truth, she wouldn't keep it a secret. "What…what do you mean?"

"I mean, I don't buy this bull about Chris being an elite runner." Drianna dropped into a deep lunge. "I passed him as I was heading back. His form looked terrible. I'm starting to wonder if you made up his athletic prowess just to impress us."

Thank God. As long as Drianna believed Brody was Chris, nothing else mattered.

"He's a good runner. He was one of the top finishers in the Blackwood Cellars 5K." April brought out her phone and pulled up the website for the race. She passed it to Drianna. "See. He's listed as first in his age group, males ages 20 to 29. Right there. Chris Rockwell."

Drianna pushed the phone away. "You could have hacked into the site and changed it. Aren't website updates a part of your job?"

Before April could object, Ollie came barreling toward the finish line, followed by Avery's husband, Hunter. Avery and her parents were close behind. Ian arrived three minutes later. Brody was nowhere to be seen.

As the Becketts went through the motions of cooling down and stretching, April noted their times on the log sheet attached to her clipboard. Later on, she'd add their stats to the Team

Beckett website. She'd created the site last Christmas as a gift to her family, and she updated it after every race. The site allowed them to share their victories and boast about their times.

"Who came in first?" Avery asked.

Drianna laughed. "Me. I told you I'd kick your ass."

"Chris was looking rough," Ollie said. "I'm not sure when he'll be back."

A blue Subaru pulled up and parked next to the line of cones. Mags emerged from it, wearing a Green Bay Packers hoodie. She opened the back hatch. "Water bottles for everyone. Plus Clif bars and bananas. I also brought towels, since you're a sweaty bunch."

"Thanks, Magdalena," said April's mom. "Much appreciated."

She shrugged. "No big deal. When Ollie and I packed up my car to bring our wedding stuff here, I tossed in supplies for the race."

As the others crowded around the car, grabbing water bottles and Clif bars, Mags motioned for April to follow her. Once they were out of earshot, she lowered her voice.

"This stays between us, but I waited 'til everyone got to the turnaround point before I headed back. Chris was a good ten minutes behind the others. I know how intense your family is, so I gave him a ride partway."

April let out a sigh of relief. "Thanks. I appreciate it."

Mags grinned. "No problem. Glad I could help."

Five minutes later, Brody appeared, breathing heavily, his shirt soaked with sweat. His time was fifty-three minutes, which wasn't anything to brag about, but it would have been worse if he hadn't gotten a ride.

"You made it," she squealed.

Brody nodded, too winded to speak. He grabbed a towel and began pacing the parking lot. Playing up the part of a devoted girlfriend, April brought him a water bottle. She would have kissed him again, just to prove how close they were, but he was too sweaty.

Once everyone had cooled down, her parents gathered the family together. April read out their times. "I'll get these up on the website once I'm home and have access to my laptop," she said. "Until the next race, Drianna is our new family champion, beating her old PR by a full thirty-five seconds. Yay, Dree!"

Everyone congratulated Drianna except her husband, Ian, who still appeared peevish. Of course, Drianna couldn't resist getting in one more dig at Brody. "Chris, if you want to be a part of this family, you're going to have to step up your game."

"Sorry," Brody said. "Next time, I promise."

AS THEY WALKED BACK to the cottage, Brody could barely stay on his feet. His body ached all over. And since he'd forgone breakfast, he was famished and craving caffeine. He leaned on April for support.

"Not much further," she said. "You can take a hot shower when we get back."

"I might need food. And coffee. Lots of coffee."

"I'm on it. Don't worry. You did great. Thanks for being such a good sport."

Guilt gnawed at him. "Umm…I didn't run the whole race. When I got to the turnaround point, I was so far behind that Mags took pity on me. She drove me part of the way back. So, I only ran about three-fourths of it."

April unlocked the cottage door. "She told me in confidence. It's fine. Although…"

He stumbled inside. "What?"

"Drianna was suspicious. She still thinks you're Chris, but she doesn't believe you're a serious runner."

He wasn't surprised. His performance had been abysmal. He

pulled a set of clean clothes out of his bag. "Is that okay? When you read out your family's times, I realized I could never keep up. Not like the real Chris could."

"Don't worry about it. I showed Drianna the race results from the Blackwood Cellars 5K, where you're listed as first in your age group. Then she accused me of hacking into the site. Like I'm this experienced hacker?" She laughed. "She's such a pain in the ass. If she doesn't let it go, I'll pull up Chris's times from a few other races. I'm pretty sure the Scripps Ranch 10K still has the results on their website."

"Okay. Good." Because no way in hell could he compete at the Beckett family level. He didn't want to either. At the moment, he was on the verge of throwing up or passing out. He went into the bathroom and locked the door.

As he was turning on the water, April's voice rang out. "Okay if we skip the golf outing? Everyone's going to Peninsula State Park Golf Course, but I'd rather not. We could use the time to check out some local wineries."

"Sounds good." Spending the afternoon touring wineries with April appealed to him far more than spending three hours on a golf course.

After a lengthy shower, he felt a little more human, especially when he caught a whiff of fresh-brewed coffee. April sat outside on the porch of the cottage, mug in hand. He went out to join her and eased himself into a sitting position.

She handed him a mug. "Brewed it in the Keurig, so it won't be as strong as your french press, but it's a start. And here." She pushed a Tupperware container toward him. "Blueberry streusel muffins."

"Are they homemade?"

"Yep. Last time I made a batch, I put half in the freezer to save for later. I brought some along, just in case."

Was there anyone more considerate than April? Coffee *and*

homemade baked goods. His personal kryptonite. "Thanks. You're awesome."

"It's the least I can do. Sorry about that stupid race."

"I'm fine now. Besides, we apparently had amazing sex last night, so it was totally worth it."

She blushed, then looked away. "That was a bit much, wasn't it?"

Not at all. The kiss was great. Except I wanted more.

Not that he'd tell her because the kiss had been part of the act. Still, he couldn't resist teasing her. "You were loving every minute of it. You have a naughty imagination, Beckett."

"It's all those steamy romances I read. A girl's got to have fantasies, right?"

"Absolutely." If they were anything like *his* fantasies, he'd welcome them.

A cheeky-looking squirrel jumped up on the porch, but April hissed at the pesky critter, scaring it away. "Not a chance, Squirrel Nutkin. These muffins aren't for you." She turned to Brody. "So...listen. If you're exhausted, no big deal, but—"

"I'll be okay, as long as we don't do anything too physical."

Except sex. If April so much as hinted that she wanted to make use of that giant bed, he'd be up for it.

What is wrong with you? His delusions had to stop.

"I did a quick search, and there's a wine-tasting tour run by a company called Door County Trolley," she said. "The trolley stops at three local wineries, and lunch is included. Badger Hollow Winery isn't a part of the tour, but we could visit it afterward. The only catch is that the tour leaves in thirty minutes."

Brody devoured his muffin in a few quick bites and reached for another. "You sure your family won't mind if you miss out on golf?"

"Nope. I'd just slow them down. As long as we join in tonight's activities, we'll be good."

He was craving a nap more than anything else. But if he got in the winery visits, he'd be able to justify his trip as somewhat work related. Plus, he liked the idea of spending most of the day with April. What with last night's dinner and this morning's race, he needed a break from her family.

"Perfect. Let's do it."

CHAPTER 12

The Door County Trolley tour exceeded April's expectations. She and Brody visited three local wineries and feasted on a hearty lunch at a farm-to-table bistro. Though Brody was dragging at first, he perked up at the Simon Creek Winery and barraged the tasting room host with a slew of questions. As promised, April took notes and photos at each winery. This way, Brody would have evidence if he needed to prove his trip was partially work related. Any awkwardness over the 10K, the shared bed, or the pre-race kiss vanished as they eased back into their comfortable friendship.

When the trolley tour ended, they took a ride-share to Badger Hollow Winery for their final tasting. Feeling sleepy and full, April would have preferred to return to the cottage for an afternoon nap, but Brody had gained a second wind.

"We don't have to spend long here, but I want to check it out," he said. "From the research I did, it's one of the best-known wineries in the area."

April's phone pinged while they were in the Lyft. Avery had sent her a text. *Done golfing and hiking. Ready for wine. Where are you & Chris at?*

As much as April wanted Brody all to herself, if she blew off her sister, Avery would give her a hard time about it later. After all, this was supposed to be a *family* vacation. She texted back. *Badger Hollow Winery in Baileys Harbor. Come join us if you want.*

She nudged Brody, who was scrolling through his phone. "Avery might be joining us. Not sure who else. Is that okay?"

"As long as I don't have to do anything competitive."

"Speaking of competitive, I should warn you about tonight," she said. "Mags is taking us to some kitschy bar for their trivia night."

She braced herself, expecting him to react with reluctance, but he grinned. "Bring it."

"What? Really? You haven't been to a bar in months."

"True, but I love trivia." He paused. "Unless it's sports trivia. Then I suck."

"Not sure what kind of trivia. But, as you've guessed, my family is incredibly cutthroat in all aspects of life."

"No problem. We can handle it."

Even if he was acting too cocky, she loved it. Loved that he was going along with everything, being a good sport, and having fun. He was the best date ever. Why hadn't she been able to find anyone like him during her numerous attempts at dating?

Because you've been fixated on him for two years. No one else comes close.

The Lyft dropped them off at the lot for Badger Hollow, which was situated off a quiet country road. Outside the winery, the patio was packed with groups enjoying the perfect fall day. April sought out a free table, but none were available. As she followed Brody into the tasting room, she shivered involuntarily. Compared to the sunny patio, the room had the ambience of a cool, dark cave. It was nearly empty, save for a group of older women, all sporting lavender hats adorned with rosettes and feathers. At the far end of the room, a curved bar made of russet-colored marble held an artsy arrangement of wine bottles, displayed against the backdrop of an exposed stone wall.

Upon approaching the bar, April stopped short. The hostess could have been Taylor's sister. Or her clone. Tall, slender, and drop-dead gorgeous, the woman shared Taylor's best features—high cheekbones, huge, dark eyes, and a glossy curtain of thick, caramel-blond hair.

Did Brody notice the resemblance? On the chance he didn't, April wasn't going to say anything.

Or maybe he did, because he appeared tongue-tied, even after the hostess asked them which wine-tasting package they wanted.

April handed the woman her credit card. "We'll do the Signature Series for Two."

"Certainly." The woman's voice was low and sultry, like Taylor's. "I'm Cecile, and I'll be guiding you through the tasting. Here's the menu for today. This brochure has information on our wine club."

"Great, thanks." April kept the brochure. She enjoyed comparing other wine clubs with the one offered by Blackwood Cellars. She nudged Brody, who stood transfixed. "What do you want to start with? Red or white?"

"Huh?" He snapped out of his addled state. "Sorry. My mind was somewhere else." He smiled at Cecile. "Why don't you start us off with the pinot noir?"

By their third sample, Brody was into his stride. Any trace of the awkward, introverted friend she'd witnessed over the past few months had vanished. Instead, he reverted to his old self as he laughed at Cecile's jokes and tried to impress her with his knowledge of wine. Bantering with her as if he'd known her for years instead of minutes. Up until Maui, it had been his default setting among beautiful women.

In the past, April had teased him about it. But as she tried to capture his attention, her discomfort grew. Didn't he realize how much he was shutting her out?

He's not doing it on purpose. He's just oblivious.

That didn't make his actions hurt any less. She tugged on his arm, but he scarcely noticed. Tears welled up in her eyes, and she blinked them away, feeling foolish. She'd wanted him to regain his old confidence, but now that he'd gotten it back, she wasn't sure she liked it.

She took a few steps back, only to catch sight of Avery and Drianna breezing through the door. Her heart sank when she saw they'd come alone. She was hoping Ollie and Mags might be with them to act as buffers.

She forced a smile as her sisters approached the bar. "Hey, guys. Glad you could join us. Anyone else coming?"

"Nah," Drianna said. "The guys went to a local brewery instead."

"Mom and Dad went back to the resort to rest up," Avery added. "We figured since you know so much about wine, you could tell us what's good and what's crap."

"It's all good." Even if April didn't like some wines as much as others, she'd never disparage them in front of the hostess. "Depends on what kind of wine you like."

"Chris, what do you recommend?" Drianna asked Brody.

Brody appeared not to hear as he chuckled over a shared joke with Cecile. April placed her hand on his shoulder. "Chris?"

He turned, startled by the interruption. "Sorry. What was the question?"

"My sisters want wine recommendations."

He pointed to the hostess. "Cecile can help them. She's the expert."

In response, Cecile gave a throaty laugh, like she'd fallen for Brody's charms. To be honest, it was a bit much.

A *lot* much.

Drianna grabbed April's arm. "We need to talk."

"Why? Don't you want to try some wine?"

Drianna gave Cecile a sickly sweet grin. "We'll be right back.

Excuse us." She dragged April over to a corner of the tasting room, near the cluster of elderly women. The one closest to them wore a name tag embellished with purple curlicues, marking her as *Lavender Lady: Iris*.

Weird. Maybe it was a Door County thing.

April tried to control the exasperation in her voice as she addressed her sister. "What's the problem?"

"Are you telling me you're okay with this?" Drianna's voice was strained with anger. "With Chris hitting on that hostess, even though you're right here?"

Trust Drianna to find her weakest spot and dig the knife in deep. "He's just being friendly."

Even to her own ears, she sounded weak. Pathetic.

"It's not cool," Drianna said. "Your man is all but drooling over her."

"I hate to admit it, but Dree's right," Avery said. "Look at his body language. He's into her."

April dug her nails into her palms. For all she knew, Brody was just excited to be out in public again, trying to win a woman over. "I'm sure it doesn't mean anything."

"No? I realize you have zero self-esteem, but he shouldn't treat you this way," Drianna said. "It's rude and thoughtless."

"Does he always act like this around other women?" Avery asked.

"No...well, sometimes." But it had never mattered before because they were friends. Not lovers. But now, the lines seemed weirdly blurred. They'd shared a bed. She'd kissed him. And—most importantly—they were pretending to be a couple.

"Are you and Chris exclusive?" Drianna spat out. "If you are, then he shouldn't be swapping phone numbers with some chick he just met."

Her voice was so loud that Lavender Lady Iris glowered at them. April moved a few steps away. She found it hard to believe that Drianna—her harshest critic—was standing up for her. She bit her lip. "I...I don't think he'd do that."

"No? Then why does he have his phone out?" Drianna demanded. When Iris clucked her tongue, Drianna bared her teeth. "What? You have a problem, *Granny?*"

Iris backed away.

In all probability, Brody was showing Cecile the Blackwood Cellars app. He loved flaunting it to other people in the industry. But what if he wasn't? What if he was getting her number and planning to hook up with her later? Maybe he thought April wouldn't care. If he was gone for the night, he'd be giving her the bed to herself, thus avoiding more awkwardness.

But she did care. Even if Brody didn't want her, the thought of him and Cecile having wild, passionate sex stabbed her like a spear through the heart.

"April, are you okay?" Avery glared at Drianna. "I think you went overboard."

"Like hell. If Chris is a cheating bastard, better she finds out now than after she makes the mistake of marrying him."

The bitterness in Drianna's tone took April by surprise. "Dree? Is everything okay with you and Ian?"

"This isn't about me. It's about you. Stop being a mouse and stand up for yourself."

April's face heated in embarrassment, which quickly turned to anger. Partly at Drianna for stirring up shit, but mostly at Brody for thinking it wouldn't matter if he flirted right in front of her. This morning, she'd done her best to act like they were a loving, passionate couple, and now he was blowing it by trying to impress a stranger.

She strode over to the bar and grabbed Brody's arm. "Finish your drink. We need to go."

CHAPTER 13

Something was up. One minute, Brody had been enjoying himself, sampling vintages and chatting with Cecile. The next, April barreled up to him, red-faced and furious, and told him they had to leave.

"But we're not done yet," he said. "We have two wines left."

"I have a terrible headache. I'm calling a Lyft. You can stay if you want, but I'm going back to the resort."

He glanced over at April's sisters, who gave him the stink eye. Whatever they'd said to her couldn't be good. Maybe they'd confronted her about his miserable failure in the 10K. He set down his wineglass and offered Cecile an apologetic smile. "Sorry. We need to take off. But thanks for everything. You were very helpful."

"My pleasure," she crooned. "Come back anytime, Brody."

Shit. Was that why April was upset? Had her sisters heard Cecile call him Brody? He'd used his real name, because he'd given her his business card on the chance Badger Hollow might be interested in partnering with Blackwood Cellars at some point in the future. But he'd feel terrible if he'd blown his cover.

"What about your sisters?" he asked. "They just got here."

"They'll be fine," April said. "Don't worry about them."

"Wouldn't you rather wait in here until our ride shows up?"

"I'm going outside. Do whatever you want."

She strode out of the tasting room at a fast clip, only stopping when she reached the entrance of the parking lot. Brody approached her like he would a wild dog, speaking softly and holding up his hands. "I'm not sure what's going on, but if I blew it, I'm sorry. I didn't mean to use my real name. But when I was talking with Cecile—"

"Talking or flirting?"

The harsh tone in her voice made him step back a few paces. "A little of both? But I don't think your sisters heard Cecile call me Brody, so you don't have to worry."

She looked away, arms crossed, then blew out her breath in exasperation. "That's not the issue. What made you think it was okay to hit on Cecile while I was in the same room?"

Why was she so upset? Hadn't she been urging him to "get back out there"? To stop obsessing over Taylor and move on? Besides, he hadn't been hitting on Cecile. Even if he'd enjoyed talking to her, he hadn't intended for things to go any further. Not when he was with April.

"I was just having fun, talking wine with a fellow aficionado," he said. "Don't you think it's interesting that Badger Hollow gets all their grapes from California? I can't believe they work with one of our vineyards in Napa. I was telling her she needs to come visit for herself."

"Is that why you exchanged phone numbers with her?"

He stared at her in disbelief, barely able to process her question. "What are you talking about?"

"My sisters saw you show her your phone."

With every passing minute, her sisters were getting harder to take. "I was showing her our wine app. The one *you* helped create. Why would I be getting her phone number?"

April's voice wobbled. "Then...you wouldn't have to share a

bed with me. Instead of pretending to have wild, passionate sex, you could actually be doing it."

His pulse sped up as he met her gaze head-on. But at the sight of tears welling up in her eyes, his fury drained away. He spoke softly. "Even if I was into one-night stands—which I'm not—I wouldn't do it here. Not while I'm pretending to be your date. Do you honestly think I'd treat you that way?"

"I don't know. But you sure seemed into her. And she looked a lot like Taylor." April wiped her eyes. "My sisters felt sorry for me, and that literally never happens."

He tried to stay calm, even as his frustration came roaring back. In the short time they'd been in Door County, April had let her sisters walk all over her. Granted, she wasn't the most assertive person on the planet, but they treated her even worse than Chris did. And that was saying a lot.

When their Lyft arrived, April greeted the driver but stayed silent once they were in the car. The tension between them made the ten-minute ride feel like an hour.

Brody waited until the driver had dropped them off at the lodge's main parking lot before he spoke again. "You might not want to hear this, but I think you only cared about Cecile because your sisters pointed it out."

"That's not true."

He clenched his hands, exasperated by her denial. "Don't you see what's going on? Every chance they get, they cut you down and make you feel inadequate. And now, when you finally bring someone home, they still can't be happy for you. Instead, they manage to convince you—in the space of ten minutes—that I'm planning to cheat on you."

April strode away so fast he had to speed walk to catch up. "This isn't about them. I was feeling shitty before they showed up."

Her words stopped him dead in his tracks. When had she

started feeling shitty? His legs protested as he rushed to follow her. The morning's race had wiped him out. "Slow down. Please."

Instead, she increased her pace, putting more space between them. By the time she reached the cottage, she was gasping for breath. Leaning on the porch railing, she pulled her inhaler out of her purse and took a quick hit. When Brody approached her, she held up her hand, forcing him to take a step back.

He waited until she put away her inhaler. "I don't understand. I thought you wanted me to be social again."

"Social, as in joining the gang for a night out. Not making a pass at some rando."

"You've seen me act this way before. It doesn't mean anything."

"It meant something to me," she said. "You made me feel like I wasn't worthy of your attention."

His head swam with confusion. For all the times he and April had gone to happy hour with the crew from Marketing, she never cared if he flirted with other women. If anything, she joined their friends in teasing him about it.

But you weren't pretending to be her date then, you dumb-ass.

Even if his actions had been unintentional, he'd hurt her. "I'm sorry."

She opened the door to the cottage. "It's okay. But can we take a breather right now? I'd like a little time to myself."

He hated leaving things so unsettled, but he didn't want to push her. "Uh…sure. Go ahead."

As she closed the door behind her, he plopped onto the porch.

Despite his best attempts, he'd screwed up twice today. First, by blowing the race, and now by hurting April.

He wasn't off to a great start.

CHAPTER 14

*B*rody sat on the porch and looked out at the lake, contemplating his next move. He considered going for a walk, but he was flat-out exhausted. Would he appear too pathetic if he curled up where he was and took a nap? Probably. And it wouldn't be a good look if any of the Becketts dropped by. He stood and walked to the main parking lot, where he'd left his rental car. The lack of sleep had given him a pounding headache.

He spent the next half hour trying to nap in his car before giving up. The sun had baked the inside of the vehicle until it was no longer tolerable. At this point, he'd sobered up enough to drive. If nothing else, he could find a shady location, pull over, and try napping again.

As he drove away from the resort, frustration ate at him. When he'd initially offered to come to Door County, he'd made the offer as April's friend. But last night, lying next to her, he'd wanted more. And that kiss before the race? He definitely wanted more of that.

Then why did you flirt with Cecile?

He couldn't deny he'd been attracted to the hostess. After three months of feeling like a loser, his ego had received a huge boost when she'd laughed at his jokes. But the thought of sneaking off with her never crossed his mind. If he wanted anyone, it was April.

But instead of telling her how he felt and opening himself up to rejection, he'd taken the easy way out. He'd focused his efforts on charming a woman he barely knew, using her approval to boost his self-esteem.

It always came down to that, didn't it? His fucking self-esteem.

Up until his freshman year of college, he'd been a short, scrawny geek. Nothing like his brother Marc, who'd been athletic and popular all through high school, never lacking for girlfriends. Brody, on the other hand, hadn't started dating until college.

He'd only turned a corner during his sophomore year, when he had a late growth spurt and started working out. Even if he wasn't tall and jacked, he'd learned how to wield his charm to capture a woman's attention. The more attractive the woman, the better he felt about himself. He wasn't proud of that fact, but it was the main reason he stuck with Taylor, even though she never treated him decently.

Losing her to someone else had demolished his self-esteem. But if he wanted to build it back up, hitting on a stranger wasn't the way to go. Not when April—the woman who'd supported him through *everything*—was by his side.

He drove along the same route he'd run during the 10K until he came to a dead end. When he pulled out his phone to check his location, the map refused to load. Not surprising, considering his phone had one measly bar. He backed up and tried to retrace his path, only to find himself on a different country road, this one running alongside Lake Michigan.

He pulled over beside an empty stretch of beach and got out of the car. For all he knew, he could have been trespassing, though there were no signs anywhere. He ventured onto the sandy beach—a slim crescent of land dotted by large white rocks —and gazed out at the water. The steady crash of the waves and the unending horizon made the lake feel more like an ocean.

As he walked down to the water, he mulled over his options. Above all, he needed to apologize to April. But what else?

He needed to talk to someone. Not anyone from work since he wanted to keep Operation Fake-Chris a secret. And not Marc, who would never understand the self-esteem issue. Not only was he the perfect older brother, but his wife, Gabi, was equally perfect. Together, they made a serious power couple.

But Gabi's younger sister, Jess—whom Brody had known since childhood—wasn't perfect. Far from it. When they were kids, he'd admired her willingness to take risks, even if her bravado often landed her in trouble. She hadn't fared much better as an adult. Last winter, she'd lost her job, her boyfriend, and her apartment. But she'd bounced back this fall, with a new job and a solid relationship with his cousin, Connor.

He brought up her number. "Jess?"

She answered right away. "Brody! Hey, bud. How's Wisconsin?"

"It's great. Really beautiful. The leaves are stunning." He took a minute to appreciate the clear blue sky, the brilliant red and gold foliage, and the sun glistening off the lake.

"I'm jealous. When I lived in Chicago, I loved having a real fall. It's too hot in Temecula. The Santa Ana winds have been brutal."

"What time is it there? Do you have a minute to talk?" He crouched down on the sandy shore to take off his shoes and socks. As he waded out into the lake, the icy water took his breath away. But the stinging pain jolted him out of his earlier lethargy.

"It's two here in California. I'm out doing some property management errands for my boss, but I can talk while I'm on the road."

"When do you start your new job?" He'd recently used his connections in the wine industry to help her secure a position with the Temecula Valley Wine Growers' Association.

"A little over a week. I can't wait. But that's not why you called, is it? What's up?"

"Did I tell you why I was in Wisconsin?"

"You didn't give me the full story, but—" She swore. "*Son of a bitch*. Don't cut me off, you dickhead!" A moment passed, and then her voice resumed its normal tone "Sorry. I'm dealing with the usual idiots on the road."

"You sure you can talk and drive?" There were times when Jess was truly a wreck waiting to happen.

"Absolutely. Give me the full scoop. Is this trip *actually* about checking out wineries? I thought the Blackwood Cellars' expansion was Marc's responsibility, not yours. Unless you're planning on joining him in Napa."

He rolled up his jeans and walked further into the water. He hadn't adjusted to the cold, but he liked the feel of the pebbles under his toes. "You heard about Napa?"

"From Gabi. She's my source for Blackwood gossip. Not gonna lie—I'll be pissed if you leave Temecula."

"You don't need me. You have Connor now."

"Don't be such a tool. Of course I need you. Friends like you aren't easy to find. And I don't want you turning into a corporate drone. Marc might treat my sister like a queen, but the guy never shuts up about marketing synergy or 'thinking outside the box.'"

Brody found it interesting that her response was similar to April's. "I haven't decided yet. But when I talked to April about it, she felt the same way you did."

"You're with her, right? What's that about?"

He could have lied to Jess, but she'd always been able to see through his bullshit. Overhead, a flock of geese flew by. After their raucous calls had ceased, he told her everything.

When he was done, she laughed. "I can't believe this. For

weeks, I've been begging you to hang out, and you always come up with an excuse. Because, apparently, you *like* being a hermit. And now you're at a destination wedding for six days?"

"I'm fully aware of the irony. Sorry I've been a crappy friend. It wasn't about you."

"I get it. But are you telling me you're pretending to be Chris for an entire week? That's a hell of a con. And it's so risky. If you get caught, it won't be pretty."

He didn't want to imagine the fallout. But if April told the truth now, she'd take so much heat. Her sisters would be merciless.

"Where's April right now?" Jess asked.

"We...umm...we had a fight. We were at a winery, having a great time, but I kind of went overboard, flirting with the tasting room hostess, and I hurt April's feelings. And then her sisters made things worse, because they convinced her I was planning to sneak out tonight and hook up with the hostess."

"Clearly, they don't know you very well. I could see Connor doing that before he got his shit together. But you—never."

"Thank you for that vote of confidence." He stubbed his toe on a rock and cursed. Hobbling out of the water, he plunked down on the shore, nursing his aching toe. And then realized he had no way to dry off his feet.

"Although..." Her voice trailed off.

"What?" He tried drying his feet on the legs of his jeans. It didn't help.

"Don't take this the wrong way, but you can be a huge flirt, especially when you use your full charm offensive."

He cringed. If Jess was calling him out on his behavior, it was worse than he thought. "My full charm offensive?"

"Yeah. Sometimes you lay it on thick, so I can see why April might be jealous. Plus, you're a real catch." She laughed. "I'm immune because I've been in love with Connor since I was twelve, but...you can be a total charmer when you want to be."

Her words boosted his ego momentarily, until he thought about April. Even if her sisters had provoked her, he was the one who'd done the most damage. "I screwed up, didn't I? It didn't help that the hostess looked like Taylor."

Jess cursed again and honked her horn. "If you want to go fifty, then get in the slow lane, Grandpa!" She let out a breath. "Sorry about that. But you've got to get over Taylor. She treated you like shit."

"I'm starting to realize that. April's nothing like her."

"Sounds to me like you're falling for April."

He struggled to pull his socks over his still-damp feet. "We're just friends. I'm here to offer her support."

"Bullshit. You don't fly all the way to Wisconsin and spend a week with someone in a romantic cottage unless you're into them."

"It doesn't matter how I feel about her. I'm not taking that risk again." He put his sneakers back on. "Whenever I put myself out there, I get my heart broken."

"Because you fall for the wrong women. You put them on a pedestal and treat them like goddesses instead of friends. That's why April's so perfect. She's your friend, not some woman you're trying to impress."

He let out a groan. "But she's not into *me*. I'm filling in for Chris, who's an elite athlete, of all things."

"Again, I call bullshit. If April wasn't into you, she wouldn't have gotten so jealous. For a computer genius, you can be a complete idiot."

If anyone else had talked to him this way, he might have hung up. But he appreciated Jess's candor. He'd been equally honest with her when she'd gotten back together with his cousin, Connor.

"Don't end up like me," Jess said. "I had a great thing going with Connor in Maui, and I messed it up because I wasn't honest with him. Thank God I smartened up. Now that we're back together, it's better than ever."

"Really?" Her words filled him with a surge of hope. Both she and Connor had once been world-class screwups. If they could find happiness with each other, then he shouldn't be so quick to dismiss the power of romance.

"Hell, yeah. We've spent the last two weekends at his place, barely leaving his bed. It's like bone central over there." She snort-laughed. "Sorry. That was so crude."

"TMI, Jess. But thanks for the pep talk."

Another horn blared in his ears, and then Jess came back on the line. "I've gotta go. This jerk's riding my tail. If you need me, text me later. In the meantime, go back to that romantic cottage and apologize to April."

Precisely what he was going to do.

CHAPTER 15

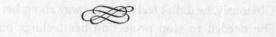

*a*pril sat on the porch of the cottage, sipping a glass of sparkling cherry juice. When she and Brody had made their purchases at the country market, she'd added it to their basket on a whim. Now she was grateful they'd bought something nonalcoholic. After all the wine she'd consumed during the trolley tour, booze was the last thing she needed. Especially since she was dehydrated from a lengthy crying jag in which she recalled every harsh word she'd flung at Brody.

How could she have treated him that way?

Here he was, trying to build up his self-esteem, and she'd laid into him. Granted, he should have toned down the flirting when they were at the winery. But all she had to do was wait until they left, take him aside, and ask him to mind her feelings. Then they could have moved on. Instead, she blew up and accused him of trying to sneak away for a one-night stand with a random woman. A ridiculous accusation. Even Chris, for all his faults, wouldn't have done something that cruel.

She wanted to blame her reaction on her sisters, who'd goaded her into confronting Brody. But it was more than that. She'd been jealous, which wasn't the norm for her. She might have resented the time Brody spent with Taylor, but only because the woman was so manipulative. Up until now, she'd never experienced the sharp pangs of jealousy she felt at the winery.

So much for not crushing on Brody. Now you're in deeper than you were before.

Obviously, he didn't feel the same way about her.

She needed to stop projecting her feelings onto him. He'd always been an affectionate friend, quick to dole out a hug when she needed it. But, right now, any PDA on his part should be attributed to his role as Chris.

A squirrel hopped up on the porch and inched toward her, but she didn't have the heart to shoo it away. As she was watching it poke around, the crunch of leaves caught her attention. Brody ambled up the path and waved at her. "Hey, April." His voice was low, tinged with sadness.

Her heart swelled at the sight of him. She resisted the impulse to rush to his side and smooth down his unruly brown hair. Instead, she held up her glass. "Hey, yourself. Want some cherry spumante?"

"No, thanks. I had enough booze earlier."

"It's nonalcoholic, remember? Tastes like sparkling apple juice, but sweeter."

He shook his head and sat beside her on the porch, close enough that she caught the scent of lake water. The bottoms of his jeans were damp as well.

Her curiosity got the better of her. "Where were you?"

"Over at the lake. Out walking. Or wading, I guess. I needed to clear my head."

Guilt ate at her. When she'd asked for some alone time, she hadn't considered his situation. He'd been stranded outside with nowhere to go. "Sorry. I didn't mean to be so selfish. There's still time for a nap if you want one."

"I'm okay for now." He placed his hand on her thigh. "But I'm sorry, too. There's no excuse for my behavior. I acted like a jerk, but I never meant to hurt you."

"I know. And I didn't mean to flip out. But it was hard watching you flirt with someone like Taylor, knowing you'd go back to her in an instant."

He frowned. "This wasn't about Taylor. It was me showing off. Flattered by Cecile's interest. But it was a dick move."

It was. But at least he wasn't trying to justify it.

"I get it," she said. "When Chris asked me out, I was amazed he noticed me, considering how gorgeous his last girlfriend was." She cringed as she remembered all the nights he dropped by, wanting a quickie, and she'd obliged without asking for anything more. She'd settled for so little.

"Are we the worst pair of losers or what?" A ghost of a smile crossed his lips. "Pour me some of that cherry bubbly, will you?"

She went into the cottage and brought back the bottle, along with another glass. As they sat together on the porch, the tension eased from her shoulders. But she couldn't shake the comment Brody had made about her sisters. His words hit close to home, bringing back painful memories. She placed her hand on his knee, letting it linger there.

"You were right about my sisters. I let them influence me more than I should."

He clasped his hand over hers. "I shouldn't have said that. Considering I met them yesterday, I don't have the right to judge."

She forced herself to meet his eyes, seeing only sympathy and compassion in their gray depths. "Whether you do or not, you totally called it. Ever since I was little, I've been trying to win their approval. Especially Drianna."

"Why her?"

"She always seemed so cool, and she didn't take shit from anyone. Whereas I was always labeled 'the sensitive one' because I cried so easily. I didn't want her to think I was just a geeky loser, when in reality that's who I was. Still am, in her eyes. There was this one time in high school…" She stopped as the memory overwhelmed her, filling her with a combination of shame and regret.

Brody tightened his grip. "You don't have to tell me if you don't want."

"No. I do. It might help you understand what I'm dealing with. It's just…I'm not proud of what I did." She drained the rest of her drink, then set the glass down on the porch. "I didn't date much in high school. But in my junior year, I had a huge crush on my chem partner—Tim—and he acted like he was into me. I made the mistake of inviting him over to work on our lab notes, and Drianna was there. After he left, she made fun of him, because he was into science fiction and on the Mathletes team."

Brody's mouth quirked up in a smile. "Hey, I was a Mathlete, too."

"I'm not surprised. For the next few weeks, Drianna wouldn't let up. So, when Tim asked me out, I turned him down, even though he was exactly the kind of boyfriend I wanted. Because I couldn't deal with Drianna's judgment. Which is so cowardly." A wave of regret washed over her. She'd spent a lot of nights alone in her room, regretting her decision.

"I'm sorry. That sucks."

"I know. I wish I'd told her to shut up and leave me alone. But that whole incident…that's kind of why I wanted Chris to come to this wedding. Not because I thought he was 'the one' or because he was the ideal boyfriend. But because he's the kind of guy Drianna and Avery would approve of. He's hot, athletic, and totally driven. I thought if Drianna saw I'd landed a guy like him —for real—she'd be impressed."

She stopped abruptly, realizing how insulting her words sounded. "Not that you aren't impressive in your own right."

Brody looked away. "I get it. I'm no Chris."

Shit. She'd made a mess of things. Before she could fix the damage she'd done to Brody's ego, the sound of footsteps stopped her cold. Her shoulders tightened, out of fear her sisters had decided to check up on her. Now that she and Brody had reconciled, she didn't need Drianna coming by to cause problems. To her relief, Ollie strolled along the lakeside trail, headed toward their cottage.

April waved at him. "Hey, bro."

Ollie approached them. "I'm not interrupting anything, am I?"

"Nope. We're enjoying a glass of cherry spumante," she said. "Want some?"

"I'm good," Ollie said. "But I came to ask you a favor. Will you partner up with us for trivia night?"

"You want me on your team?" No one ever chose her for anything. In her own family, she was the perpetual last-kid-picked in gym class.

"Yeah. You weren't around the last time we did one of these, but Avery and Drianna challenged me and Mags, and they kicked our butts. I need payback, especially since the stakes are even higher. Are you in?"

"What kind of stakes are we talking about?" she asked. "I mean, besides bragging rights."

"Whichever team scores the most points pays the other team's bar bill. And it's margarita night."

Though she might work for a winery, margaritas were April's personal catnip. She shot a grin at Brody, who gave her a thumbs-up.

"We're in," she said. "But can we invite Ginger? She texted me earlier and said she needs an escape. Otherwise, she's stuck doing dinner with the parents."

"You bet. We can have up to six teammates. But we need to demolish Drianna's team. She was insufferable the last time she won."

"How unlike her," Brody whispered under his breath.

April gave him a hard nudge. "We'll do our best."

"Great. Okay if we get a ride-share? Then no one has to drive."

"Sounds good to me," she said. Brody agreed.

Once Ollie left, she turned to Brody and punched her fist into her palm. "We *have* to win. I want to grind my sisters into the dirt and make them pay for all my margaritas."

"Whoa. Who's competitive now?"

"They beat me at everything. For once, I'd love to come out on top. And with you on our team, we should kick ass."

Brody held up his hands. "Um...I might have sounded a little *too* confident earlier. I'm not that much of an asset. Unless the categories are movies, computers, or comics."

"Oh. Shit." She blew out a long breath. "We're sunk, aren't we?"

Like he said. A couple of losers.

CHAPTER 16

*A*fter knocking off the rest of the cherry spumante, April took the empty bottle and the glasses back into the cottage. Brody followed her inside. Claiming exhaustion, he crashed out on the bed and fell asleep immediately. With the softest of touches, April smoothed down his messy hair and set his glasses on the nightstand. He looked so sweet and vulnerable her heart went out to him. Yes, he'd screwed up at the winery and hurt her feelings. But he'd also apologized and owned up to his behavior, rather than making excuses.

While he slept, she looked up trivia questions on her phone, scrolling through dozens of examples. But planning ahead was useless. Some categories, like movies and books, were doable. Anything in the sports realm was beyond her abilities.

They left the cottage at six and joined the others in the lodge's main parking lot. From there, they took a couple of ride-shares to the Salty Crow, located in the nearby town of Sister Bay. Outside the pub, the chalkboard listed "Taco Tuesday" specials, which included two-dollar tacos and half-price pitchers of margaritas.

The pub was decorated in a funky pirate theme, with a Jolly

Roger flag hung over the bar, weathered maps on the wall, and skull candleholders at every table. Above them, plastic skeletons, colorful glass floats, and fishing nets hung from the rafters. A rusty cannon occupied one corner of the pub, next to a giant treasure chest. The whole place had a spring-break-in-Florida vibe.

"Okay, troops," Mags said after they filed in. "We're all registered. Our team is Grape Expectations." She beamed at April and Brody. "In honor of you two being wine experts. I'm hoping there's a wine category."

"We're Victorious Secret," Avery said. "Because we're guaranteed a victory." She high-fived Drianna.

Drianna smirked at Mags. "Hope you brought your credit card because we plan to run up a huge tab. I'm ordering top-shelf tequila."

"Have fun with that, seeing as how you're going to end up paying for it," April shot back.

"You're that confident?" Drianna asked. "Maybe we should up the stakes."

April stared down her sister. To be honest, she wasn't that confident, especially since she and Brody were so weak in categories like sports and current events. But she wasn't about to back away from a challenge.

Ollie held up his hands. "Um...the stakes are plenty high already."

"What's wrong, little bro?" Avery said. "Can't handle a Beckett-level challenge?"

"We can handle it," April said. "Tomorrow we're all going to the Door County Creamery, right? To buy Wisconsin cheese? The losers buy *all* the cheese."

Knowing that Brody was a fellow cheese lover, she flashed him a conspiratorial smile, but his uneasy expression unnerved her. Once again, she might be putting a *little* too much pressure on him. But before she could back down, Drianna spoke up.

"You're on," she said. "Tonight's tab *and* tomorrow's cheese-fest. Good luck, losers."

Given the silence that descended on her team, April regretted her bravado. She followed Brody, Ollie, Mags, and Ginger to their table, while Avery, Drianna, and their husbands occupied the one to their right.

Before their group could mull over the pricey stakes they'd agreed to, Mags cheered them up by ordering a pitcher of margaritas and a round of tacos. Though April had already consumed a *lot* of wine during the trolley tour, she couldn't resist a margarita. The icy tequila and sweet lime made her shiver with pleasure. Cold, tart, and delicious, her first drink went down far too easily. But it loosened her up and helped her shake off her insecurity.

Ginger took a carne asada taco from the platter. "Thanks for letting me crash the party. It got me out of a painful dinner with the folks, enduring another lecture about my questionable life choices."

"Your hair?" Mags said. "I think it looks fabulous."

"Nah. They've gotten over the hair." Ginger poured herself a margarita. "Mom hates that I'm still working as a nanny and selling jewelry on Etsy. In all fairness, maybe French studies wasn't the most practical major, but she won't let up. She keeps nagging me to go back to school and get a teaching degree."

"Would you be into that?" Mags asked. "If you're a nanny, you must be good with kids."

Ginger shuddered. "I'm good with two or three kids, max. Preferably under the age of five. Teaching high school French would be my worst nightmare. Plus, the guys would be a foot taller than me."

"What do you want to do with your degree?" Brody asked.

"No idea. I'd be happy living in France and working there." She gestured to April. "You're so lucky. Graphic design's not the most marketable field, but you landed a job in the wine industry." She winked. "With that hot tech guy, Brody Blackwood."

Brody laughed. "I hear he's kind of a dick, though. Steals all her ideas."

"It's a great job, but my parents aren't on board," April said. "My dad keeps bugging me to go back to school and get an architectural degree. He won't be happy until I follow in his footsteps."

"Are you even interested in architecture?" Mags asked.

April had considered it a few times, even going as far as researching the classes she'd have to take, but the thought of designing buildings didn't excite her. "It's not for me. Besides, I like working at Blackwood Cellars. I had a blast developing the wine app, even if it meant putting up with that annoying Brody Blackwood." She gave him a sly smile.

At seven, a burly, bearded guy dressed in full pirate garb strode up to the front of the pub and stood behind a table outfitted with a microphone and a small sound system. "Avast, me hearties! It's time for Pirate Pete's Trivia Night!!"

"Yikes," Ginger muttered under her breath. "This could be rough."

"No kidding," April whispered. Still, she was willing to play along since Mags seemed all in.

"Alright, ye scurvy sea dogs," Pete called out. "There be ten teams competing for the grand prize tonight. Our wenches be passing out answer sheets and pencils to each table. We'll have six rounds, with six questions each. At the end of each round, I'll be posting the leading teams on this here scoreboard." He pointed to a standing chalkboard next to the table.

"High-tech outfit, isn't it?" Brody said.

April smacked his arm. "Shh. They didn't have PowerPoint during the Golden Age of Pirates."

"If ye would, please be placing yer phones into the basket on each table. If I catch anyone cheating, they'll be doing time in the brig!" Pete pointed to a small table, decorated with a stuffed parrot and a pyramid of plastic skulls. "The first round be—football. Green Bay Packers football, if ye please."

April caught Brody's eye. They were sunk. But Mags pumped her fist. "In the bag."

"Mags is a huge Packers fan," Ollie said.

"My family makes it to a few home games every season. And we never miss a game on TV." Mags took a swig of her margarita. "Trust me, I can handle it."

April did. Because as Pirate Pete reeled off six questions about the Packers, including one about an Ice Bowl—whatever the hell *that* was—Mags wrote down the answers without hesitation. When April peeked over at her sisters' table, they were bickering with their husbands.

After the scores were tallied, their team was in the lead. As were four other tables. Apparently, the Green Bay Packers were a huge deal in Wisconsin.

"We didn't help much," Brody said to April. "But we didn't hurt, right?"

"Right. Besides, we don't have to win. All we have to do is beat my sisters' table."

Pirate Pete rang a dinner bell, calling them back to attention. "Second round, me hearties! And the topic be—video games!"

Brody rubbed his hands together and grabbed the team's pencil. "I'm on it."

"I didn't realize you were a gamer," Ollie said to him.

Oops. April should have warned Brody to tone down the gaming talk. But before she could speak up, he course corrected. "It's something I don't mention a lot. I don't want to come off like a total nerd."

April let out her breath in relief. Beside them, Ginger snorted with laughter.

"First question," Pirate Pete called out. "Which theme park

was inspired by the video game series *World of Warcraft* and *Starcraft?*"

Jeez, the questions were harder than she thought. But Brody smiled and wrote something down. "World Joyland. It's in China. I'd love to go there."

"Nicely done," Ginger said, topping up her margarita. "And for the record, *Chris*, you're a giant nerd."

Pirate Pete's voice rang out. "Shiver me timbers, it's time for the next question. What classic video game did Tony Stark catch a member of S.H.I.E.L.D. playing in the first Avengers movie?"

Brody slid the paper over to her. "You're the Stark fan, sweetie. Go for it."

She filled out Galaga on the answer sheet. She'd seen *The Avengers* five times, including a Marvel marathon she'd done with Brody over a long weekend last winter. They'd had so much fun reciting their favorite lines and indulging in different snacks for each movie. During the slower scenes, they'd taken turns napping on her couch.

Between the two of them, they swept the video game questions. At the nearby table, Avery and Drianna were shooting daggers at them. "You rigged the game," Drianna called out to Mags.

Mags shrugged. "Not possible. Pirate Pete has his own agenda."

True enough, because the next category was golf, which set them back. Between the five of them, they could only answer three questions. Drianna took the opportunity to mock them, claiming her table had aced the entire category. Thankfully, round four was European geography, which Ginger dominated, because she'd done her junior year abroad in Paris. They lucked out with round five—food and wine. Together, April and Brody answered all six questions.

By now, their team was leading by two points and ahead of Drianna's table by three. As long as they didn't get another sports category, they might beat them. Better yet, they might win the whole thing.

"Avast, ye swabs! Grape Expectations be taking the lead. But will they be stumped by the final round? It be—animated movies!"

Brody shot April a devious smile. "All you."

As someone who'd spent four years studying graphic design, she appreciated good animation, particularly the Disney classics. Another facet of her personality her sisters had teased her about for years.

Not anymore, bitches.

"What the hell!" Drianna's voice carried over the crowd. She pointed to Mags. "You totally rigged this."

Pirate Pete thumped his fist on the table. "Settle down, little lady. Don't be making a ruckus, or you'll find yourself in the brig."

"This is a fucking sham," Drianna said. "How much did they pay you?"

"To the brig!" Pete called out. "Wenches, take her away!"

"Screw you." Drianna stood and glared at her table. "You're all a bunch of losers. I'm leaving."

The pub remained silent as she stalked out the door, and then Brody started laughing. Full-belly, uncontrollable laughter. "I'm sorry. I can't help it."

April joined in. "That's Dree for you. If she's not winning, she's not happy."

"This is awesome," Mags said. "Free margaritas, here we come."

Pirate Pete continued as if nothing had gone awry. "There won't be any mutinies on *my* ship. Now, if ye may, let me pose the first question. What were the names of Cinderella's evil stepsisters in the 1950 Disney animated version of the movie?"

"Oh my God. What are the chances?" Ginger grabbed the

pencil and filled out Anastasia and Drizella, then grinned at Brody. "My pet names for April's sisters."

"Perfect," Brody said.

"Arrr—time for question two," Pirate Pete called out. "Which Studio Ghibli movie was based on a children's book by British author Diana Wynne Jones?"

Ginger handed April the pencil. "No idea."

She filled out the answer sheet. When it came to fantastical animation, *Howl's Moving Castle* was one of her personal favorites. The last four questions were tricky, but she knew them all. As she wrote down her answers, her exhilaration grew.

So, this is what victory feels like.

As the winners, their team received medals and felt pirate hats. Given that they didn't have to worry about their bar tab, they stayed on at the pub, toasting each other with another round of margaritas. April was not only high on victory, she was up for anything.

One bed? No problem.

CHAPTER 17

$\mathcal{B}$rody stumbled along the trail to the cottage, trying to find his way in the dark. His only source of light came from his phone, which proved a poor excuse for a real flashlight. Beside him, April leaned on his shoulder, so drunk she could barely stay upright. If he guessed correctly, she'd had three margaritas over the course of four hours. Or was it four margaritas in three hours? Either way, she was plastered. Whereas he'd only allowed himself one drink before switching to ice water. After his meltdown at Marc's wedding, he'd vowed never to get that drunk again.

On their ride back to the resort, April had regaled him with a medley of sea shanties. As if a switch had been flicked, she started up again. Loudly.

He tightened his grip around her shoulder. "April, shhh. People are sleeping."

"Idiots. Why waste the evening?" She started singing the theme song from *Popeye*. Her enthusiasm would have been adorable if they weren't at risk of waking everyone around them.

When they reached the porch, he propped her up against the

side of the cottage. He searched his pockets but couldn't find his key. "You brought your key, right? Do you have it in your purse?"

"I dunno." She thrust it at him. "See for yourself."

As he rifled through it, she grabbed his arm and looked into his eyes. "Brody? I have a serious question."

"What is it?"

"Have you ever wanted to be a pirate?" She dissolved into a fit of giggles.

He fished out the key and turned it in the lock. "Not really. I mean, most pirates were kind of dicks. Lots of pillaging, looting, and ravaging of women. Not a good look."

She poked him in the shoulder. "You're too much of a gentleman."

Did that mean she wanted him to ravage her? Or at least take the initiative in bed?

Don't even go there. She's drunk. It's probably one of her romance novel fantasies.

He helped her inside. "Why don't you get ready for bed? And maybe drink some water? Otherwise, you're going to have a nasty hangover."

"Okey dokey." She staggered to the bathroom and slammed the door behind her.

He grabbed a bottle of water from the mini fridge and set it on her nightstand. More than anything, he wanted to crash out for a full eight hours, since he still hadn't recovered from the morning's grueling race, but he needed to take care of April first. If he could get her to hydrate, she might not feel as miserable in the morning.

When she emerged from the bathroom, she'd stripped down to her camisole and a tiny pair of underwear. Atop her head was the pirate hat she'd won at the pub. He tried not to ogle her full breasts, which peeked out of the lacy pink camisole.

She flopped down on the bed. "Wow. I am done for the night."

He swallowed, forcing himself to look away. Her near

nakedness was far too enticing. "I'm going to get ready. Make sure you drink some water before you pass out."

She saluted him. "Aye-aye, Captain Blackwood!"

He went into the bathroom and took his time prepping for bed. With any luck, April would drift off before he was done. She was too drunk for him to contemplate doing *anything*.

But when he came out, she was still awake, looking up at the ceiling. She twisted the pirate hat between her hands. "Do you want to wear it? You didn't get one."

He eased into bed, putting two pillow shams between them to serve as barriers. "I'm good. Like I said—not into the pirate thing."

"No?" She leaned toward him until her face was inches from his. Her tequila-laden breath wafted over him. "Because you know what would be really hot?"

He was afraid to ask.

"If you fucked me wearing nothing but that pirate hat."

He tried to control the lust coursing through him, but his traitorous dick sprang to attention. Now that she'd said it, the image was lodged in his head. Riding her sweet, sexy body. Whispering roguish comments into her ear as she clutched him and cried out his name. Though he had no experience with sexual role-play, he'd gladly act like a lusty pirate captain if it was what April wanted.

"Come on, Captain Blackwood. Don't you want to have a little fun?" She leaned closer and brushed her lips against his.

And then she was kissing him, with far more passion than she'd shown that morning. Her tongue tasted of margaritas, sweet and salty, twisting against his. He returned her kiss, threading his hands through her thick, wavy hair. As he claimed her mouth, his desire outweighed all rational thought. He wanted to strip off his clothes, pin her to the bed, and fulfill her every need.

But she was wasted. And just because she'd lost her

inhibitions didn't mean she wanted this in real life. Hadn't she mentioned, just hours ago, how impressed she'd been with Chris's physique and athleticism? He couldn't compete.

With every inch of willpower he could summon, he broke away. "April. No."

She pouted. "You don't want me?"

"Of course I do. You're sexy as hell. But you're drunk." He pushed her back onto her side of the bed, resisting the urge to cover her body with his own and run his hands along her tantalizing curves.

"Am not," she muttered. "Just a little tipsy."

"Drink some water. Please."

She rolled her eyes but sat up and uncapped the bottle. After she'd swigged half of it, she glared at him. "Satisfied, Mr. Killjoy?"

He stared her down. "Finish it."

"Nope. Otherwise, I'll have to pee again." She placed it back on the nightstand. "You're no fun. And you're not satisfying my needs."

"Not tonight." Before she could lure him into another kiss, he sprang out of bed, angling his body so she couldn't see his erection. "I'm going to take a shower."

"It's so late. Stay in bed with me."

"Good night, April."

He escaped into the bathroom and started his third shower of the day. But if he didn't find a way to relieve the pressure, he'd be tempted to take April up on her fantasies. And no matter how much he desired her, he didn't want to do something they'd both regret in the morning.

BRODY WOKE SLOWLY, his head in a fog. Even with the drapes pulled tight, a little daylight had seeped into the room. Beside him, April slept soundly. Her bare shoulders peeked above the blankets, reminding him that, underneath, she was nearly naked. Naked and far too tempting.

More than ever, he was glad he'd opted to take a lengthy shower last night. He'd gotten himself off, imagining April the entire time, as visions of ravishing her sexy body raced through his mind. By the time he returned to bed, she'd clocked out for the evening. He was able to drift off, feeling proud he'd resisted her.

Today, however…

Let's just say, if she propositioned him again, he'd be all in.

Or was that the worst idea ever?

Things between them were good. Even if they were hiding a massive secret, they were having fun together. Yesterday, they'd moved past the jealously issue and talked through the self-esteem problems that plagued them both. Did he want to throw a wrench into things? They had such a great friendship. Sex would complicate that immensely.

But maybe that was what lovers were supposed to be. Friends. Not someone you idolized. Not someone who forced you to hide your faults. But someone who loved and accepted you for who you were, flaws and all.

She might be your friend, but she'll break your heart in the end. They all do.

He wanted to have faith in her, but what if Chris came back into her life once she was home from the wedding? Would she be strong enough to resist him? If she went back to him, Brody would end up gutted and miserable. And alone, without anyone to lean on.

Enough.

He needed to get out of his head. And he couldn't do it if he was still in bed, lying next to the object of his desire. He got up quietly and peeked out the drapes. Another perfect fall day, with plenty of sunshine. He went to his suitcase and retrieved his running gear.

Oddly enough, now that he wasn't worried about humiliating himself in front of the Becketts, he wanted to run again. Although yesterday's race had been a painful experience, he liked the idea of getting back into running. He loved the way it allowed him to challenge his body while also freeing his mind.

He threw on his clothes, laced up his sneakers, and went outside. The brisk morning air and the heady scent of pine invigorated him.

Perfect. He'd get in a few easy miles, and then head home.

This time, he remembered to stretch. As he was doing lunges on the porch, a voice called out to him. "Hey, Chris."

Ollie jogged over to the cottage, with Mags trailing behind him. Both were dressed in running shirts and fleece joggers. "Want some company?" Ollie asked.

Shit. Brody's legs couldn't handle a Beckett-level run. Before he could bow out, Mags spoke up. "Only if you don't mind a slower pace. I'm still feeling the effects of last night's margaritas."

Brody offered up a silent thank-you for her request. "Sounds good. I haven't recovered from the 10K yet."

"You feeling better?" Ollie asked. "No lie, you looked like shit out there."

"It wasn't my best effort," Brody said. "That's why I eased up on the booze last night."

Mags twisted her curls into a ponytail and secured it with a hair tie. "How's April doing? She drank us under the table."

"Still sleeping," Brody said. "But she'll be feeling it today."

"That's rough. You'll have to give her lots of TLC."

If only.

"Let's run into town," Ollie said. "It's about a three-mile loop, there and back."

They took off jogging, with Ollie leading the way. Thanks to Mags, the run was more like the one Brody had taken when he first arrived. Within five minutes, he'd warmed up and could keep pace. It was a good feeling.

"You should get April to come with you," Mags said. "I'll bet she'd enjoy it if you didn't turn it into a competition."

"I doubt it," Ollie said. "The last time she tried running with us, it didn't go so well."

April had never mentioned running with her family before. When Brody had helped her create the Team Beckett website, she told him how much her family loved to compete, but she told him she didn't participate. At the time, she blamed her asthma.

"What happened?" he asked.

"It was rough," Ollie said. "She came in last, but she was trying. And she was thirteen, which was an awkward phase for her."

Brody remembered thirteen—he'd been skinny and gawky, with a mouthful of braces and a face full of acne. Not his best look.

Ollie continued. "When April got to the finish line, she tripped and sprawled all over the place. She wasn't that hurt, but her fall was so klutzy it looked like something you'd see in *America's Funniest Home Videos*. Dree filmed the whole thing on her phone."

They came to a stop, waiting to cross the wide country road. Brody was glad for the break, because he was so pissed he could barely focus. "What's Drianna's problem? Why does she treat April like shit?"

A break in the traffic came up, and Ollie motioned for them to follow. Once they'd crossed the road, they resumed running.

"They've never been that close," Ollie said. "When we were kids, April and I always stuck together. It was the two of us against Avery and Dree. But Dree was never outright mean. Things changed when April got really sick."

"April was sick? How sick?" She'd shared a few childhood stories with Brody, but she'd never mentioned a serious illness.

A passing car honked as it sped by. Brody couldn't tell if it was a friendly honk or a warning for them to get out of the way. He inched closer to the side of the road.

"She was twelve, I think," Ollie said. "Her lungs aren't the greatest—she has asthma, and she used to get bronchitis a lot. This time, it turned into double pneumonia. She had to go to the hospital for a week. Or maybe it was longer—I can't remember. Our parents took turns visiting her, but Drianna resented them for being gone so much. It was her junior year, and she was having some boyfriend crisis. But no one cared. Then, one day, when she was in the kitchen, pissed about Mom being gone all the time, she said, 'What does it matter if April dies? You still have three other kids.'"

Mags gasped. "That's horrible."

"It was bad. My mom grounded her for a month. Forced her to miss prom. So, her loser boyfriend took someone else. After April got better and came home, Dree ignored her, for the most part. But lately, she's gotten worse."

It explained a lot. Still, that was twelve years ago. Some grudges were understandable, but not this one. What was one prom in the scheme of things? Drianna should have gotten over herself by now.

Whatever the case, Brody felt even more protective of April. And if he had any qualms about pretending to be Chris, they were gone. No way would he reveal the truth during their vacation. Not if it gave Drianna a chance to dig the knife in deeper.

He was going to protect April at all costs.

CHAPTER 18

*A*pril groaned as she came into full consciousness. Why had she ever thought she could handle that much tequila?

Mindful of her pounding head, she sat up slowly and did a quick self-assessment. She was clad in nothing except a lacy pink camisole and matching panties. Her ensemble would have been acceptable if she'd been flying solo, but she'd worn it while sleeping with Brody.

Not sleeping *with*. Sleeping next to. Big difference.

Brody's side of the bed was empty, and the bathroom door was wide open. His absence was probably for the best since she was in no state to be sociable. As she scanned the room, trying to recall the details of the previous night, dread crept over her. A sense that in her inebriated state, she'd crossed a line of no return.

On her nightstand was a half-filled water bottle. She chugged the rest of it, desperately needing to hydrate. When she saw the pirate hat on the floor, the memories came flooding back.

She'd asked Brody to wear the hat. And she'd asked him to…
Oh God.

Maybe she was confused. After all, the last book she'd read had been an old-school historical romance, set on a pirate ship.

Nope. She could remember all of it now. She'd propositioned Brody. And he turned her down.

As she eased out of bed, her stomach lurched. She staggered into the bathroom and dry heaved over the sink. Nothing. At least she hadn't vomited in front of Brody last night. That would have added to the humiliation.

She took two ibuprofen and turned on the shower. As she stepped into the warm spray, she told herself her drunken antics hadn't meant anything. She'd been letting loose after the thrill of winning trivia night.

You wouldn't have asked him for sex if you didn't want it.

Maybe she'd wanted it, but he hadn't. End of story.

From here on, she'd have to rein in the drinking. And no more kissing, even if she was trying to convince her family they were lovers. The last thing she wanted was for Brody to take her aside and gently remind her what she already knew. They were just friends. She wasn't his type. And he'd *never* feel that way about her.

The awkwardness would be off the charts.

When she was done in the shower, she changed into leggings and a flannel shirt. As she was firing up the Keurig to make her first cup of coffee, Brody came into the cottage, dressed in running garb and dripping with sweat.

He wiped a hand across his forehead. "Morning."

"Were you running? Voluntarily?" She hoped he didn't think he *had* to run in order to prove he was Chris.

"I got in a few miles with Mags and Ollie."

April sat on the edge of the bed and dried her hair with a towel. "And you enjoyed it?"

"Yeah. I actually like running. It's competing that stresses me out." He gestured to the bathroom. "Are you done? I'm going to grab a shower."

She chewed on her lip. As much as she wanted to pretend her drunken escapades had never happened, she had to say something. "Sorry if I was kind of pushy last night. I had too much to drink."

"It's no big deal."

Maybe not to him. But she couldn't stop thinking about it. "I might have said or done some things I didn't mean. Inappropriate things." She cringed. "Sorry."

He shrugged. "Don't worry about it."

That was it. He went into the bathroom and shut the door behind him. A few minutes later, the water started running.

Obviously, he wanted to move past last night's fiasco. Definitely for the best.

If he didn't want her, she wasn't going to remind him she'd asked him to have sex. They could stay friends and keep things platonic.

So why did she feel so disappointed?

She grabbed a blueberry muffin and took it outside with her coffee. But after sitting in the bright sunlight for all of five minutes, she went back inside and fetched her sunglasses and another bottle of water.

She needed to talk to someone about last night. Someone who knew her and would listen to her nonsensical ramblings as she tried to make sense of this—whatever it was—between her and Brody. She texted Ginger. *You around?*

The reply was instant. *I wish. Heading out for breakfast with the folks followed by mini golf. My life is a nonstop thrill ride.*

Okay then. She couldn't call her office-mate Delilah—her usual go-to whenever she had a romantic crisis—because it was 7:00 a.m. on the West Coast, and Delilah was *not* a morning person.

But Victoria Blackwood was. She might be Brody's cousin, but she and April were friends in their own right. Though they worked in different departments at Blackwood Cellars, they'd bonded when they joined the company's book club. The club's coordinator had turned out to be an egotistical blowhard who favored literary fiction over all other genres. He quickly dismissed April's love of romance novels and Victoria's passion for mysteries. The two women salvaged the evening by going out for drinks after. Since then, they usually met up once a month to bond over booze and book recommendations.

"April?" Victoria answered on the first ring, sounding slightly winded.

"I didn't wake you, did I?"

"God, no. I'm finishing up a five-mile run. Walking the last bit to cool down. Is everything okay?"

"Sort of?" April moved away from the porch in case Brody had finished in the shower. "I don't remember if I told you, but I'm in Wisconsin right now for my brother's wedding."

"Right. How's it going? Are your sisters annoying the hell out of you?"

"No more than usual." She hesitated for a moment, wondering how much she should reveal. "If I tell you something, can you keep it a secret?"

"Is it about Brody?"

April sucked in her breath. "What makes you think it's about Brody?" She wandered behind the cottage, seeking out a shady spot beneath a pine tree.

"He went with you, right? I was over in Marketing yesterday, grabbing some brochures for our Fall Open House, and Delilah told me Brody went as your plus-one. What's up with that?"

April glanced around. No sign of Brody yet. Chances were good he wouldn't seek her out until he'd downed his first cup of coffee. Speaking softly, she spilled the entire story, including the awkwardness of sharing a bed, especially now that she'd made a drunken pass at him.

When she finished, the long pause that followed made her worry they'd been cut off. "Victoria? Did I lose you?"

"I'm still here. Processing everything you told me. It sounds like one of your romance novels."

"If it were, Brody wouldn't have held back last night. It's obvious he doesn't want me. I should back off. Right? Tell me I should back off." She took a long drink of water. "Let's face it, I'm nothing like Taylor."

"Which is a good thing. She was terrible for Brody. And such a snob. Which means a lot, coming from me."

True enough. Though April enjoyed Victoria's company, she couldn't deny her friend had a snobbish streak. The first time she'd visited April's apartment, Victoria had drawn back, like a vampire facing a cross. "My God," she said. "I've never seen so much IKEA furniture."

April picked up a pinecone and tossed it at a nearby tree, hitting it with a resounding thwack. "I don't know if he's over her yet."

"Maybe not. But he offered to be your date. *At a wedding.* And we all know what happened at the last wedding he went to. It was a shit storm of epic proportions."

"So I've heard."

"But even after all that, he volunteered to come with you. For an entire week. I think he likes you."

As a friend.

But as she was about to say it, another memory came to light. When she'd kissed Brody last night, he hadn't pushed her away at first. Instead, he'd kissed her back. Passionately. And what had he said when she claimed he didn't want her? *Of course I do. You're sexy as hell. But you're drunk.*

If she'd been sober, would he have kept going?

Then again, if she'd been sober, she wouldn't have been that bold.

"You think he's into me?" she asked Victoria. "Has...does he ever mention me?"

"He actually mentions you a lot. Mostly when he's talking

about work. But he's also raved about your baking skills. And he wouldn't shut up about that damn app. He was so proud of it, like the two of you had climbed Mt. Everest or something."

The words gave April a warm glow, especially when she remembered the way he'd spoken up for her at dinner.

"April?" Brody peered around the corner of the cottage. "What's up?"

"I'm...just...sitting in the shade. The sun was giving me a headache." After Brody left, she whispered into the phone. "I should go. Thanks for listening."

"I'm not sure I was much help," Victoria muttered. "If you need to talk again, I'm around most nights. My social life is practically nil."

April was struck with a rush of guilt. Chris might have been self-centered, but he had nothing on Victoria's ex-fiancé, Ben, who'd recently dumped her for another woman, three months before their big society wedding. "Are you doing okay?"

"It's been rough. After Ben kicked me out of his condo, I had to move back home, which—as you can imagine—was absolutely *delightful.*"

"I'm sorry. That's terrible."

"The worst part is all the pity. Either that or the friends who've completely fallen off the map. Like they're ashamed to be associated with me now that Ben's marrying someone else."

April shuddered. "Forget them. How about we go out for drinks as soon as I get back?"

"Perfect. Then you can fill me in on the rest of your trip, and I can live vicariously through your antics."

Despite her uncertainty, April couldn't help but laugh. "I doubt there'll be much to tell. But you'll be the first to know."

After she hung up with Victoria, April ambled back to the front of the cottage where Brody sat, drinking coffee and munching on a blueberry muffin.

He gave her an affectionate smile. "These muffins are the best. Thanks for bringing them."

Her heart melted a little bit more.

Yep, she definitely had it bad.

ONCE SHE AND Brody finished their coffee, April checked in with her family. They had a jam-packed itinerary but nothing involving any level of competition. They visited the Cana Island Lighthouse in Baileys Harbor, which provided a perfect backdrop for a slew of group pictures. Then it was on to the Door County Creamery in Sister Bay, where they indulged in six kinds of cheese and visited adorable goats. April delighted in purchasing the fanciest, most expensive cheeses she could find, knowing that Drianna and Avery were footing the bill.

By now, Brody appeared comfortable with her family. Even Avery had warmed up to him after they bonded over a true-crime podcast they both loved. Not April's idea of fun, but she was glad they'd found common ground. Only Drianna seemed indifferent to Brody's charms, but she'd been sniping at everyone because she was still bitter about trivia night.

After lunch, they parked at Cave Point County Park and set off on a hike. Thanks to a post-lunch espresso, April's brain fog had cleared up. She'd also been rehydrating all morning, since Brody had brought along a couple of stainless steel bottles filled with ice-cold water. Brody, Ollie, and her father led the pack as their family walked along the lakeside trail. Below them, the waves crashed against the limestone cliffs, producing a fine spray that sparkled in the sunlight.

April took so many photos of the rock bluffs she fell behind. She scrambled to catch up to her mom and Avery, who were at the back of the group.

"So, April…" her mom said.

She braced herself. Whenever her mother took that tone, an interrogation was sure to follow.

Her mom gestured to the group ahead. "Chris seems nice. Are things getting serious between you two?"

Serious? Where had that come from? "What do you mean?" April asked.

"You've never brought anyone home before," her mom said. "Not even for a weekend."

"Yeah, Chris took off a week to be with you," Avery said. "That's huge."

"And he's meeting all of us at once," her mother added. "That shows real commitment."

April swallowed, overwhelmed by their two-pronged assault. "Umm...commitment's a big word. We've only been dating since May."

Her mother reached over and gave her a side hug. "Sweetie, no one's saying you need to marry him. Not yet, anyway. But at least you're taking the first step. I'm not a fan of this whole 'hookup' culture." She used air-quotes around the term, causing her daughters to roll their eyes.

"It's not like I was hooking up with tons of guys." There had been exactly four since April graduated from UCLA and moved to Temecula. But her mom was right in that none of them had been serious. Though April had been seeing Chris for five months, she'd never deluded herself that she was in love with him.

Not the way she loved Brody.

Oh God. Was she falling in love with him?

No. She loved him as a friend. A work buddy. Someone who had her back when she needed him. She wasn't *in* love with him.

The trail led them into a shady forested area. Below them, tangled tree roots and fallen logs made the path more challenging. April watched her footing, not wanting to sprawl on her face in front of her entire family.

"Hey, kid." Avery nudged her. "Don't stress. You still have two years before you have to say 'I do.'"

"What?" She stopped short, her voice so loud that Mags and Drianna, who were a few paces ahead, turned around. She waved them on to keep walking.

Avery stepped over a fallen tree blocking their path. "You know the drill. We Becketts get married every two years. First me and Hunter. Then Dree and Ian. Now Ollie and Mags."

April wiped her forehead, suddenly warm, despite their cool surroundings. "Please don't repeat this in front of Chris. He might freak out."

"I doubt it," her mother said. "It's obvious he cares about you. I'm just so glad you're in a mature relationship, like an adult."

Like an adult. This had been one of April's goals when she initially invited Chris to Door County. To show her parents she was capable of a real relationship. To prove she wasn't a kid anymore. And it was working.

"Have you thought about Thanksgiving?" her mom asked.

Thanksgiving? April stared at her in shock. Her foot caught the edge of a thick tree root, and she stumbled forward.

Avery grabbed her arm. "Careful."

"Thanks. I...was just caught off guard. Thanksgiving's ages away."

"It's next month, silly," Avery said. "You should bring Chris home with you. That way he can compete in the Turkey Trot with us."

Another Beckett family tradition. The Turkey Trot was a 5K race, held at 7:30 a.m. on Thanksgiving morning. Their family was always among the top finishers in their age groups.

"Umm...Chris might be doing Thanksgiving with his parents," April said. "They live in Napa."

"Well, tell him he's invited," her mom said. "We'd love to have him."

Except I won't be dating him anymore.

Why hadn't she considered the long-term ramifications of this scenario? Once this week was over, Operation Fake-Chris would be at an end. And she'd be single again, like always.

What would her parents think if she came home without Brody? Would they be disappointed in her?

She was so screwed.

CHAPTER 19

After returning from Cave Point County Park, Brody was pleased to learn they had the rest of the afternoon free. Though he'd grown more at ease around April's family, he was craving a break from their tightly planned schedule. Their next group outing wasn't until eight, when they were supposed to go to a fish boil. The concept of boiled fish didn't appeal to him, but since it was part of the itinerary, he'd go along with it.

In the meantime, the sunny weather was ideal for kayaking. When he asked April if she wanted to take a couple of kayaks out on Lake Michigan, he hadn't thought anyone else would be interested. Big mistake. Avery and Drianna immediately offered to join them, since their husbands were going golfing. Brody tried to respond with enthusiasm, even though he could barely tolerate Drianna. Maybe she'd paddle on ahead since she possessed a pathological desire to come first in everything.

They left the cottage at three, after April had tucked away their purchases from the Door County Creamery. As they walked down to the sandy beach that ringed the resort, Brody took her hand. She'd been acting skittish ever since they got back. "You okay?"

"A little nervous. I've never been kayaking."

"It's easy. If there's a double kayak, we'll take it, and I can steer. You just have to help paddle." He squeezed her hand. "How's that sound?"

"Okay. I guess." Her voice lacked conviction.

He gave her hand another squeeze. Once he got her out on the lake, he hoped she'd shake off her fears and enjoy herself.

On the beach, gentle waves lapped the shore. Avery and Drianna stood waiting for them, dressed in t-shirts, jeans, and baseball caps. Avery pointed to four colorful kayaks lined up along the sand, along with four life jackets. "All the double kayaks were taken, so the outfitting company dropped off four singles. We need to have them back onshore in two hours."

April nudged one with her foot. "They don't look too sturdy."

Drianna rolled her eyes. "Don't be such a baby." She grabbed one of the life jackets and secured it, as did Avery. Brody took one and handed the other to April.

But when she put it on, the clip wouldn't snap. "Guys? I can't get this life jacket to close over my boobs."

"Maybe this is the universe's way of telling you to lose a few pounds," Drianna said.

"Rude." April's face reddened as she tried to adjust the setting. Brody came over and fiddled with the straps, but it was no use. The life jacket hadn't been designed for a woman with a generous amount of cleavage.

He placed his hand on her arm. "Do you want me to go back to the lodge and ask if they have another size available?"

She shook her head. "It's fine. I'm a decent swimmer."

"But—"

"It's fine," she said.

He didn't want to push the issue, not when she seemed so uncomfortable with her sisters watching. But he also wanted to give her an easy out. "If you'd rather not do this, I understand. There's no pressure."

"You've kayaked before, right?" she asked.

"Loads of times. And we're not in a race. We can go at any pace you like." As he said this, he looked right at Drianna, who gave him another eye roll. He focused on April instead. "If you get in your kayak first, I can push you out into the water. That way you don't have to worry about tipping over."

She twisted the strap of her life jacket. "Is it easy to tip over?"

"Only if you stand up or move around a lot. If you're worried about tipping, leave your phone here."

"You're a lot more patient than I am, Chris," Drianna said.

Would she ever let up? "That's because I care about April, and I want her to be happy." Which was one hundred percent true, even if he wasn't her boyfriend. The more Drianna picked on April, the more his protective instincts kicked in.

Avery pointed to her sweatshirt, which she'd set on the beach. "April, you can put your phone under there. That way, it'll be safe."

"Thanks." April took her phone out of her pocket and tucked it under the sweatshirt. Brody helped her into the kayak, handed her the paddle, and took off his shoes. Barefoot, he waded into Lake Michigan, his skin tingling at the chill. He pushed her kayak into the water. "Hang tight for a minute. I'll catch up."

Avery and Drianna set out next, but Brody took his time. Once April's sisters had made a little headway, he eased himself into his own kayak and pushed off from shore, paddling until he reached April.

"How are you doing?" he asked her.

"I'm okay." She clenched the paddle in a death grip. "But I can't drop this. If I do, I'll be stuck out here."

"Relax. Watch me paddle. Side to side. See? We can take it nice and slow." He grinned at her. "It's better if we don't catch up to your sisters, because they'll turn it into a race."

She offered up a small smile. "Good point."

He led, moving slowly, his paddle slicing through the water.

The warm sun seeped into his skin, making him glad he'd left his sweatshirt at the cottage. He inhaled the familiar smell of lake water, bringing back memories of Big Bear Lake. Even if Marc had teased him that the smell he loved was caused by algae and weeds, Brody never tired of that scent.

He waited until April caught up before starting again. "See? It's easy. And relaxing."

"It's nice. I thought I'd be terrible. I suck at most physical things."

He should have let her remark go, but he couldn't. Not after what Ollie had told him about her failed attempt at running. "Why do you say that?"

"Isn't it obvious? I don't run. I'm out of shape. I can't keep up with anyone in my family."

"Not all physical activity is about competition. Like hiking. Or yoga. What about that Zumba class you took with Delilah? I thought you liked it."

"It was fun, but…" She looked away, shame coloring her cheeks. "Chris came to pick me up once, after class, and said it was the dumbest thing he'd ever seen. A bunch of uncoordinated women trying to keep the beat."

If possible, Brody's loathing for Chris grew stronger. "I'm no fitness guru, but whatever you enjoy—that's what you should do. Screw everyone else."

She kept quiet, paddling alongside him, and he worried he'd gone too far. He didn't want to bully her the way Chris and her sisters did. But he didn't want her to dread trying new things either.

When she spoke up again, her voice had a teasing lilt. "I'll try Zumba again if you go with me."

He splashed her lightly with his paddle. "No way."

She brushed water droplets off her bare arm. "Come on. One class."

"Fine. I get something in return."

"What do you want?"

A loaded question. After last night, he knew exactly what he wanted. But he wasn't about to share his desires with her. "Come running with me. Just once."

"Bro-dy."

"A gentle jog. A couple of miles, max. I'll take you out for breakfast after."

She paused, then gave him a quick grin. "Okay. I'll give it a shot. But after we're done, you're taking me to Cork Fire Kitchen, and you're paying. I'm having the brioche french toast. *And* a side of bacon."

"You've got a deal."

Rather than venture out too far, Brody stayed close to the shoreline, hoping April would feel more comfortable that way. Above them, tall trees decked out in orange and gold bowed out over the lake, casting dark reflections. Lazy dragonflies skimmed the water's surface. He let out a long breath, feeling more relaxed than he had during the entire trip. Best of all, Avery and Drianna were far off in the distance.

"How'd you learn to kayak?" April asked.

"My family has a lodge up in the mountains at Big Bear Lake. When we were kids, we used to go there for two weeks every summer. We owned a speedboat and a bunch of kayaks, so we spent a lot of time on the water."

"Your family owned a *lodge*?" she said. "How big was it?"

He tried not to flaunt his family's wealth, but he didn't want to lie. "Huge. Kind of over-the-top. But we used to vacation with my cousins, so there were nine of us staying there." A group of kayakers passed them, and he waved, feeling a kinship with anyone who was out on the water. "We always had a great time. Plus, we hung out with this other family who stayed at the cabin next door. Have you ever met my sister-in-law, Gabriela Chavez-Blackwood? She helps run the Sales division in the Napa office."

"Didn't she come down from Napa for our big app

presentation? She was *so* intimidating. She asked us a bunch of hardball questions."

He laughed. "That's Gabi, all right. We first met when we were kids. She and her sister Jess used to come up to the mountains at the same time we did. We had so much fun together." When he'd been at Big Bear with his cousins and the Chavez girls, his status as a geeky loser didn't matter. They'd all banded together, playing games and spending hours on the lake.

"Does your family still own the lodge?" April asked.

"Yeah. I made us a customized calendar app so we can keep track of everyone's weekends there. You should come with me sometime."

Though he'd spoken without thinking, the idea appealed to him. He'd wanted to take Taylor, but she had no interest in spending time in the mountains. Their last vacation had been an expensive weekend at a luxury spa in Ojai.

"I'd love to go," April said. "I bet it's beautiful up there."

He wiped his forehead, feeling suddenly awkward. Had he invited her as a friend? A date? The lines were starting to blur. "Uh…yeah," he said. "I'll see when it's free."

No turning back now. And if she wanted to keep things platonic, the area offered plenty of outdoor activities. Since the lodge had five bedrooms, they wouldn't be forced to share a bed.

Above them, an eagle circled the treetops. The lake was still, other than the steady shush of their paddles. Brody could have stayed out on the water for hours, but he didn't want April to push herself too hard. "Time for us to turn around."

Following his lead, she turned when he did. Her face was slightly flushed, her smile like a beacon of sunshine. "I like this. It's peaceful. And it's so beautiful out here. Thanks for being patient with me."

Her sweet smile weakened his defenses. Why was everyone so hard on her? Why couldn't her family appreciate her the way he did?

"You've been so supportive," she said. "I'm glad you're here with me. You're enjoying it, right?"

"I am. This was definitely the right decision—for both of us." Despite his unfulfilled lust and his stress over playing the role of Chris, he was having more fun pretending to be April's date than he'd had in months. By the time their trip was over, he might be back to his old self.

As they approached the shore, he caught sight of April's sisters, pulling up their kayaks. *Damn.* Drianna was no doubt hoping April would screw up.

"When we get close to shore, I'll go on ahead," he said to April. "Wait 'til I've beached my kayak and gotten out, then paddle forward. I can bring you in so you don't tip over."

She frowned but kept her voice even. "Okay. Thanks."

He paddled to shore, eased himself out, and dragged his kayak onto the beach. Drianna regarded him with amusement. "How'd she do?"

"She was fine." He shucked off his life jacket and waded out again, wincing at the bracing feel of the water. "Come on in," he called to April. "You don't have far to go."

"I can't." Her voice was strained. "There's a bee."

A bee had landed on her bare upper arm. One of those sluggish, late-fall bees, looking for a place to land. He couldn't imagine it posed much of a threat. "Just brush it off."

Avery shook her head. "She's terrified of bees." She held up her hand and called out to April. "Don't move! It'll fly off."

"I…can't. I need it off me. Now!" April wriggled around, rocking the kayak back and forth. When the bee zoomed toward her face, she batted at it, shifting her weight to one side.

"April—stop. Don't!" Brody yelled.

Too late. With a splash, the kayak tipped over, sending April plunging into the waters of Lake Michigan. She shrieked as she went under. Before Brody could dive in after her, Avery grabbed his arm. "She's fine. It's not over her head."

Seconds later, April emerged. The water was only up to her waist, but she was drenched, her t-shirt and leggings sticking to her skin. A tangle of weeds trailed from her shoulder. "It's...it's so cold." She lumbered toward Brody, stumbled, and fell onto her knees. By the time she reached him, she was visibly trembling.

Brody eased the sopping life jacket off her shoulders and tossed it on the ground. He put his arm around her, shocked at how intensely her body was shaking. "We need to get you back to the cottage. You don't want to catch hypothermia."

Drianna scoffed. "This isn't the Arctic. The water isn't *that* cold."

April turned on her. "How would you know? It's not like you fell in."

"Because I'm not clumsy like you are."

"Dree. That's enough." Avery gestured to April's kayak. "Leave it there. I can wade out and bring it in. And we'll make sure the kayaks get picked up. Go get April warmed up."

April shivered uncontrollably, her teeth chattering. Goose bumps pricked her arms. "I...I'm so cold. I can't stand it."

Brody hustled her along the trail, eager to get her as far from Drianna as possible. "Come on. Once we get to our cottage, you can take a hot shower."

"I...I can't."

"A little further." Was it his imagination, or did her skin have a bluish tint?

Their walk to the cottage took forever, with him encouraging her every step of the way. Once they were on the porch, he unlocked the door, shut it behind them, and led her into the bathroom. He turned on the shower. "Think you can take it from here?"

"No. My...my hands are numb."

"Okay. Hang on." He didn't want to be a perv, but the longer she stood in wet clothes, the worse she'd feel. He peeled her flannel over her head, then helped her out of her leggings. He tried not to stare at her, but her bra and panties were translucent.

You're supposed to be helping her, damn it. Not objectifying her.

"Stop. I can go in like this." April pulled aside the shower curtain and stepped in, sighing as the hot water hit her skin. Within seconds, her wet bra and panties came sailing over the curtain rod and landed on the bathroom rug with a squelch.

Don't think about the fact that she's naked. Do not think about it.

"Okay...so...I'll leave you to shower," he said. "Meanwhile, I'll make a fire and fix you something warm to drink."

"See if there's any cocoa." Already, her voice had perked up a little.

Phew. If she was asking for hot chocolate, she wasn't in too much danger of going into shock from hypothermia. Closing the bathroom door behind him, he went to his suitcase and changed into a t-shirt and sweats. The fireplace came with a couple of Insta-Logs, so the flames shot up immediately. Perfect.

What wasn't perfect was his reaction. As much as he'd wanted to take care of her, he'd been aroused by her semi-naked body.

What the hell is wrong with you?

The truth was, in the past two days, he'd realized how much he *liked* April. He'd always enjoyed working with her, and he treasured their movie nights, but he was suddenly seeing her in a different light. Not just as a friend, a movie buddy, and a fellow nerd. But as a woman. A sweet, sexy woman who was as desirable as anyone he'd ever dated. He couldn't believe it had taken him this long to figure it out.

He wished he were Chris. Not actual Chris, the d-bag. But the Chris of April's dreams. The hot, athletic stud who turned her on and satisfied her needs.

How was he ever going to last the rest of the week?

CHAPTER 20

April stood in the shower, basking in the warm spray, as the feeling ebbed back into her fingers and toes. She wished she could stay immersed for the next few hours. Leaving meant facing Brody and apologizing for all the trouble she'd caused.

Until that stupid bee encounter, she'd been doing so well. Brody was proud of her for trying something new. Hell, she was proud of herself. She enjoyed being out on the water, savoring the gorgeous fall afternoon. But, once again, she screwed up and humiliated herself. In front of her sisters, no less.

With a sigh, she turned off the water and dried herself with a huge, fluffy towel. She grabbed her bathrobe and wrapped her wet hair in another towel. When she couldn't delay the inevitable any longer, she left her sanctuary, shivering as she emerged from the cloud of steam.

In the main room, flames crackled in the stone fireplace. Brody sat beside it, dressed in a Berkeley t-shirt and sweats. He looked up at her. "Are you all right?"

"Better now." She joined him on the carpet, luxuriating in the heat of the fire.

He handed her a mug. "You're in luck. The coffee station had four types of hot chocolate. I made a wild guess and chose the salted-caramel flavor."

"Perfect. Thanks." She took a sip, sighing as the sweet drink warmed her from the inside out. Taking a deep breath, she looked Brody in the eye. "I'm sorry."

"For what?"

"For falling in. For making you drag me back to our cottage. I feel like such an idiot."

He placed his hand over hers, reassuring her with his touch. "Everyone tips their kayak at some point. I've done it a bunch of times."

"You have?"

"Sure. But in the summer when the water wasn't as cold."

Though his words placated her, she regretted the way she'd overreacted. *To a bee.* Like she was a little kid instead of a grown woman. "I would have been okay, except—and this is going to sound stupid—I'm terrified of bees. They're my biggest phobia." She sipped her hot chocolate. "It's the one thing Avery doesn't tease me about, because she's afraid of spiders."

"What about Drianna?"

"She's not scared of anything. Except coming last in a race."

"For what it's worth, I hate getting shots. And needles in general. I have to psych myself up just to get a flu shot. And I'll probably never get a tattoo."

She couldn't help grinning. "Too bad. You'd look like a total badass."

"Really?"

Laughter bubbled out of her. "No. Be serious. You'll never be a badass."

She released her hair from the towel and let it hang, damp, around her shoulders. With her fingers, she fluffed it out in front of the fire. Outside, the sun was setting through the cottage's picture window, painting the sky with pink and orange streaks.

As she finished her hot chocolate, a satisfied glow overtook her whole body. She needed to set her anxiety aside. Brody wasn't upset about her kayak fail. If anything, her mishap had brought them closer. They were alone in an adorable cottage, with a fire burning, and she was wearing nothing but a bathrobe. She couldn't envision a cozier, more romantic scenario.

But if she propositioned Brody again, would he respond with enthusiasm? Or would he turn her down?

A second rejection would sting worse than the first. Especially since she was sober this time. If he didn't want her, she'd have to spend the next four nights lying next to him in that huge bed, knowing he felt as awkward as she did.

You're not his type.

Maybe that had been true six months ago when he was still involved with Taylor. But what if he'd changed? What if this vacation was making him see her in a new light?

She had to take her shot. If she passed up this opportunity, she'd spend months regretting it.

"Were you serious about Big Bear?" she asked.

"About spending the weekend there? You bet. But it's late in the season for kayaking. Winter comes early in the mountains."

Was he trying to deter her? He'd tossed off the invitation so casually she wasn't sure if he meant it. She pushed him a little more. "Can you go up there in the winter?"

"As long as the roads are clear, it's totally doable. The mountains get a ton of snow—like a Christmas card. And the skiing is awesome. Do you ski?"

She scoffed. "Do I look like someone who skis?"

"That's okay. There's other stuff to do, like snowshoeing or sledding. Or sitting by the fire and reading. The lodge has a huge kitchen. You could bake up a storm."

The conviction in his voice gave her hope. He *wanted* her there. "I'd love to go."

"I'll find out when it's free. Depending on traffic, it's only about two hours from Temecula."

She could imagine all of it—the mountains, the snowfall, the cozy fire. But before her imagination ran away with her, she had to take the next step. "Would this be a platonic trip? As friends?"

His hand still covered hers, binding them together. But his voice wavered. "Do you want it to be?"

She shook her head. And prayed he didn't pull away.

Instead, he leaned forward and pushed a damp wisp of hair from her face. His free hand curved along her cheek, making her shiver, despite the heat from the fire, and his lips found hers. A gentle kiss—soft, coaxing, tasting of hot chocolate.

When he broke away, his expression showed uncertainty. Like he wanted to retreat into his shell. Her heart went out to him. How could he think he was pushing things too far? Especially since she'd thrown herself at him last night.

"Was that okay?" he asked. "Because—"

She didn't let him finish. Instead, she took the initiative and kissed him back. His hand cradled the back of her head, bringing her closer, and the sensation of his tongue against hers filled her with longing. She placed her arms around his neck, scooting up against him until she was almost in his lap. He deepened the kiss, claiming her lips like he couldn't get enough of her.

This wasn't a perfunctory peck, but a kiss that sent her nerve endings ablaze. But she wanted more. She pressed her thighs together, trying to stem the throbbing ache building up inside her.

He pulled away, his breath ragged. "April, do you want—"

"To have sex? Yes. Absolutely."

His look of surprise stopped her cold.

Nope. Definitely not what he was asking.

CHAPTER 21

april covered her face with her hands. "Oh my God. Forget I said anything."

"Are you kidding? No backsies, Beckett."

His smug expression made her laugh. "What were you going to ask me?"

"If you wanted to close the drapes so we'd have more privacy. But your suggestion is a million times better. Besides, I was hoping you'd proposition me again."

Her cheeks blazed with heat. "What...what exactly did I say last night?"

"I believe you said, 'It would be really hot if you fucked me wearing nothing but that pirate hat.' Not that I've been playing that request back in my head nonstop or anything."

She should have been mortified, but his grin was so infectious her shame melted away. "And you turned me down? What the hell, Blackwood?"

He placed his hand over his heart. "I solemnly swear I wanted you with every fiber of my being. But you were wasted. I was hoping you'd make me another offer when you were sober."

Her earlier hurt resurfaced, needling at her confidence. "I thought maybe you didn't want me."

"April Beckett, I have wanted you since the moment I saw that bed. I've spent the last two nights dreaming about it. Pirate's honor."

She tried to keep her voice light, even though her heart was beating in double time. "Pirates don't have honor."

"This one does." He leaned in again, placing gentle kisses along the curve of her neck, his lips whisper-soft on her skin. Pushing the collar of her bathrobe to one side, he kissed her shoulder. His hand slipped under the robe and stroked her breast, making her gasp with unexpected pleasure. Her nipples perked up in response, craving his touch. But he stood abruptly, leaving her aching for more.

"Wait. Where are you going?" She sounded like a needy child, but she couldn't help it. They were just getting started.

Again with that smug smile. As though he knew *exactly* what he was doing by making her wait. "We're not going any further until I close those drapes. I don't want everyone out on the water to get a full show."

As she readjusted her robe and got to her feet, her insecurity kicked in. Was she making a terrible mistake? Did he *actually* want her, or was it because she was available, he wanted to get laid, and they were in a romantic situation? What would happen to their friendship if they had sex? Would it mean they were a couple? Or would this just be a fun, onetime fling during their stay in Door County?

Stop. If you overthink this, you'll ruin everything.

To hell with it. This was her vacation. Damned if she wasn't going to enjoy every minute of her time with Brody.

She joined him next to the picture window as he pulled the drapes, darkening the room. The only light came from the flicker of flames in the fireplace. She expected him to take her in his arms, but he stepped back a pace, his brow creasing with concern.

"Everything okay?" she asked.

He rubbed the back of his neck. "Shit, April. I...I'm not prepared for this."

"Emotionally?" Like a dope, she took a minute to realize what he meant. "*Oh*. Wait a sec." She dashed into the bathroom and rooted through her toiletries bag.

Please let them be there.

She exhaled in relief when she found a few condoms buried under a travel pack of Kleenex. She'd packed them months ago, back when she and Chris had spent the weekend in Oakland for his triathlon. He'd been so worried about overexerting himself they hadn't used them. She placed them on the nightstand. "Got you covered. Literally."

He raised his eyebrows. "Thinking ahead?"

When she looked away in embarrassment, he laughed gently. "I'm kidding. I'm glad one of us is prepared. I can buy more tomorrow."

"I have three."

He gave her a devious grin. "Like I said, I can buy more tomorrow." He crossed the room to meet her beside the bed and set his glasses on the nightstand. Without them, he looked vulnerable, making her realize he had as much at stake as she did.

Her heart pounded as he untied the sash of her robe. The thought of being completely exposed excited and terrified her, but she wasn't about to turn back now. She reached for his t-shirt, tugging it over his head, then ran her hands along his chest, feeling the ridges of muscles under her fingers. "You look really good with your shirt off."

"I believe the expression you used was *really hot*."

"Whatever. But you look good. And feel even better." She kissed his throat and shoulders, tasting the slight saltiness of his skin. He smelled of lake water and eucalyptus.

He eased the robe off her shoulders, letting it fall to the floor. And then she was naked. So very naked. She resisted the urge to cover herself. Especially since he was looking at her with a raw desire that made her ache for his touch.

"You're so sexy," he said. "I can't believe I slept next to you for two nights and didn't do anything."

"You were a gentleman."

"Not anymore." He tugged off his sweats and kicked them away. His boxers followed, leaving him as exposed as she was.

And, wow, Brody Blackwood was even hotter when he was totally naked. She couldn't stop staring.

His eyes danced with amusement. "You like what you see?"

She looked away as a rush of heat set her cheeks aflame. But any awkwardness vanished when he took her in his arms and kissed her again. The warmth of his skin was a tantalizing aphrodisiac, heating her more than the fire. She broke their embrace long enough to pull back the covers and push the annoying pile of pillows out of the way. When he lowered her onto the bed and melded his body against hers, she sighed at the very rightness of it. How they fit together so perfectly. She stroked his back, meeting his mouth for another long, hungry kiss.

When his tongue flicked over her nipples, she moaned, tangling her hands in his thick hair. Just as she'd suspected, it did feel amazing beneath her fingers. He took his sweet time, tasting and teasing, until she was ablaze with need. She'd forgotten how much she loved foreplay.

She wanted to taste his skin on her lips, but he kept her pinned to the bed, taking control as his mouth traveled lower down her body. He parted her legs, kissing the inside of her thighs. Kisses that promised more. Her body tensed with anticipation. It had been so very, very long since she'd been the recipient of such generosity.

"Oh, yes," she murmured. "Yes, please."

A sharp rap at the door struck her like an arrow to the heart. She went deadly still, hoping—*praying*—Brody had locked the door behind them.

"Yes?" she called out.

"It's Avery. I wanted to make sure you're all right?"

All right? She was naked, with Brody's head between her legs. She'd never been more all right in her life. "I'm good. Great! Thanks!"

Brody looked up at her with a bemused expression. She flushed under his scrutiny. "Sorry," she whispered. "I'll get rid of her."

"Take your time," he murmured. "I can do this all day." He teased her again with featherlight kisses that danced along her inner thighs. She squirmed under him, aching with desire.

Avery's voice rose. "Can I come in? You left your phone on the beach."

For the love of God, Avery.

April struggled to control the wobble in her voice. "I...I'm not decent. Leave it on the porch, okay? Thanks!"

"Sounds good. Fish boil's at eight. Meet us in the parking lot by 7:45."

"Will do!" She waited a beat, hoping her sister would take the hint. After a minute passed, she let out a long breath. "I think we're safe."

"Good," Brody said. "Because I'm not close to being done."

He curved his hands under her bottom, holding her firmly as he used his tongue to find her sweet spot. She twisted her hand around the pillow, clutching it for dear life as she writhed in his grasp, scarcely able to bear the exquisite sensations coursing through her. Her breath came in gasps as she climbed higher, so close to the edge she could hardly stand it. When she finally crested the mountain, she lost control, crying out Brody's name as her body shuddered in ecstasy. She was still trembling when he came up for air and reached for the condom on the nightstand.

She propped herself up on her elbows to get a good look at him. His lean, muscular body. His hard length, aroused and ready for her. She wanted to take him in her mouth and make him groan in submission. "Wait. Let me return the favor."

"Another time, I promise." He gave her a wicked smile. "If I don't get inside you right now, I'm going to explode."

"Allow me." She took the condom, unwrapped it, and rolled it over him, taking her time to stroke him properly. And then he was covering her body with his own and parting her legs again—and, *oh*—did he feel good inside her. She buried her face into his shoulder. "Oh yes, Brody. Yes."

He groaned her name, then pushed in deeper. Her body responded to his, arching up to meet him with each thrust. As the pleasure built, she dug her nails into his back, wanting to bring him closer. When he stopped, she tensed up, worried she'd done something wrong. "What is it?"

His stormy gray eyes captured hers. "I don't want to rush this. You're so fucking gorgeous when you're excited."

No one had ever looked at her that way during sex. Like she was special. Worthy of more than a quick tumble on the couch.

She whispered his name and then he was sliding into her again, but slowly this time, drawing out each stroke, stopping to brush his lips against her skin and tease her nipples with his tongue. She whimpered as he stoked the fire within her, little by little, until she was near to combustion. He quickened his pace, and she moved with him, rolling her hips with each thrust. As waves of pleasure engulfed her, she cried out, the heat inside her igniting into an all-consuming flame. Seconds later, he groaned in release and then lay still, his body pressed against hers.

For a moment, they lay together, foreheads touching, breathing heavily. She couldn't find the words, not when her impossible fantasy had come true. The man she'd dreamed about for two years had finally made love to her, and the sex had exceeded her wildest expectations.

He eased himself off her, removed the condom, and wrapped it in a Kleenex. But unlike most of her dates, he didn't rush off to shower or dash out the door. Instead, he took her in his arms. She curled up against him, resting her head on his chest and listening to the drumbeat of his heart. He murmured her name, like a gentle caress, and she was all but ready to drift asleep, cozy and secure in his arms.

Even without the pirate hat, it was absolutely, one hundred percent perfect.

CHAPTER 22

If Brody had his way, they would have stayed in bed the rest of the evening. True, they'd get hungry at some point, but they had enough wine and cheese in the cottage to sustain themselves. He could think of nothing more appealing than spending the next few hours satisfying April's every need. He wanted to hear her cry out his name again, to feel her nails digging into him as he drove himself deep inside her. He couldn't believe they'd had sex. And that it had been so incredible.

April nestled in closer, her body warm and soft against his. He was glad he'd resisted her last night. This way, their first encounter wasn't a hazy, drunken blur but a searing memory neither of them would ever forget.

He kissed the top of her head. "What *is* a fish boil? Do we have to go?"

"Not sure. But yes, we need to be there. It's another Door County tradition Mags wants us to experience. I don't want to let her down."

"Fair enough." He curved his hand around her bottom. "Can we come back here afterward? Like, right away?"

"We'll take your car. That way we can leave as soon as

humanly possible." She looked up at him, a naughty smile crossing her lips. "I take it you want more."

"Without question. We should find a drugstore tomorrow. Or maybe tonight. Because we only have two condoms left." He chuckled. "You underestimated me."

"I didn't know we'd be having sex." She ran her hands along his back. "Not that I didn't dream about it."

"For how long?"

"Umm…"

"Come on. Spill."

She let out a lengthy sigh. "Honestly? I've had a crush on you since day one. Even though we dated other people, I always had these Brody fantasies tucked away in the back of my mind."

Damn, if that wasn't an ego boost. "I love that I was the focus of your daydreams."

She gave him a gentle shove. "Don't let it go to your head. I also envisioned a lot of scenarios involving Robert Downey Junior and Chris Hemsworth."

"Even better. You're putting me in the same category as two of the Avengers."

Before this trip, he'd always thought she was cute and enjoyed her company; a few times, during their late-night movie marathons, he'd wondered what would happen if he crossed the line and kissed her. But he never pursued her. Instead, he wasted so much time and energy chasing after girls who made him work for it. Aloof, high-maintenance women who looked great on his arm but never understood him the way April did. He'd been so stupid. So egotistical. All along she'd been there, and he'd completely missed the boat.

Not anymore.

〜

BRODY SNUGGLED in bed with April until they could no longer delay the inevitable. After they changed into sweatshirts and jeans, they walked to the main parking lot to rendezvous with the rest of the family. Now that the sun had set, the chilly air had a definite bite, making Brody glad April had warmed up properly. He kept his arm around her, relieved he could act as affectionate as he wanted without worrying he was going too far.

As usual, they were the last to arrive. Brody expected Avery to chastise them for being late, but her tone was gentle. "Glad you two made it. April, you sure you're okay?"

"I'm good," April said. "Thanks for dropping off my phone."

Mrs. Beckett came over to April and placed her hand on her daughter's arm. "Honey, I was so worried when Avery told me what happened."

"I'm fine, Mom. Chris helped me get back to the cottage. But it was scary at the time."

Drianna was ready, her claws out. Her mouth twisted in a sneer. "Scary? It was waist-deep."

Mags glared at her. "This isn't California. Lake Michigan's freezing cold this time of year." She offered April a sympathetic smile. "I'm sorry you fell in."

April leaned into Brody, who tightened his grip around her. "No worries. But next time, I'm going to make sure I have a life jacket that fits. I'm lucky it didn't go flying off me. If the water had been deeper, it would have been a lot worse."

Mags drew in her breath. "You should never go out on Lake Michigan without a proper life jacket. Even if you're a good swimmer."

Brody caught Drianna's eye and gave her a pointed look. He was partly to blame because he hadn't pushed the issue. He could have gone back to the lodge and found April a bigger life jacket. But he'd let her make the call, and she'd only capitulated after Drianna mocked her.

In turn, Drianna let out a huffy breath. "Let's go. If we don't hurry up, we'll be late."

They piled into various cars, with Brody making certain he and April drove alone. Following the others, they drove to the White Deer restaurant, located in the nearby town of Fish Creek. According to Mags, fish boils were a key part of the Door County foodie experience. Most restaurants in the area offered them multiple times a week during the height of the tourist season.

Outside the restaurant, wrought-iron patio tables encircled a bricked-in area. At the center was a burning pile of logs that held a large cast-iron kettle. Clouds of steam wafted from it. Brody inhaled, taking in the strong aroma of woodsmoke.

Mags staked out a couple of tables. She pointed to a burly man standing near the fire, who resembled Pirate Pete, minus the garb. "That guy's the boil master. Once the water's boiling, he'll add the potatoes and onions. The whitefish comes last. The best part is at the end, during the boilover, when he pours kerosene on the fire, and it goes up in a giant blaze." She licked her lips. "I hope you brought your appetite because the fish and potatoes are served with melted butter. And every meal includes a slice of homemade cherry pie."

Brody's mouth watered. As he sat beside April at one of the tables, he spoke softly so only she could hear. "Forget I complained about the fish boil. This sounds fantastic."

"We definitely worked up an appetite," she whispered back. "I'm ravenous."

Ginger walked over to them. "I'm going to the bar. April, will you come with?"

"No drinks for me," April said. "I had too much tequila last night."

Ginger leaned over her chair, fire blazing in her eyes. "Then you can order a soda. Because you need to come with me. *Now*." She raised her eyebrows. "Excuse us, *Chris*."

April gave him a shrug, but she stood and accompanied her cousin. "Do you want anything?" she called back.

"I'll take a beer. Something local, if they have it on tap." Watching her go, Brody gave a deep, satisfied sigh. They'd had amazing sex, they were about to feast on a delicious meal, and they'd follow it up with more sex. Life didn't get much better than this. Around him the Becketts were laughing and talking, all except Drianna's husband, Ian, who was once again absent.

Brody allowed himself to relax. Pretending to be a couple was so much easier now that they were *actually* a couple.

But the minute he let down his guard, Drianna was at his side, taking April's seat.

He kept his tone light. "Sorry, but April's sitting there."

"I saw her and Ginger head for the bar," Drianna said. "They'll be a while."

He nodded and focused his attention on the boil master, who was in the midst of his spiel. Apparently, the earliest fish boils originated in the 1800s, brought to Door County by Scandinavian immigrants. Drianna waved her hand in front of his face. "Earth to Chris. I'm talking to you."

He let out his breath. "What is it?"

"It's not my fault April tipped her kayak, so don't go acting like I'm the one to blame."

"I never said it was your fault. No one did. But you could have been more sympathetic."

"You think I'm too hard on her?" Drianna was all but baring her fangs.

He hated to bring up the past, but he was troubled by what he'd learned. "Ollie told me what happened back when April was twelve. When she got sick."

"You don't know anything about it."

"I know I wouldn't have reacted the same way if it was *my* brother stuck in the hospital for a week."

"Huh." She leaned back in her chair, appraising him coolly. "April told me you were an only child."

Shit. Another facet of Chris-knowledge he'd forgotten about. "I...ah...do have a brother. But I don't talk about him much. We had a falling-out, a while back. We're estranged."

Even to his own ears, he sounded like an actor on a bad TV drama. He tried to pivot, channeling the confidence the real Chris would have shown. "Sounds like April talked about me a lot. I guess I should be flattered."

"Oh, she talked all right," Drianna said. "Because every time she mentioned you, I hit her up with more questions. To make sure you weren't fake, like Sam Jameson."

What a pain in the ass.

"As you can see, I'm very real." He desperately wished someone would swoop in and rescue him, but the Becketts were caught up in their own conversations.

"You might be real, but something's off. Because you're nothing like the guy April told us about."

He wiped his forehead, aware of how much he was sweating. Did he look as flustered as he felt? "You mean because I tanked in the race? I had too much to drink."

"It's more than that. April told us you'd fit right in because you love to compete. But you can barely hold your own."

"What are you talking about? We kicked your butts in trivia night."

"Because you dominated the video game category. Another factoid April never shared with us. Ollie said it was your dirty little secret."

Brody tried for a casual shrug. "It's not something I brag about. Wouldn't go with my image."

Where was April with his drink? He moved as if to stand, but Drianna gripped his arm. Hard. Her voice was like flint. "I've also been watching you eat. Your diet is for shit. If you were doing

Paleo before this trip, you'd be sick to your stomach after all the crap you've eaten."

She was watching him eat? She'd officially turned from annoying to creepy.

"Hey." April stood over them, drinks in hand. Beside her was Ginger. "Can you move over, Dree? I'm sitting there."

"I'm done." Drianna placed two fingers in front of her eyes, then pointed them at Brody before skulking off to spread her misery elsewhere.

April set a pint glass in front of Brody. "Here you go. Spotted Cow. The bartender said it's a big thing here, and you can only buy it in Wisconsin." She sat down beside him, a can of Diet Coke in hand.

Ginger sat across from them. "What did Drizella want?"

Brody took off his sweatshirt and draped it over his chair. Either the fire or Drianna's interrogation had raised his body temperature a good ten degrees. "She suspects something's up with the fake-Chris scenario."

"Oh, shit," April said. "You didn't break, did you?"

"No, but I inadvertently mentioned I had a brother. Sorry. I forgot Chris was an only child. I tried to backtrack, but—"

"Oh my God, you guys," Ginger said. "Confess and be done with it. Especially since you're *actually* together now." She lifted her wineglass in a salute.

"You told her?" Brody asked April.

She gave him an apologetic smile. "She guessed it herself. I didn't want to lie."

Ginger rolled her eyes. "It's stunningly obvious. But also kind of cute. I'm rooting for you."

"I don't want to tell my family the truth yet," April said. "Not with the wedding coming up. We'll come clean after."

And then what? Did her words imply she wanted them to continue on this path? That they'd still be a couple after this week? He hoped so.

At some point, they needed to talk about their relationship. But not now, with Ginger sitting beside them. Ollie and Mags joined their table a few minutes later, and the conversation turned back to trivia night. They paused when the boil master worked his magic. As he doused the logs with kerosene, the fire erupted into a blaze of bright-orange flames, drawing the crowd's attention.

Though the meal that followed was delicious, Brody couldn't recapture the contentment he'd felt earlier. He was too aware of Drianna's gaze drilling into him like the evil eye of Sauron, waiting for him to stumble.

CHAPTER 23

*A*pril woke to the sound of rain drumming on the roof. The gloomy weather came as a welcome relief, because she could think of nothing she'd like better than a low-key day. Yesterday's kayak ordeal and the subsequent bedroom shenanigans had worn her out.

Not that she had any complaints.

She pressed her body against Brody's, relishing the warmth of his bare skin. Though they'd exhausted themselves last night, her desire was already stirring. She couldn't remember the last time she'd felt this *wanton*. With Chris, she'd gotten used to his pattern of "one and done." When she was with Brody, they couldn't get enough of each other.

When her lover opened his eyes, she nuzzled his shoulder, inhaling the scent of cedar and eucalyptus. "Good morning."

"Morning." Placing a chaste kiss on the top of her head, he pulled away. He sat up and retrieved his glasses from the nightstand. "I'm off to get us some coffee. Real coffee, not that Keurig crap."

Disappointment gnawed at her. It had been so long since she'd been with anyone who spent the night. She missed the delicious ease of morning-after sex. She spoke up, hoping she didn't sound too needy. "There's no rush. If you want, we can stay in bed a little longer."

"I'd love to, except we're out of supplies." He gave a rueful shake of his head. "You were very demanding last night."

"Oh, right." They'd burned through all three of her condoms. That had to be a PR. "Are you going to get more?"

He quirked an eyebrow at her. "Is that a trick question? I'm buying an entire box."

Her insecurity vanished, replaced by the thrill of anticipation. "Perfect. And if you're going for coffee, I'll take a latte."

He hopped out of bed and went over to the picture window, where he pulled back the drapes. "It's pouring. I might have to do a little work this morning. Check my email, touch base with the marketing team, that kind of thing. I'll type up your notes from the wineries."

"Sounds good. I'll check in with the fam. I'm not sure what they had planned, but it's fine if you take a day off from being Chris. At least until tonight." She grabbed her phone from the nightstand and checked her calendar. "I have the bachelorette night at six, and you're supposed to leave for Ollie's pub crawl around the same time."

He pulled a flannel shirt and jeans from his suitcase. "Are you sure I'm invited? I'm not in the wedding party or anything."

"Ollie wants you to go." She wagged her finger. "But don't stay out too late. I'll wait up for you."

Once he left to get coffee, April lay back in bed, allowing her mind to wander. After the fish boil, they'd rushed back to the cottage, barely able to keep their hands off each other during the drive. Then they made love in front of the fire at a slow, leisurely pace, touching and teasing and taking their sweet time. They ended the night with a final romp in bed. She couldn't believe they'd had sex three times in one day. When she got up to use the bathroom, her legs wobbled like Jell-O.

But that was nothing compared to the giant wobble in her heart.

You're falling in love with him.

Brody hadn't mentioned love, but the way he treated her implied he cared. And he'd invited her to his family's lodge at Big Bear Lake in a decidedly non-platonic way. But she still wasn't sure if he was ready to commit to a real relationship.

Why not? You're already friends. Why can't you take things to the next level?

They needed to talk about it, but she didn't want to spook him, not after the heartbreak he'd been through with Taylor. At the same time, she didn't want a friends-with-benefits situation, either. She'd had her fill of that with Chris. She wanted romance. Commitment. Someone who included her in every aspect of his life.

But Brody had yet to make a final decision about the Napa offer. If he accepted it, he'd be living eight hours away from her. And he might not be up for a long-distance relationship.

All this angst was ruining her morning-after buzz. Since there was no urgency, she could wait to broach the subject.

SHE WAS STILL LOUNGING in bed when Brody returned, a half hour later, with a couple of lattes and a large box of condoms. After they finished their coffee and tested out one of the condoms, they indulged in a long, sensual shower. April could have spent the entire morning in bed, but she forced herself to get dressed and face the day. While she'd been in the shower, Ollie had sent her a text, letting her know the family was planning a cutthroat game of Monopoly in the lodge's community room. Because the Beckett clan couldn't do anything without turning it into a high-stakes endeavor.

Leaving Brody to his emails, she grabbed her sketchbook and

pencil case, along with the large golf umbrella supplied by the cottage. As she stepped outside, she inhaled the earthy scent of wet leaves. Though the umbrella sheltered her from the worst of the downpour, her canvas sneakers were no match for the large puddles underfoot. Navigating the trail took twice as long, since the rain had made the path extra slippery.

She found the community room on the ground floor of the lodge in a space furnished with tables and chairs, comfortable couches, and bookshelves filled with puzzles and games. At one end, a stone fireplace offered up a roaring blaze. A row of picture windows provided a view of the lake, now obscured by mist and rain. The Becketts had commandeered the table closest to the fire, with the Monopoly board already laid out.

"Hey, April," Avery said. "We set up the game. You can partner with Mom if you want."

April usually partnered with Ollie, but today Mags was at his side. Avery and Drianna never partnered with anyone. And her mom always worked in tandem with her dad, but he wasn't at the table. "Doesn't Dad want to play?"

Her dad waved from a couch by the window. "I'm sitting this one out. I need to review a few projects for work."

"I'll join you." She held up her sketchbook. "I'd rather draw than engage in a Monopoly war."

She sat on the other end of the couch, with her legs curled underneath her. Outside, the rain beat down in a steady onslaught. The perfect day to laze around indoors. She flipped to her most recent sketch, one she'd started during the flight to Green Bay.

After a half hour of drawing in comfortable silence, punctuated by the occasional outcry from the Monopoly table, she set down her sketchbook and fished through her pencil case for a sharpener.

Her dad took off his glasses and rubbed the bridge of his nose. "Good Lord. This could put anyone to sleep."

"Environmental impact report?"

"It's a doozy." He gestured to her sketchbook. "Nice to see you're still drawing."

"I try to fit it in when I can. But these days, I don't have much time for it." When she was younger, she drew all the time. Now, she only sketched when she had the chance to relax. But she couldn't give it up completely. Something about drawing on paper rather than using a computer, felt so freeing.

"I remember when you were home sick for all those weeks," he said. "You never stopped drawing. Other kids might have been bored, but you filled an entire sketchbook."

A bittersweet memory, given how ill she'd been. She'd spent nine days in the hospital, fighting off a severe case of double pneumonia. After she was discharged, she had to stay on bed rest for another two weeks because her lungs were so weak. But her dad made a point to visit her every night after work. He'd spent hours reading to her, looking over her day's sketches, and drawing alongside her.

"Can I see what you're working on?" he asked.

She passed him the sketchbook. Most of her compositions featured superheroes in various poses. At first, she'd gotten inspiration from her comics collection, but lately she'd been creating her own characters. She set them in full-page panels, complete with elaborate backdrops.

Her dad chuckled. "I see you haven't outgrown your obsession with superheroes."

She braced herself, expecting his criticism. Both her parents thought Marvel movies were childish and predictable. A ridiculous opinion, given their passion for sports movies. Nothing was more predictable than a film where a ragtag team surged to victory in the final moments of the big game.

As her dad flipped through the pages, he stopped at one and offered an encouraging smile. "The detail on this spread is unbelievable. You must have spent hours on it."

One of her older compositions, drawn six months ago. At the time, she'd been holed up in her apartment, alone and miserable after Brody canceled another movie night.

He handed back the book. "You have so much talent. I don't understand why you don't try for more."

His words cut into her, making her feel like she'd disappointed him by not choosing a more challenging career. "I like my job. It's fun. I get to work on all kinds of projects."

"But it's so ephemeral. Logos, digital images, social media. None of it has any lasting power."

She stretched out her legs. "I dunno, Dad. Wine's been around for centuries. Since the Roman Empire at least. And Blackwood Cellars owns ten percent of the global wine market. It's not like I'm working for a startup."

He laughed. "That's not what I meant, and you know it. I'm talking about the lasting power of creating a building—a museum, a monument—versus online content that comes and goes in the blink of an eye."

Ollie strolled over to join them. "But digital content is the future. Think of how many digital applications you use. I can't imagine doing my research without them."

April scooted over to make room for her brother. "Shouldn't you be helping Mags beat Avery and Dree in Monopoly?"

He sat beside her. "She kicked me out after I told her Baltic Avenue was a waste of money. Apparently, I was messing with her strategy."

All the more reason April was glad she'd opted out of the game.

"And Drianna's being a huge pain in the butt," he said. "She keeps checking her phone. She totally missed it when Mom landed on one of her properties."

"Boardwalk?" her dad asked. Drianna always went for the big-ticket monopolies.

"With *two* houses," Ollie said.

April still couldn't figure out why her sister was more on edge than usual. "Why was she so distracted? Work stuff?"

"I guess. Something to do with that Gary guy. *Again*." He scanned the room. "I take it Chris isn't a big Monopoly player?"

"He had to catch up with work. And he was kind of tired after last night."

"Where'd you go, anyway?" Ollie asked. "Mags went to find you after the fish boil ended, but you'd mysteriously vanished. We hit up a bar in Fish Creek."

"We...wanted to get back to the cottage. To...you know— rest?" She stifled a grin. She didn't want everyone in her family to think she and Brody spent all their free time having sex. Especially after she'd played up the role of the oversexed girlfriend before the 10K.

Ollie nudged her. "You've got it bad, kiddo."

"Can we not?" She cast a subtle glance at her father.

"Sorry. Hey, speaking of Chris, can you send me his phone number? I want to make sure I have it for the bar crawl tonight. He's coming, right?"

Without thinking, she almost shared Chris's number from her contact list but stopped herself in time. If Ollie called it, he'd find out the real Chris was thousands of miles away. Instead, she looked up Brody's number, carefully typed it into a text, and sent it to Ollie. "Here you go. He'll be there, I promise."

"Great. I also wanted to tell you Mags and I downloaded your Blackwood Cellars app. We figured this way we'd have a clue when we shop for wine. Most of the time, we opt for whatever's on sale. Either that or Mags picks the bottles with the cutest logos."

April beamed, thankful for his support. "See, Dad? I'm helping Ollie become a savvier consumer."

"I'm not sure how important apps are in the grand scheme of life," he countered.

"I'll bet your phone has lots of apps you use on a daily basis,"

Ollie said. "Spotify, Netflix, Fitbit, Venmo. You and Mom are addicted to Map My Run."

He held up his hands in surrender. "You win. Those running apps are great. All I'm saying is April should consider aiming higher than creating digital content. With her talent, she shouldn't have to settle."

But I'm not settling.

Still, if her dad was willing to drop the argument, she'd let it go.

For now.

CHAPTER 24

$\mathcal{B}$rody sat on the bed with his laptop beside him. He'd returned six emails, called the office to deal with a technical issue, and typed up April's notes from the wineries. He sent them off to Marc, even though he wasn't sure if his brother had considered expanding Blackwood Cellars into the Midwest. At least this way, he was covering his bases.

He opened his latest email from Jimmy, the programmer he'd hired to help manage the app development team. According to Jimmy, the latest update was proving troublesome. Normally, Brody would have relished the chance to dive in and debug the code, but he was having a hard time focusing on the issue.

He was having a hard time focusing on *anything*.

Except April.

His mind kept wandering as he recalled every detail of the previous night. Making love to her in front of the fire. Watching the firelight dance on her naked skin as they lay together in blissful exhaustion. Holding her close as they drifted off to sleep. They'd created more memories this morning, with another round of sex, followed by a steamy, passionate shower.

His phone rang, startling him out of his daydream. He glanced at the screen, surprised to see his brother's name. "Hey, Marc. What's up?"

"How's Wisconsin?"

"Great. Really relaxing." Any doubts he'd harbored about accompanying April on this trip had vanished. His offer to join her might have been impulsive, but it was the best decision he'd made in years.

"What's the deal with the winery notes? Uncle Brian and I met yesterday to discuss our expansion into Washington state, but he never mentioned anything about Wisconsin. Is this a new initiative I don't know about?"

Trust Marc to worry he was out of the loop. The guy liked to be on top of everything.

"Not really," Brody said. "There are some decent local wineries, but nothing to justify investing in Wisconsin. Since I was going to be out here, I figured I'd do a little recon for you and…" He trailed off, feeling guilty. When he'd told Marc he was going to Door County, he hadn't given him a real explanation.

"Cut the shit," Marc said. "You're there because of April."

Brody froze. He'd never divulged the details of his friendship with her. As far as Marc knew, she was just his coworker, someone he'd bonded with when they created the Blackwood Cellars app. "How…how did you know about April?"

His brother chuckled. "You talk about her a lot. So, when you mentioned this trip—out of the blue—I had to dig deeper and find out why you were taking a week off to go to Wisconsin. Luckily, Victoria was able to fill me in."

Victoria. Brody groaned. He'd completely forgotten his cousin and April were friends. No doubt April had confided in her, probably over wine or margaritas. "What did she tell you?"

"She said you went with April as her date for a family wedding."

Brody let out a long exhale. Maybe April hadn't shared *all* the details of the trip with Victoria. Like the fact he was pretending to be Chris. "She didn't mention anything else?"

"Why? Is there more?"

Damn it. He had to be careful. He had no intention of sharing his ruse with Marc. His brother was so sure of himself he'd never pretend to be someone else. "That about sums it up."

Marc laughed. "Dude. I can't believe you're willingly submitting to another destination wedding."

Brody flinched. The Maui wedding would haunt him forever. "I'm trying to keep a low profile. I'm staying away from the booze. And I'm not offering to give any speeches. I don't want to fuck things up like I did at your wedding."

"You know I'm not mad about any of it, right? My rehearsal dinner might have been a disaster, but it all ended well."

"No thanks to me."

"Don't beat yourself up. It's over. And I'm not trying to bust your balls about this trip. It's great you're moving on. Taylor didn't deserve you."

A rumble of thunder diverted Brody's attention, making him wonder if he'd heard Marc correctly. He'd assumed his family had been impressed with Taylor since she was so far out of his league. "What?"

"None of us liked her. She treated you like shit. You're better off without her."

Marc's words hit him like a smack upside the head. "Why didn't you say anything?"

"Because you were so proud of yourself. Like landing her was this huge accomplishment. You wouldn't have listened."

Brody cringed. He'd bragged about her to everyone in his family, desperately craving their approval. But they'd seen right through him. Needy Brody, always looking for ways to bolster his self-esteem.

He spoke quickly, wanting to defend himself. "This is different. April's not like that."

"I figured as much. Hell, even Victoria likes her, and you know how critical she is." Marc waited a beat, then asked, "So…is it working out? With April?"

"Yeah. Better than I imagined." His gaze fell upon the fireplace. The scene of the crime, as it were. One of their crimes. They'd now had sex in the bed, the shower, and in front of the fireplace.

"You there?" Marc said.

Brody got his head together. "Sorry. Listen, can you keep this quiet for now? April and I are still…figuring things out." He didn't want his parents thinking he was involved with someone new, only to dash their hopes if it didn't work out.

"No problem. Is this a vacation thing or…something more?"

"I don't know. But I'd like it to be more. April's amazing, and I don't want to lose her."

"Does that mean you're going to stay in Temecula?"

Brody let out his breath. He'd put the Napa opportunity out of his mind after talking to April and Jess. But their words had resonated with him.

"Would you be disappointed if I stayed?" he asked.

"I won't lie, it would be great to have you up here. But not if you don't want it." Marc paused for a moment. "I guess the question you should ask yourself is whether you'd take the job if April wasn't in the picture."

"A fair point. But I was having doubts regardless. I like what I'm doing. I just don't want to let Dad down."

"Are you kidding? Dad thinks you're a fucking genius. He always brags about that app to anyone who'll listen. The stuff you do? It's way beyond any of our abilities."

His dad had bragged about him? "But then, why offer me this job?"

"To give you a chance to get away from Temecula. Maybe try something different. He was worried about you. Taylor messed with your head. Real toxic shit. But we just want you to be happy."

The rush of relief that coursed through Brody was so overwhelming he couldn't speak, for fear his voice would break. No one was disappointed in him. They didn't think he was a loser.

They just want you to be happy.

"Brody?" Marc said. "You still there?"

"Yeah. I'm doing better now, thanks to April."

She hadn't just responded to his romantic overtures; she'd also helped him see what he really wanted. To be his own person, without changing to fit anyone's ideals. Not Taylor's. Not Marc's. Not his parents'. To use his skills to shine at things he enjoyed.

"Good to hear," Marc said. "I should get going. Have fun with April. You deserve it after the hell you went through in Maui."

He *did* deserve it. And he planned to enjoy every minute of their time together.

By FIVE, the rain let up, and the sun peeked out in time for their evening activities. April went to join the ladies for the bachelorette party. Brody followed soon after, meeting Ollie and his crew in the lodge's parking lot, where a Door County Trolley stood waiting to take them on their pub crawl. Of the group, the only people he knew besides Ollie were Hunter and Ian, who were talking about golf, yet again. The rest consisted of Ollie's groomsmen and a posse of his college buddies. Brody felt like the odd man out until he connected with a couple of Ollie's friends from grad school—both of whom were hard-core gamers.

The third bar on their itinerary was the Salty Crow. Still as pirate-y as ever, although their "Tropical Thursday" specials included mai tais and piña coladas. In the background, Jimmy

Buffet tunes added to the vibe. As a waitress sauntered by, wearing a pirate hat, Brody's memory was jarred back to April's drunken request. If she was still awake when he got back to the cottage, he'd offer to fulfill her fantasies. With another drink or two, he could easily muster up the balls to play the role of Captain Blackwood.

He went up to the bar and ordered a Spotted Cow lager. He'd developed a taste for them after the fish boil. Pirate Pete was on duty, looking far less flamboyant than he had on Tuesday.

"No pirate garb tonight?" Brody asked.

Pete set his pint glass on the counter. "Only for trivia night. That's more than enough."

The germ of an idea stuck in Brody's head. "You wouldn't happen to have an extra pirate hat back there? I wanted to take a selfie." The request made him cringe, but his embarrassment would be worth it if the photo produced the desired effect.

Pete let out a long breath. He reached behind the bar and pulled out a felt pirate hat. "Knock yourself out."

"Thanks." Brody perched it on his head, took a quick photo, and placed it back on the counter. He sent April a text. *Brace yourself, wench. Captain Blackwood's coming into port tonight.*

Cheesy, yes, but April replied seconds later with a string of emojis, including a smiling devil face and a honey pot. A fiery heat suffused his body, and his groin tightened as he imagined what awaited him. He shoved his phone in his pocket when Ollie approached the bar.

Ollie clapped him on the shoulder. "Need anything? We've got two tables in the back, and we're going to order wings."

"I'm good, thanks." Not that he was a spice wimp, but the wing flavors listed on the chalkboard sounded like tongue-burning torture, with names like BBQ Volcano and Dead on Arrival.

After Ollie ordered a beer and three baskets of wings, he leaned against the bar, waiting for his drink. "Thanks for coming, man. I appreciate it."

"No problem. Your family's been great."

"Glad you think so. My sisters can be a giant pain in the ass. Not April, but Avery and Dree turn everything into a contest. Mags was intimidated at first, until she challenged them to a 'friendly' soccer game." Ollie chuckled. "That was a match for the ages."

Brody's mind drifted for a moment as he imagined being a part of April's family. Surprisingly enough, the idea appealed to him. He might have tanked in the 10K, but he'd redeemed himself by helping Ollie's team win at trivia night. Other than Drianna, the Becketts seemed to have accepted him.

Ollie's next words took him by surprise. "April said you played baseball in high school. Your team went to State twice."

What the hell, Chris? Couldn't you be a normal athlete?

Unlike Chris, Brody hadn't played a single sport in high school, although his robotics team had made it to the World Championships. Not something he'd mention now. But if Ollie wanted to talk about baseball, he was screwed.

"What position did you play?" Ollie asked.

"Uh...shortstop?" Not exactly a lie. In college, when he realized sports could be fun, he joined an intramural baseball team. Last summer, he also played for Blackwood Cellars in the Temecula Valley Winery League. Since the league was strictly amateur, the pressure was minimal, other than some good-natured trash talking.

"Excellent," Ollie said. "That's Ian's position, but he's got other plans. The dude's obsessed with golf. Avery will be relieved we've got a shortstop for the game."

The game?

His shock must have been evident, because Ollie laughed. "April didn't tell you? We have one more tradition. The family softball game. Us versus Mags's family. The last two weddings, the Becketts came out on top. We don't want to break our streak."

Brody gestured to the two tables at the back, overflowing

with Ollie's buddies. "Wouldn't you rather recruit some of your friends?" *All* of them appeared to be more athletic than he was.

"Family first. That's Avery's rule. And you're practically family." He grinned. "At least, as far as April's concerned."

The music switched from Jimmy Buffet to a louder steel-drum band. Brody leaned in, unsure if he'd heard Ollie correctly. "What do you mean?"

"My sister's crazy about you."

"She said that?" He sounded like the world's biggest wuss, but he wanted to know what April had told her family about him. Not the Chris stories she'd spun before, but the stuff she was telling them now. About *him.*

The bartender set a pint glass in front of Ollie. He took a long drink of his beer, then nodded. "April's easy to read. She's got it bad. And she's never brought anyone home before. She seems happy, too."

Was that Brody's doing? If so, he'd take the win. A warm glow came over him. "She's incredible. I'm lucky to have her."

Ollie tipped his glass toward Brody. "Good to hear. But don't hurt her. No one messes with my little sister."

He swallowed. Ollie was an easygoing guy, but he had at least five inches and thirty pounds of muscle on Brody. Though, to be honest, no one struck as much fear into his heart as Drianna.

"I'd never hurt her. I'm in love—"

Shit. He'd almost said it.

I'm in love with her.

Ollie slapped him on the back. "Dude, you are so whipped."

He was. Well and truly.

CHAPTER 25

B rody jogged along Pine Drive, only slowing when he reached the entrance to the North Bay Resort. He eased into a walk, taking deep, even breaths as his runner's high ebbed away. Another gorgeous, sunny day, and he'd greeted it by getting in a quick run while April was sleeping. He hadn't wanted to wake her, not after he'd kept her up until two in the morning. Last night's pub crawl had ended at one. When he returned, April was sitting up in bed and reading another romance novel. Naked.

The next hour had been entertaining, to say the least. Inspired by his stop at the Salty Crow, he'd worn April's pirate hat. A fair amount of role-play was also involved. Never in a million years would he have guessed April's mind held such wicked fantasies.

When he reached the porch of their cottage, he stretched into a deep lunge. Two days left. After today, the final hurdle was the wedding on Saturday afternoon, when all of April's family would be in attendance. If they could pull that off, they could consider Operation Fake-Chris a success.

Except Brody didn't want things to end. His slipup at the pub had forced him to face the truth. He was falling in love with April. A huge leap, to be sure, but she'd been an integral part of his life for the past two years. Through all the highs and lows, she'd been there, offering up baked goods and sympathy, sharing stories and jokes, and bonding with him over countless movie nights.

After losing Taylor, he'd sworn not to get in so deep. He couldn't take another heartbreak like that one. But his heart operated on its own terms, and, right now, it was telling him he was past the point of no return.

So be it. He still had to talk things over with April. Though he wasn't sure where she stood, he knew what he wanted. To keep their relationship going. To not allow this sexy, adorable woman to slip from his fingers, not when he'd wasted two years chasing after women who were entirely wrong for him.

He sat on the porch and took off his running shoes, setting them aside to air out. When his phone buzzed, he pulled it out of his armband and answered it quickly, not bothering to check who was calling.

"Brody?"

Bad mistake. If he'd waited one second longer, he would have read the name on the display first. *Taylor Calloway.*

"Brody? Are you there?"

For weeks after she left him, he'd dreamed of this moment. At first, all he wanted was a chance to win her back. As the weeks passed, his pathetic neediness changed to anger. He longed for the chance to tell her off.

But now? He was done with her.

He was tempted to hang up, but his curiosity got the better of him. "Hey, Taylor."

"Are you at work?"

"No…I'm…" He didn't want to reveal anything about his personal life. Not Operation Fake-Chris. Not his relationship with April. He didn't want Taylor to take his joy and twist it into something ugly. "I'm in Wisconsin. Checking out wineries for Blackwood Cellars."

"Wisconsin? Sounds dreadful. Isn't it cold there? I thought grapes needed sunlight."

He wasn't going to dignify her ignorance with a response. If he recalled correctly, she had no interest in any place she considered "fly-over country."

"It's...never mind. Everything okay?"

Why the hell are you calling me? And why now?

"I...no." Her voice trembled. "It's not."

Guilt stabbed at him. Even if she'd broken his heart, he could treat her with decency. "What's wrong?"

"It's Pierce. He...he hasn't been treating me right."

Pierce was the rich bastard who'd stolen Taylor away from him. The guy she'd been seeing on the sly, even as she promised Brody she'd join him in Maui for his brother's wedding. In Taylor's eyes, Pierce was a better catch, because he was wealthier and more connected.

He hated Pierce with every fiber of his being. "Did he hurt you?"

"Not physically. But he's been so mean lately. Treating me like I'm some hanger-on instead of the woman he pursued for months. I think he might be seeing someone else."

Hurts like hell, doesn't it?

But he didn't say it. Instead, he continued listening, like a friend would. When the breeze stirred up the leaves on the porch, he watched them swirl into the air. A sense of melancholy overtook him, as he remembered all the hours he'd wasted pining over Taylor.

"Brody? Are you listening?" Her voice was needle-sharp, slicing into him, reminding him of the agony she'd caused.

"Sorry. What were you saying about Pierce?"

"I thought he was the one. Otherwise, I wouldn't have left you. But last night, he said some horrible things and stalked out of my apartment. I started drinking again."

"Oh, Taylor. I'm so sorry." His heart went out to her. As the daughter of an alcoholic, she was terrified of falling into the same patterns as her father. "Have you checked in with your sister? Or any of your friends?"

"Not yet. I wish you were here. You're always so understanding."

He stared out at the lake, wincing at the bright sunlight reflecting off the water. In the distance, he spotted a few kayakers. He'd considered asking April if she wanted to go out again, this time in a tandem kayak, but now, all he could think about was Taylor. A few times, she'd gotten so drunk she blacked out completely.

"I don't want you to do anything desperate, okay?" he said. "You shouldn't be alone."

"That's why I need you. When are you coming back?"

Now she needed him? The irony was unbelievable.

"I fly in on Sunday," he said. "We can meet for coffee on Monday if you want. But if it gets worse, you need to call your therapist."

When she spoke again, her voice was choked by sobs. "You're being so nice. And I was so horrible. I'm sorry, Brody."

She hadn't apologized before. She'd broken up with him via text, but when he tried calling her back, she didn't even have the courtesy to pick up the phone. Instead, she responded with another text: *Leave me alone. It's over.*

He took a deep breath. Back in July, her response had gutted him, but he wasn't the same guy anymore. "It's fine. I'm okay now."

Her sobs grew in intensity, sending slivers of pain into his heart. "It's not okay. I feel awful. I should have come to Maui with you."

He paused for a moment, not wanting to respond in anger. No matter how badly she'd hurt him, he didn't crave revenge. This trip with April had healed him. Being with her made him realize how liberating it was to love someone who allowed him to be his true self.

He kept his tone gentle. Soothing. "It's in the past. Consider yourself forgiven."

April popped her head out the door. "Good morning. I'm going into town to grab us some coffee. What would you like?"

"Hang on." He focused his attention back on Taylor. "I need to go. I'm sorry."

"Can I call you back later?" she said. "There's something else I wanted to talk about."

His heart sunk like a deflated balloon. He didn't want to deal with her. Not on this trip. But he didn't feel right about ignoring her when she was hurting this badly. "Okay. I'll text you when I know my schedule."

After ending the call, he turned to April. She frowned. "Was that work? Is there some crisis you need to deal with?"

Lying would be the easy way out. But he was already lying to enough people by pretending to be Chris. "It was Taylor."

"Oh." She leaned back against the door, as though she'd had the wind knocked out of her. "Does she call you a lot?"

He knew how hard it was for April to ask. To make herself vulnerable. "No. That's the first time she's called since Maui. It's been over three months."

"Why now?" April's voice held an edge.

He stood up and rubbed his arms, chilly now that he'd cooled off. "She's having problems with Pierce."

"The guy she was seeing behind your back? When she cheated on you? *That* Pierce?"

"Yeah. I was trying to be a friend. That's all."

"Okay." She let out her breath, then forced a smile. "So...coffee?"

"Definitely. Can you get me an Americano? And a pastry?"

"Sure." She poked his shoulder. "I'd ask you to come with, but you're too sweaty for public consumption."

He grinned, glad they were back on a stronger footing. "You're lucky I didn't wake you up and ask you to join me. You still owe me a run."

"Only after you join me in Zumba, Captain Blackwood." She winked at him and sashayed off, putting a little swing in her walk.

The words "Captain Blackwood" were a trigger, bringing back a host of erotic memories. Which was good, because he'd rather focus on last night's delightful antics than Taylor's unexpected cry for help. As he went into the cottage and stripped down for his shower, he realized he could call Taylor back if he wanted. With April going into town for coffee, she'd be gone at least twenty minutes.

But he didn't want to talk to Taylor. Or get drawn into her web of self-pity. With any luck, she'd call her sister or one of her friends, and use them as a sounding board for her drama. If she still needed to talk later, he'd call her back.

But only if absolutely necessary.

CHAPTER 26

$\mathcal{A}$s April drove into town, her hands clutched the steering wheel in a death grip. She willed herself to calm down, but her pulse raced unevenly.

Why now?

Three and a half months ago, after Brody returned home from his brother's wedding in Maui, the first place he went was her apartment. There, he spilled the details of his miserable breakup. Though she wanted him to be happy, she secretly hoped he'd never get back together with Taylor.

By now, April assumed he was done pining over her. But what if—all along—he still wanted her back?

Ridiculous. Besides, Taylor hadn't asked to come back. She was trying to work things out with Pierce. She probably called Brody because he was a decent human being. The kind of guy who'd offer support, even if it meant consoling the woman who'd shattered his heart.

April found a local coffeehouse in the nearby town of Baileys Harbor, where she ordered their drinks and picked up a couple of scones. By the time she returned to the cottage, Brody had showered and changed. He sat on the porch, looking out at the lake with a tranquil expression on his face. Like he was at peace, without a care in the world.

Maybe she'd been wrong to worry about Taylor. Maybe he was truly over her.

She sat beside him and passed him the Americano. "I got us dried cherry scones."

"Yum. Door County cherry?"

"Naturally." She handed one to him, wrapped in a napkin. For a moment, she allowed herself to relax as she sipped her latte and basked in the warmth of the sun. The morning was still and quiet, save for the steady chirping of the sparrows flitting in the trees above them. When Brody reached over and threaded his hand in her hair, she gave a sigh of contentment.

"What are you thinking?" she asked.

"Just enjoying being with you. Thanks for the coffee."

Her heart flooded with affection. She was falling so damn hard. "My pleasure."

"Do we have any free time this morning?"

"We have until two. The big softball game's this afternoon. The Becketts versus the Flores family. I warned you about that, right?"

He took a bite of his scone. "This is good. Almost as good as those lemon blueberry scones you made last spring."

She couldn't help smiling. "Do you remember everything I make?"

"Remember? I write it down. I have a whole list of April Beckett 'Treatday Thursday' favorites." He wiped the crumbs from his mouth. "But to answer your earlier question, no, you did *not* warn me about the game. Or if you did, it was only in passing. Ollie filled me in last night."

Guilt gnawed at her. She'd considered telling him on their first day, but she hadn't wanted to overwhelm him. Given everything that had happened since then—especially all the sex—she'd forgotten about the game until this morning.

"Sorry," she said. "You play, right? I thought you played for Blackwood Cellars in the winery league."

"I'm surprised you remember. I don't recall seeing you at many of the games."

His tone held an edge, as if to remind her of all the times he'd asked her to come, and she'd declined. But Taylor had always been in the stands, cheering him on. A girl could only take so much. "I only went to a few. Chris wasn't into it because he didn't think the games were very exciting. He played in high school."

"So I heard." Brody shook his head, as if to chastise her, but a small smile played at the corner of his mouth. "You should have come. I crushed it as shortstop."

"In the same way you 'crushed' the Blackwood Cellars 5K?" By teasing him, she felt like they were back on familiar ground.

"You'll see. I had a shot at the team's MVP. I might have gotten it, if my cousin Darren hadn't hit that grand slam home run in the playoff game." He let out his breath. "The bastard stole all my thunder."

"Okay, Blackwood. You'd better bring it." She stretched out her legs. "After the game, we have a little free time, but not much, because the rehearsal's at six. I have to be there since I'm doing a reading. Dinner's at the lodge—the same place we ate the first night."

"Sounds good." He gestured to the lake. "Any chance you'd want to go out again? I called the rental place, and they have a double kayak available."

She drew in her breath. Falling in Lake Michigan had been a terrifying experience. But spending time on the water with Brody would cement their connection. "Just us?"

"No one else. And we'll make sure our life jackets fit properly. But if you don't want to, I understand completely."

She appreciated the effort he was making. And the way he didn't push her. "Let's do it."

~

BRODY HAD SUGGESTED KAYAKING to get his mind off Taylor. He also wanted April to have another chance on the water. His plan succeeded, and they had a relaxing morning on Lake Michigan without a single mishap. Upon their return, April suggested they celebrate their successful kayak outing by having sex, and he gladly obliged. When he held her in his arms, his stress and uncertainty vanished. He couldn't imagine wanting anyone else but her.

At one thirty, while they were sitting on the porch, nibbling on crackers and cheese from the Door County Creamery, Avery cruised by on a bike. Slung over her shoulder was a small duffel bag. She skidded to a stop and tossed them a couple of t-shirts. "Here. Wear these for the game."

The shirts were red, bearing the Team Beckett logo April had designed for the family's website. Brody took a shirt and passed the other one to April.

"Why am I getting a shirt?" she asked. "Don't you want me to keep score like I usually do?"

"I wish," Avery said. "But we're down two players. Ian's out golfing, and Dad's shoulder is acting up again. We're so desperate we recruited Ginger to play left field."

April groaned. "You're making me play catcher, aren't you?"

"You'll be fine. I'm pitching, so we'll work together. Try not to drop the ball if it comes to you." She hopped off her bike and pulled a couple of mitts and a softball out of her duffel bag. She handed them to April. "Why don't you practice before you come over to the field? And don't worry. It's a friendly game."

April gave a short laugh. "No game in our family is ever friendly."

After Avery left, April went back into the cottage to grab a couple of baseball caps. Brody's phone buzzed. This time, he had the foresight to glance at the screen. *Taylor.*

Shit. He'd forgotten to text her to let her know when he'd be free. Or maybe he'd subconsciously avoided it, hoping she wouldn't need him again. He declined the call. With the family softball gaming looming, he couldn't talk to her now. He'd wait until April was at the rehearsal.

He sent a quick text. *Sorry. Busy. I'll call at six.*

In response, she sent him a string of heart emojis.

April returned, caps in hand, and Brody pocketed his phone. They walked to a flat stretch of ground behind the cottage, under a small grove of evergreens. Scattered leaves and pinecones covered the area. He paced off until he was sixty feet away from April and lobbed her a few soft pitches. She caught them easily and flung them back with a surprising amount of force. Enough force that he staggered back after catching one. He paced off another ten feet and threw harder, but she missed very few.

He stared at her in disbelief. "I thought you said you couldn't play."

She cocked her hip to one side. "I can't. All we're doing now is throwing the ball back and forth. It's easy because there's no pressure."

"So—what, you choke up when you're in a game?"

"Sometimes?" She gave a sad shrug. "I'm not terrible, but I suck compared to the rest of my family. They're all *so* good. Ollie was on a traveling team in high school. Both my sisters spent years in rec leagues. Mom played in college. And my dad was the best player in his over-fifties league, until his old shoulder injury acted up."

Brody's stomach churned. Just because he'd been one of the better players on the Blackwood Cellars team didn't mean he could hold his own with April's family. He let out his breath in a long exhale.

April walked over to him. "What's wrong?"

He took off his cap and raked his hand through his hair. "I am so fucking doomed. You think the 10K was bad? This is going to be worse. We should leave now. Hop in that rental car and drive like hell. Tell them we'll be back in time for the wedding."

Her smile bubbled into laughter. She reached over and smoothed his hair. "Sounds perfect, but it's not going to happen."

"Apologies in advance if I tank. I can't even use sex as an excuse this time."

She took his hand and pulled him toward her, pressing her body against his. "You know one of the things I like about you?"

He clasped his arms around her waist. "That I overestimate my athletic abilities to an embarrassing degree?"

"That you're nothing like my family." She leaned in and kissed him gently. Soft kisses, on his lips, his cheeks, his forehead. "You're sweet, and smart, and just as geeky as me. You're trying your damnedest to fit in with the Beckett clan. And you've been one hundred percent here for me since the moment we arrived."

If he hadn't been sure of it before, he was now. He was totally, completely all in with this woman.

"Hey, lovebirds!" Drianna's voice was like a knife to the heart. She peered over her bike, glowering at them. "Get your asses over to the field! Mom's about to lead us in a warm-up."

Brody broke away from April. "Where are we playing?"

"There's a baseball diamond on the west side of the resort," Drianna said. "For corporate retreats and stuff like that."

April glared at her. "Ease up, okay? We'll be there in a few minutes."

"Try not to screw up the game," she muttered.

"I wouldn't have to play if Ian would bother to show up. What's his deal anyway?"

Drianna's eye twitched. She clenched her jaw. "None of your damn business. Hurry up and get there." With that, she pedaled off on her bike, reminding Brody of Almira Gulch, the Kansas counterpart for the Wicked Witch of the West in *The Wizard of Oz*. Brody could still remember cowering in terror when the

Wicked Witch made her first appearance in the movie. To be fair, he'd been five at the time.

"Something's up with Ian," April said. "Even for Drianna, that was an extra level of hostility."

"Probably best not to bait her," Brody said. "Like you're not supposed to tease the bears at the zoo."

She took his hand and squeezed it. "Thanks for doing this. In return, I'm fully on board with tonight's fantasy."

He couldn't wait. When he'd suggested a role-play inspired by the James Bond films, she'd eagerly agreed to play the part of a sexy Soviet agent. "Did you memorize a few Russian commands?"

"Did I? You'd be amazed at what you can learn on YouTube." She gave him a cheeky grin. "Get ready for your interrogation, Mr. Bond. Should be fun."

Whatever happened with the softball game, he didn't care. Not when he had a steamy reward waiting at the end of the night.

CHAPTER 27

*W*hen the dust settled, the Becketts had beaten the Flores family seven to three. Though April had been anxious about Brody, he held his own. A few of his catches were vital to the game, including his role in an all-important double play that brought the fourth inning to a close. At bat, he managed to knock off two singles and a double. Even April enjoyed the game more than she usually did because the Flores clan didn't possess the same all-consuming, cutthroat spirit as the Becketts.

After a round of beers from Ollie's cooler, April and Brody walked back to their cottage. With precious little time before the rehearsal was scheduled to start, April took a quick shower, *without* Brody to distract her. She changed into a burgundy lace minidress and a black cardigan, then emerged from the bathroom, bringing her toiletries bag and the hair dryer with her.

"Hey, Brody, bathroom's all yours," she said.

He wasn't in the cottage. When she peeked out the window, he was standing on the porch, talking on his phone. From the way he gestured with his hands, he appeared to be deeply engaged in the conversation.

Her stomach plummeted. Without asking, she knew who was on the other line. *Taylor.*

As much as she wanted to go outside and confront him, she reined herself in.

Act like an adult. And give him the benefit of the doubt.

The minutes ticked by as he continued his conversation. April's hands trembled as she dried her hair. Applying her makeup was nearly impossible. When she tried putting on mascara, she slipped and left a black smear under her eye.

Please don't let him go back to her.

She couldn't stand the thought of losing him to Taylor again. The first time had been painful enough. But now? After the passion they'd shared? She'd be devastated.

Stop it. You're overreacting.

Was she? Because she remembered how much Taylor's rejection had gutted Brody. How he'd schemed to win her back for a month, often texting April to ask her advice. Ever the supportive friend, she'd tried to be helpful, even if she was secretly glad he was free of the woman who'd torpedoed his self-esteem.

Having Taylor come crawling back had to be a huge boost to his ego. How could April compete with that?

She checked her phone. The rehearsal was starting in five minutes. Wiping her clammy hands on her dress, she went onto the porch as Brody ended the call.

He gave her a nervous smile. "Sorry about that. You look great. Cute dress."

She wouldn't let him distract her with compliments. "Was that Taylor?"

He rubbed the back of his neck. "She's going through a rough time right now. In her defense, she finally apologized for what she did to me in Maui."

About time. The incident in Maui had taken place three and a half months ago. April took a deep breath, bracing herself for the worst. "She wants you back, doesn't she?"

"Yes, but don't—" He froze, frustrating her, until she turned and saw Mags and her sister within earshot, walking up the trail to the cottage.

"Hey, April," Mags called out. "We thought we'd come snag you since you're perpetually late." She flashed a grin at Brody. "I assume you're to blame for delaying her."

April's chest tightened. "Can...can I join you in a few minutes?"

Mags shook her head. "We've only got the minister for a half hour, because he has a seven-o'clock wedding in Sister Bay. We need to hustle. You can text Chris when it's time for dinner."

April stood fixed in place, too overwhelmed to move, until Brody placed his hand on her arm. He pulled her closer and kissed her forehead. "Don't worry about it," he murmured. "We'll talk later."

She wanted to stay in his arms until her anxiety passed. Until he reassured her, without a shadow of a doubt, that he wasn't planning to leave her for Taylor. But she couldn't keep the others waiting. "You promise?"

"Of course. I'll see you at dinner. Okay?"

She couldn't ask for any more details, not with Mags and her sister hovering nearby. "Okay. See you soon."

As she followed Mags down the trail, she peeked back at Brody, who gave her a friendly wave. He wasn't acting like someone who planned to break her heart. And he'd been nothing but supportive over the past five days. She needed to trust him.

But when she took a second look, he'd already turned away, his head bent over his phone. Like he was calling Taylor back.

She clenched her fists and tried to breathe evenly. Under no circumstances could she lose her shit. Not until she and Brody talked things over.

"April? Everything okay with you and Chris?" Mags asked.

"He…he was dealing with work. His boss called and wanted him to run some numbers, and I overreacted. But he hardly ever takes vacation, so he deserves a break. I don't want him to miss dinner."

The lies rolled off her tongue far too easily. Then again, she'd been lying about Brody for five days, so maybe her skills were improving.

Mags and her sister offered up their sympathies, which led to a shared rant about bosses from hell. A good thing, because April couldn't stop thinking about Brody. And that phone call.

What else had Taylor asked for? And what had Brody promised her?

The wedding ceremony was scheduled to take place outside the main lodge, on the grassy lawn facing Lake Michigan. Right now, the area was empty, save for a few stanchions marking where the seats would be placed. On Saturday, the lawn would be lined with wooden chairs; at the front, an arbor decked in fall leaves would serve as the altar.

The rest of the wedding party milled around, waiting for them. Guilt tugged at April's conscience. She needed to work on her time-management skills.

Her mom approached them, wearing a navy blue dress and heels. She beamed at Mags. "This is such a beautiful location. I love that you're getting married right on the lake."

"The weather came through for us," Mags said. "Sometimes fall in Wisconsin can be miserable, but tomorrow's supposed to be sunny and clear, with highs in the sixties. If it had rained, we could have held the ceremony inside the lodge. But this is nicer."

Nicer, though a little chilly with the breeze coming off the lake. April shivered and pulled her cardigan tighter around her, wishing she'd worn her coat. As the wedding party moved into place, she stepped away and pulled out her phone, hoping Brody had texted her.

All she wanted to hear from him was "I'm done with Taylor. Forever." No long explanations were needed.

But if he was going back to her, he wouldn't tell you in a text.

Instead, he'd take her aside and apologize profusely. As she imagined the painful conversation, her eyes welled up with tears. She blinked rapidly, knowing that if she wiped them, she'd smear her makeup. When her mother called her to attention, she rejoined the crowd, smiling brightly.

"Are you all right, hon?" her mom asked.

"Weddings make me sentimental. You know?"

"Huh," Drianna said. "You didn't cry at *my* wedding."

"She's probably imagining her future wedding. To Chris." Mags clasped her hands together. "You two are such a cute couple."

April gave a short laugh. "Ah...we're not there yet. He's a little...commitment-shy."

"But he seems so into you," Mags said.

April's dad came over to the women, gesturing for them to get into place. "Ladies, please. Let's get this show on the road."

April fished into her purse, bringing out the sheet of notepaper where she'd written out her reading. For the actual ceremony, she'd have a laminated piece of parchment, but this would suffice for now. When it was her turn to read, her voice held a slight wobble. She hoped her family would chalk up her shakiness to emotion rather than uneasiness. As soon as she was done, she hustled back to her place in the audience and peeked at her phone. Nothing.

Stop being so paranoid. Brody will be here soon. You can talk then.

The minutes dragged by as Mags and Ollie recited their vows, Mags's friends sang a duet, Ginger recited a romantic French poem, and Drianna did another reading. Although April tried to appear calm, she somehow twisted her sheet of notepaper into a ball. She unfolded it and tucked it into her purse, hoping no one had noticed.

When the rehearsal ended, she quickened her pace as they made their way through the Bay Breeze restaurant. At the far end was the private dining room, where the rehearsal dinner was taking place. The room shared the same Northwoods theme, with a fieldstone fireplace, mounted fish and deer antlers, and dark wood paneling. Four tables displayed autumnal décor worthy of Pinterest, with hunter-green tablecloths, burlap-wrapped mason jars, rustic centerpieces composed of fall foliage and mini pumpkins, and candle holders made of natural wood. At each place was a large pinecone with a name card tucked on top.

Since the rehearsal had gone overtime, the other guests were already seated. Ollie, Mags, and the rest of the bridal party were at one table. The Flores family occupied two others. The fourth table was reserved for the Becketts. April's chest loosened in relief when she saw Brody seated at her family's table. But she suppressed a groan at the sight of Drianna's name card, right next to hers. She couldn't switch the cards either since Drianna was close on her heels.

She sat beside Brody and smoothed her palms on her dress. When he reached under the table and took her hand, she shivered.

"You feel so cold." He rubbed her hand between his. "You didn't bring your coat?"

"I didn't think it would be so chilly outside."

"Here." He set a glass of red wine by her place. "I got you a drink."

A few sips of the wine helped soothe her jangling nerves. He was always so thoughtful. How could she ever imagine he'd leave her?

The moment was ruined when his phone buzzed with a text. He clicked on it carelessly, then stared at the image on the screen long enough for April to catch a glimpse. A photo of Taylor, dressed in black lingerie.

April's stomach hit bottom. This was worse than she expected.

He shoved his phone into the pocket of his suit coat. "I can explain."

Explain what? Like the fact Taylor was sexting him when he was supposed to be April's date? His phone buzzed again. When he took it out and peeked at it, his face reddened.

"Sorry. I...I'll put it on airplane mode," he said.

April let out a ragged breath. She wanted so badly to trust him. To believe he wouldn't have gone from sleeping with her to swapping sexy texts with Taylor in the space of a few hours. But the evidence was right there in front of her.

He leaned in closer. "I'm sorry about the pictures, but—"

The tap of a wineglass drew their attention to the bridal party's table. Ollie stood and addressed the guests. "Good evening, everyone."

April forced herself to focus on her brother. As stressful as her situation was, she didn't want anything to detract from his speech. After he thanked the guests for coming, he praised his bride-to-be, made a few jokes about the softball game, and then ceded the floor to Mags. In turn, she was gracious and funny, promising that the next time the two families got together, they'd compete in a soccer game instead.

Once the speeches were done, a crew of waiters entered the room, bringing individual Caesar salads and baskets of rolls for every table. Though April loved a good Caesar salad, she pushed her plate away. For the first time since she'd arrived in Door County, her appetite had vanished.

Brody reached for her hand again. "Can we talk alone for a minute?"

Aware Drianna was looking their way, April kept her voice low. "It's fine. We can wait until after dinner."

It wasn't fine. But if his news was bad, she didn't want to risk a potential meltdown. Not with her whole family in attendance.

"I'd rather not wait," he said. "Let's slip outside. Then I can explain everything."

Before she could respond, the door to the private dining room burst open. She assumed the waiters had arrived to serve the appetizers.

She was wrong.

Standing at the doorway, flowers in hand, was Chris.

CHAPTER 28

What the actual hell?

Had April gone so loopy with stress she was imagining things?

How was it that Chris Rockwell, her ex-boyfriend and former wedding date, was *here*? In Door County, Wisconsin? He was supposed to be two thousand miles away in Southern California.

He strode over to their table like he owned the place, carrying an oversized duffel bag and a large bouquet of roses. However many hours he'd traveled to reach the North Bay Resort, he looked unruffled and as devastatingly handsome as ever. Though no one at the other tables appeared to notice him, the guests at *her* table couldn't help but gawk. All heads turned to face her as Chris set down his bag and knelt in front of her chair.

"April, my love. I've missed you *so* much."

Words failed her. She could only stare, astonished Chris had materialized out of thin air.

"April? I know this is a shock. I don't have any right to ask for a second chance. But I'm here, hoping you'll forgive me and take me back." He stood and handed her the bouquet. "For you."

She took the roses but still couldn't manage a reply.

I'm having a bad dream. Any minute now, I'm going to wake up.

"What's going on?" Drianna's shrill voice carried through the room, alerting everyone to the spectacle taking place at their table. She pointed at Chris. "Who the hell is this?"

April's face flamed with heat. This was it, her own personal boilover.

Kill me now.

Chris extended his hand to Drianna, giving her a smarmy smile. "You must be one of April's delightful older sisters. Charmed to meet you."

"But who *are* you?" Drianna said.

"Isn't it obvious? I'm Chris Rockwell—April's plus-one. We've been dating for five months."

Drianna let out a triumphant cry. "I knew it!"

April hid her face in her hands. In her worst nightmares, she couldn't have imagined a more degrading scenario.

"Hang on." Avery pointed to Brody. "I thought *this* was Chris Rockwell."

"Honey, what's going on?" her mom asked.

April set down the roses and placed her hand on Brody's arm. She forced herself to raise her voice, loud enough for her whole table to hear. "This is Brody Blackwood. We work together at Blackwood Cellars."

"The Brody Blackwood who stole your ideas?" Avery said. "The guy who takes credit for your work?"

Brody took off his glasses and cleaned them on his napkin, looking more vulnerable than April had ever seen him. "It's...not like that. We're actually friends."

Ollie and Mags approached their table, drawn in by the commotion. Mags looked from Chris to Brody to April. "What's with the love triangle?"

April grabbed her napkin and wiped her forehead. If she didn't stop sweating, her makeup would melt into a full-on, raccoon-eyes disaster. "I..."

Drianna turned on Brody. "I knew you were fake. I just knew it." She gave a loud cackle. "You tanked so badly in that race. It was pathetic."

Chris turned to Brody, realization dawning in his eyes. "You were pretending to be me? What the hell, man?"

April couldn't let Brody take the blame. Not when he'd done so much to support her. She stood and held up her hands. "Stop!" By now everyone was staring at her. *Everyone.* All the tables, all the guests, even the waiters who had come to refill their water glasses. Drianna had her phone out, recording the scene.

"This is all my fault," April said. "Not Brody's. And, just to be clear, he never stole my ideas at work. We're friends." She pointed to Chris. "This is the real Chris Rockwell. He's the guy I bragged about—a triathlete, a sports junkie, and an elite runner. But he's also the same guy who gave me a week's notice when he decided to bail as my date for the wedding."

Chris opened his mouth, as if to interrupt, but she glared at him and plowed on ahead. "I couldn't show you any pictures to prove he existed, because he refuses to post anything on social media. I figured if he didn't show, you'd think I made him up. Like Sam Jameson."

Everyone at the table nodded like they hadn't forgotten the Sam Jameson incident.

No one ever would.

"I couldn't handle a full week of teasing, so I recruited Brody to come with me and act like Chris," she said. "In retrospect, it was a terrible idea. I'm sorry I lied. I should have told you the truth and explained that Brody was here as my friend."

"Wait," Ollie said. "You two aren't a thing? But—"

"Of course not," Chris said. "She's with me."

"I'm not *with* you," April said. "I told you we were over."

Chris got down on one knee again. "And you had every right to." He placed his hand over his heart. "April Beckett, I'm so sorry I let you down. And I'm sorry I was afraid to commit. After you left for Wisconsin, I realized what a horrible mistake I'd made." He glanced around the room as if to gauge the audience. "I was such a fool."

"I'll say," Ginger muttered from across the table.

Chris took April's hand and kissed it. "I love you, April, and I want you back. Yes, I said it. I love you. That's why I flew here at the last minute. I'm hoping you'll give me another chance."

April gaped at him, too shocked to react. Never in her wildest dreams had she imagined a scenario like this one. Beside her, Brody appeared equally stunned, his mouth half-open, as if trying to process what he was seeing.

But her sisters had no qualms about expressing their reactions. Loudly.

"Oh my God," Avery said. "This is a grand gesture. For real."

"It's like one of those rom-coms where the hero pulls out all the stops," Drianna added. "Like *The Wedding Singer*. But I've never seen anyone do this in real life."

Avery clasped her hand over her heart. "He loves you, April." She turned to Brody. "Not that you didn't do a hell of job convincing us you felt the same way."

"Yeah, you totally fooled us," Mags said.

"It was just...an act." April's voice shook. "But I shouldn't have let it get this far. I'm sorry."

~

IT WAS JUST AN ACT.

Brody swallowed past the painful lump in his throat. April might have shared his bed for a few blissful nights and made him feel whole again. But all along, she'd wanted Chris. And he'd delivered. In the most spectacular way possible. The grand gesture of every woman's dreams.

Are you going to let him get away with this?

He wanted to challenge Chris. To tell that smug bastard he

had no right to April, not after the way he'd treated her. But she'd suffered enough public humiliation. If he started lobbing accusations at Chris—who'd clearly won the crowd over—he'd look like the asshole in the situation. And he'd make April feel worse.

Time to bow out while he still had an ounce of dignity left.

Taking a deep breath, he stood and set his napkin on the table. "I guess my work here is done. Nice meeting all of you."

April stared at him in shock. "Wait. Brody. *No*."

He gave her a fleeting smile. "It was fun while it lasted. But I assume you'd rather have the real thing."

Chris laughed and slung his arm around April's shoulder. "You got that right."

Giving them a quick nod, Brody turned to go. April called out to him, but he kept walking. A stronger man would have stayed long enough to hear her out, but he'd reached his breaking point. Above all, he did *not* want to lose his shit in front of the Becketts.

He strode through the restaurant at a fast clip, not looking back, not pausing, just keeping his feet moving. Through the bar, out the door, into the cool fall air, and across the trail. He secretly hoped April would chase after him in a grand gesture of her own. She'd grab his arm, beg him to stay, and tell him she was in love with him. But by the time he reached the cottage, he'd given up hope. He leaned against the doorframe as the grief sliced into him, sharp as a knife.

He'd lost April.

To Chris, the jerk who'd taken advantage of her for the past five months. Who thought it was perfectly acceptable to show up in Door County at the last minute, as though a bouquet of roses would make up for his late arrival.

Brody would have been better off if he'd holed up in his apartment all week, debugging code on the Blackwood Cellars app. Why had he opened his heart again? Had he learned *nothing* from his experience with Taylor?

It struck him as cruelly ironic that both disasters had happened right before a wedding. He'd been an idiot to think he could break his curse. Clearly, he needed to avoid weddings like the fucking plague.

He glanced at his phone and saw it was still on airplane mode. As he switched it back to normal, he prayed he'd see a text or a call from April, begging him to come back.

Nothing.

He had to accept the facts. Operation Fake-Chris was over.

He'd been replaced by the real thing.

CHAPTER 29

*A*pril stood in stunned silence, unable to believe Brody was gone. Even though she'd called out to him, he hadn't turned around or acknowledged her.

He'd just left, as if Operation Fake-Chris was nothing more than a job. A role. And now that he'd fulfilled his role, he was ready to move on.

But wasn't she more than an obligation? They'd had sex. Glorious, passionate sex. They'd snuggled and talked and teased each other. She'd secretly hoped they would stay together once they got back from Door County.

But that was before Taylor came back into the picture.

Was that why Brody had conceded to Chris without argument? Maybe the unexpected interruption had worked in his favor. Now he could go back to Taylor without a shred of guilt.

You don't believe that, do you?

At this point, she didn't know what to believe. Or who to trust.

Chris pulled her closer, his warm breath tickling her ear. "Nice of Brody to fill in, but he's no substitute for the real thing."

She flinched at his touch, wanting to put space between them.

Oblivious to her discomfort, Chris turned to face her family and gave them a sheepish grin. "Sorry to interrupt your dinner. But I had to follow my heart. I'm so glad April gave me another chance."

Their enthusiastic response made her stomach churn. Didn't they see how he was manipulating them? Grand gestures might be acceptable in romantic comedies, but in real life, they were questionable as hell.

Why hadn't Chris warned her he was coming? And why show up now? She'd been in Wisconsin since Monday, and he hadn't given her any indication he wanted to join her. No phone calls. No texts. Nothing.

Something about his declaration of love rang false.

He sat down in Brody's chair, a smug expression on his face. Like he'd bested his opponent and planned to enjoy the spoils. When Avery leaned over and asked him about his last triathlon, he gave her his full attention, eagerly launching into a detailed recap of the race. Even though he'd traveled two thousand miles to win April back, he no longer seemed to care that she was seated right beside him.

As she watched him charm her sister, a sudden rush of clarity struck her. His grand gesture wasn't about love. It was about *winning*. He was a man who cared about winning above all else, and she was just another trophy.

For months, she'd been grateful for the crumbs of his attention, because she'd thought she wasn't worthy of him.

The truth was, he didn't deserve *her*.

But Brody did. And she'd let him get away. Maybe he was planning on going back to Taylor, but she wouldn't know unless she asked him and told him how she felt.

She had to text him before he left. As she took her phone out of her purse, Drianna snatched it away. "No phones at the table, remember?"

"What about yours? You recorded every minute of Chris's grand gesture."

"You'll thank me for it later when we play the video at *your* engagement party." Drianna set April's phone in the center of the table, just out of reach.

As April lunged for it, she knocked over her water glass. The icy liquid cascaded onto the table and drenched her phone.

No.

She grabbed the device, popped it out of its case, and wiped it on the sleeve of her cardigan. Before she made things worse, she turned it off so that it wouldn't short-circuit. She fixed Drianna with a murderous glare. "You *bitch*. This is your fault."

Her sister smirked. "Hardly. You're the clumsy one."

"You ruin *everything*." She scrambled to her feet, intending to rush back to the cottage. It wasn't like Chris would care, seeing as how he hadn't even noticed her altercation with Drianna.

Her mother's stern voice stopped her in her tracks. "*April Beckett*. Sit down and wipe up that mess."

She swallowed tears of frustration. "Mom, please. I need to go back to the cottage. My phone isn't working."

Her mom blew out a breath. "You can deal with it later. Right now, your place is here, with your family. You've already caused enough trouble, disrupting dinner with all your drama. Show some respect, for God's sake."

April hung her head in shame. Even if Chris's attention-seeking gesture hadn't been her fault, it had still derailed her brother's big night. "Sorry, Mom."

She was trapped. In the rehearsal dinner from hell.

BRODY COULDN'T STAY in the cottage, not when Chris probably planned to turn it into his own personal love nest. At the thought of Chris and April enjoying the king-size bed, his stomach twisted into a pretzel. Grabbing his backpack, he scanned the room for his belongings.

The first thing he packed was the box of condoms on the nightstand. No way was he leaving them for Chris.

It's strictly BYOC, asshole. If you didn't bring any, too fucking bad.

He went through the cottage systemically, gathering his laptop, his spare glasses, his razor. He shoved everything into his suitcase, including his foul-smelling laundry bag, filled with his running gear. For the next fifteen minutes, his packing fell into a rhythm—pack a few things, check his phone. Pack. Check. Pack. Check. But as he filled his suitcase to the bursting point, his phone stayed silent.

When he was done, he stood for a minute, unable to take the final step.

Are you really giving up this easily?

Chris had obviously blindsided April, and her sisters hadn't helped with the way they'd swooned over his obnoxious gesture. Maybe once April recovered from the shock, she'd see through Chris's act. And maybe—*just maybe*—if Brody sent her a text telling her how he felt about her, she'd choose him over Chris.

No. He was done putting his heart on the line. Besides, at least twenty minutes had passed since he'd left the restaurant. If she wanted him, she would have texted. Or called. Or come after him, for fuck's sake. She'd done nothing.

Dragging his suitcase behind him, he gave the cottage a final look, trying to block out the memories. He placed his key under the mat on the porch. As he walked along the trail, an owl hooted in the distance. Over the lake, the moon was round and full.

Grief washed over him, painful and raw. April didn't want him. The Becketts probably hated him for all the lies he'd told. And he'd lost out to Chris.

He shouldn't have tried to pretend he was Chris in the first place. How had he ever thought he could compete with a guy like that? Given the choice, what woman wouldn't opt for a triathlete, state baseball MVP, and all-around winner?

Once he got to the parking lot, he put his suitcase in the trunk of his rental car and placed his phone on the seat beside him. He needed to book a new flight home. Tonight, if possible. Fortunately, Blackwood Cellars had a corporate membership in a 24-hour travel service. Though he'd never used the service before, his brother had raved about it. When Brody called to make his request, the hold time was twenty-five minutes, so he left a voicemail.

Then he punched in the address of the Green Bay airport on his phone and pulled out of the lot.

Goodbye, Door County.

CHAPTER 30

*A*pril endured the rest of the rehearsal dinner in misery. Chris was firing on all cylinders, charming the table with the same personal magnetism that had first won her over. Telling stories about his races. Real stories, with impressive times. Sharing tales of his high school glory days as a baseball legend and a cross-country god. Naturally, her family ate it up. With a fucking spoon. *This* was the guy they'd been waiting to meet. Someone who was as athletic, driven, and competitive as they were.

By now, a full hour had passed. Maybe more. Time had no meaning when April was trapped in her own personal circle of hell. She wanted to break away, but she couldn't risk upsetting her mom again.

When Chris excused himself to use the restroom, she placed her head down on the table, wishing she were anywhere else. At least Drianna had stopped focusing on her now that Ian had shown up. They'd been bickering at a low volume for the past hour.

April was tempted to sneak over to the bar and order a round of shots—just for herself—but she'd eaten so little she'd be wasted in minutes. And she didn't want to be drunk around Chris. She had no intention of *ever* having sex with him again, but if she was drunk, he might press his advantage. He'd done it before.

Ginger came around to her side of the table and leaned over her chair. Her voice was an angry hiss. "How could you let Brody go?"

She lifted her head to face her cousin. "I didn't let him go. He walked away."

"But why didn't you try to stop him?"

"I wasn't expecting him to leave, just like that. Besides, I didn't know if he still wanted me. His ex called him today. *Three times.* She wants him back."

If she was expecting sympathy, Ginger wasn't dishing it out. "Then go fight for him. Brody loves you."

"No, he doesn't." April's voice trembled. She steeled herself not to cry. "I was stupid to think it could ever work out."

Ginger scowled. "So, you're going to stick with Gaston? Big mistake."

"Are you kidding? Everyone here adores him."

"Do *you* adore him? That's what matters."

April shook her head. Despite his grand gesture and his obvious charisma, she did not.

"Then what are you waiting for? Dump his ass—*again*—and go after Brody."

April aimed a pointed look toward her mother. "I tried leaving earlier, but my mom—"

She stopped abruptly, realizing how childish she sounded. Like a kid desperate for her parents' approval. Why was she letting everyone walk all over her? Not only Chris but her family, as well. She needed to stop acting like a doormat.

"You're right," she said. "As soon as Chris gets back, I'm out of here. But my phone died, so I'm not sure how to reach Brody."

"Your cottage has a landline, right? If not, you can use the one in my room. I'll head back there as soon as they serve dessert. In the meantime, I can distract your mom for you." She walked over to April's mom and leaned down to talk to her.

April took a deep breath. She wished she'd been this bold an hour ago. As soon as Chris came back from the restroom, she stood and took his arm. "Grab the roses. We're leaving now."

"Can't wait, huh?" Chris grinned. "I feel the same way." He waved to April's family. "Good night, all."

Good night, all, my ass.

She was done letting everyone push her around.

As BRODY DROVE off from the resort, his misery and frustration ebbed away, replaced by a bone-weary exhaustion. He hadn't intended to stop until he reached Green Bay, but after he almost dozed off behind a slow-moving truck, he pulled over at a gas station. Though he desperately needed caffeine, he couldn't handle bad convenience-store coffee. Instead, he bought a can of Dr. Pepper and a couple of Hershey bars. As he was returning to his car, his phone rang.

His heart leapt in pathetic hope, only to sink like a stone. Not April. Just the travel service, calling him back.

"Mr. Blackwood? Sir? This is George Dobson with Encompass Travel Services. I do apologize, but I'm not able to process your request."

The guy had an upper-crust British accent. Like Brody's own personal Jeeves.

"Do you need my credit card info?" Brody asked. "It should be on file. Under Blackwood Cellars—it's an American Express."

"It's not that. The airport in Green Bay doesn't appear to have the same level of traffic as the San Diego International Airport. There are no flights to the West Coast at this late hour. Your only options are a flight to Chicago or Minneapolis. Otherwise, I could reserve a spot for you on a plane to San Diego tomorrow morning at 6:10 a.m. Fair warning, it makes two stops along the way. Would you like me to book it?"

Getting up that early sounded like hell. And two layovers? There had to be a better option. "Not yet. For now, can you find me a hotel room in Green Bay? A Hilton or a Marriott would be ideal." Blackwood Cellars had accounts with both chains.

"Will do, sir. I'll ring you back momentarily."

"Great. Thanks."

He got back into his car and let out a long breath. Instead of spending the night with April in the cozy cottage, acting out another role-play fantasy, he was going to be stuck in a faceless chain hotel in Green Bay. Tomorrow, he'd have to fly home without April and return to his lonely apartment. And then head back to work on Monday.

Work.

How was he supposed to work with April after everything that had happened? No doubt she'd feel guilty at tossing him aside for Chris, and he'd have a hard time controlling his resentment. The awkwardness would be off the charts.

Maybe he should consider the Napa offer after all. Even if he didn't want the job, he'd be making a clean break from all of it. Taylor. April. Temecula.

He could start out fresh. Devote himself to his new position. And avoid all romantic entanglements for the foreseeable future. Even if he was a loser in love, he could transform himself into a managerial superstar.

When his phone buzzed with a text, his pulse raced. But it wasn't April. Instead, Taylor had sent him *another* photo. A selfie, with her wearing the red lingerie he'd given her last year for Valentine's Day. Underneath it, she'd texted: *See what you're missing out on?*

He set down the phone and rubbed his hands across his face. She needed to stop.

No matter how many photos she sent him, he wasn't going back to her.

But you could if you wanted. You don't owe April anything now.

The problem was, he wasn't in love with Taylor anymore. He was in love with *April*. Which made her decision even more frustrating. After everything she'd told him about Chris—the way he shamed and criticized her—why had she given in to him again?

Because you never told her you were done with Taylor.

Guilt surged through him as he recalled his last conversation with April. He'd asked her if they could talk alone, but he hadn't yet given her the reassurance she needed. As soon as those photos had shown up on his phone, he should have let her know she had nothing to worry about. *Immediately*. Instead, he'd made her wait in agony.

And you should have admitted that you've fallen in love with her, you idiot.

Instead, he'd left her feeling vulnerable and uncertain, easy prey for someone else to swoop in and take advantage. And now he was paying the price.

CHAPTER 31

Upon leaving the restaurant with Chris, April wanted to lash out at him, but she forced herself to hold her tongue. She wanted to get as far from her family as humanly possible. Outside, the night air held a brisk nip. The breeze chilled her bare legs and whipped her hair into her face. Shivering, she pulled her cardigan more tightly around her body.

Her heartbeat accelerated as they reached the porch. At her first attempt to unlock the door, she dropped her key and scrambled to retrieve it. With trembling hands, she opened the door, scarcely daring to breathe. If Brody hadn't left, she still had a chance.

But reality sunk in all too quickly. His suitcase was gone. The nightstand on his side of the bed was empty. All his personal things had vanished, including the box of condoms. She clenched her hands, trying to stem the tears building up inside her.

"Nice place." Chris dropped his duffel bag on the bed and set the roses beside it.

April ignored him. She scanned the cottage, relieved when she caught sight of a beige phone sitting atop the dresser. She inched toward it but stopped short when Chris looked up at her. "Where'd Brody sleep?"

Oh God. She did *not* want to be having this conversation. "Um…in the bed?"

Chris gave a hearty chuckle. "Must have made for some boring nights. The guy's such a dweeb."

I had better sex with that dweeb in two days than with you in five months, you big jerk.

Not that she'd ever say it. If she gave in to her dark side, she'd end up like Drianna. Besides, she didn't want to hurt Chris. More than anything, she wanted to make him understand they were well and truly over.

"Chris—what's going on? I broke up with you last week and you haven't contacted me once since then. Why are you *really* here?"

"Like I said, I wanted to win you back by any means possible." He flashed her a dazzling smile—the same smile that had always weakened her defenses whenever he stopped by for a booty call.

She wasn't falling for it. "Why didn't you warn me?"

"Because I wanted to make a grand entrance. Otherwise, your family might have been pissed I waited until the last second to show." He smirked. "It worked like a charm. They adored me."

He was *so* arrogant. In the past, she'd admired his confidence since it was something she lacked. But now she saw him for what he was—a braggart who placed his own needs over everyone else's.

She forced herself to speak clearly. "I'm sorry you came all this way, but this isn't going to work. I need you to leave."

Naturally, he hadn't heard a word she said. He wasn't even looking at her.

"Chris? Are you listening? It's over. You can't stay here."

Still oblivious, he was bent over, rooting through his duffel bag. "I brought something for you. Give me a minute to find it."

He dumped out the duffel bag on the bed, shoving aside magazines, energy bars, rolled-up socks, and—

Son of a bitch. Was that a race packet?

She'd seen enough of Chris's race packets to know what they looked like. She snatched it off the bed. "What's this?"

From the pile, he pulled out a lacy black negligee. He held it up. "Here, babe. I was going to wrap it, but I thought you'd want to put it on right away." When he saw the packet, he blanched. "I...can explain."

She pulled a race bib and map out of the packet. "The Fall 50? Is that why you're here?"

"I'm here for *you*. But I thought since I was going to be in Door County, that—"

"Don't lie to me."

"April..."

Her anger escalated, sending her pulse racing. "Tell me the truth. *Now.* Or, so help me, I will take all your racing gear and throw it into Lake Michigan."

"Okay. Sorry." He raked his hand through his hair. "When you first invited me to the wedding, I was going to say no. But then I found out about the Fall 50. It's a fifty-mile race across the length of the Door County Peninsula, usually run in teams of four or five."

Still scowling, she gestured for him to speed things up.

He continued. "A college buddy of mine lives in Milwaukee. Nate. He's a competitive runner, mostly half-marathons. He's done the race before as part of a team. I asked him if I could be on his team if I came to Door County with you."

"That's why you agreed to come?" She let out her breath, her rage escalating into a rolling boil. She'd been so stupid. *None* of this had been about her.

"It's not the only reason. I figured the sex would be great." He reached out his hand, aiming for her cheek. "It always is with you, babe."

Clenching her teeth, she batted his hand away. "Keep talking."

"His team was full. But one of his runners was having knee problems, so he promised he'd keep me in the loop. I decided I'd take the chance and go with you to Wisconsin anyway, but last week, I—"

"You what? Got cold feet? Decided I wasn't worth the trip?"

He had the decency to look sheepish. "Something like that. Like I said, a family wedding is a big level of commitment. And we're not about that."

No kidding.

She didn't hide her sarcasm. "Let me guess what happened next—the injured team member dropped out at the last minute? How convenient."

"Exactly. I thought, why not kill two birds? Great sex with you and a chance to be part of an epic race. It's a win-win."

Fury built up inside her, fueling her adrenaline. "What was all that shit about being in love with me?"

He held up his hands. "I didn't want your family to hate me. But that's not the only reason I said it. I might not be in love with you, but I definitely want you back."

"You do?" She recoiled, more confused than ever. The race was something she could understand. But Chris wanting her back?

He approached her as though she were a wild tiger, visibly relaxing when she allowed him to touch her. He stroked her cheek, his clear blue eyes locked on hers. "I've never been with anyone like you before. Most women are so high-maintenance. They expect fancy dinners and elaborate, thoughtful gifts. They insist on planning things weeks in advance. But with you, it's so easy. I can come over any night, and you'll be there for me."

Had she been that pathetic? "That's horrible."

"No, it's great. No strings, no lies, no unrealistic expectations. Just smoking-hot sex and a lot of fun."

Did he think the sex had been that hot? Half the time he

finished before she was close to feeling satisfied. She couldn't believe she'd put up with him for five months.

"Come on. I realize you're upset about the race, but we can still have fun." He brandished the negligee. "This will look *so* sexy on you. Though we can't go overboard because I'm running fifteen miles tomorrow morning."

"Are you kidding me?" She snatched the negligee from his hands and tossed it onto the floor.

He frowned. "What's wrong with you?"

"I'm sick of your bullshit. I want you out of here. Now."

"You can't kick me out. I flew thousands of miles to get here." She stared him down. "For a race."

"You're still mad. I get it. But I need a place to sleep."

"I'm sure you can find a hotel somewhere," she said. "Door County's full of them."

He looked down. "Well, actually...they're all full. I tried making a reservation, on the chance you might not take me back. But the Fall 50 is huge. And it's peak tourist season in Door County. Not to mention the big Packers game on Sunday. There's nothing from here to Green Bay. Nothing decent, at least."

Asshole. "So, you came here for a free bed?"

"And the chance to be with you. Don't discount that." He placed his hand over his heart. "I might have lied about the love and commitment stuff, but not about the sex."

That's all she was to him? A free room? A quick booty call? As if her self-esteem couldn't get any lower. "I'm not having sex with you ever again. Got it?"

He threw up his hands in submission. "Fine. But I still need a place to stay. And I've got to crash soon, because I have to be at the starting line by seven in the morning." He pointed to the bathroom. "I'm gonna grab a shower. You're welcome to join me."

How could anyone be so self-centered? If she had to spend another minute with him, her head would explode. She pointed to the bathroom. "Go."

She didn't want him to stay. He wasn't even her friend. He was just a guy who used her when he needed her. And she'd let him do it for months.

But if she kicked him out, he'd have nowhere to go. And at this point, she cared more about salvaging her relationship with Brody than punishing Chris.

She'd screwed up royally by letting Brody go. But she wasn't going down without a fight. The minute the bathroom door closed, she bolted over to the landline and grabbed it, intending to call him.

And blanked.

Because she couldn't remember his number.

How could she have forgotten it? She'd texted it to Ollie *yesterday*. In her mind's eye, she could see the first three digits, but the rest was a blank.

Think, damn it.

She needed help.

She needed Ginger.

But now she couldn't remember her cousin's number either. Fortunately, she had a workaround. She picked up the phone, called the resort's reception desk, and asked to be connected to Ginger Beckett's room.

It was high time she came up with a grand gesture of her own.

CHAPTER 32

*B*rody sat in the gas station parking lot, cursing his stupidity. Why hadn't he explained—right away—that he'd turned Taylor down? Why had he left the resort without trying to win April back? He'd all but handed her over to Chris.

He needed to make a game plan, but he had no clue what his next move should be. When his phone rang, he startled, spilling Dr. Pepper on his khakis. Without glancing at the screen, he guessed the caller wasn't April.

He was right.

"Mr. Blackwood?" The travel agent's voice lacked confidence. Like he was about to deliver another piece of bad news.

Bring it on. This shit show can't get any worse.

He wiped the soda off his pants. "I'm here."

"I do apologize, sir, but I couldn't find any Hilton or Marriott hotels with vacancy in Green Bay. In fact, there were no moderately priced hotels available."

He'd have to splurge. "How about expensive hotel rooms? No price limit."

"Sorry, sir. I checked those, too. I had no luck."

Jeeves was seriously letting him down. "None? How is that possible?"

"There's quite a bit going on this weekend. Fall happens to be prime tourist season in Door County. There's also the big Fall Fest in Green Bay. And a rather important Green Bay Packers game on Sunday at noon. They're playing their hated rivals, the Chicago Bears."

Shit. Brody didn't want to sleep in his car. Or at the airport, his body draped over a couple of uncomfortable seats. "Isn't there *anything?*"

"The Green & Gold Motel has rooms available. But TripAdvisor only ranked it number forty-eight out of all the hotels in Green Bay."

"That's not terrible. How many hotels in Green Bay are there?"

The pause that followed made him suspect the worst. "Forty-eight, sir."

He was screwed. But he needed a place to stay. "That's fine. Can you make a reservation? Then text me the address? Thanks."

"You're very welcome, sir."

Brody finished the rest of his Dr. Pepper and ate one of his Hershey bars. All he'd eaten since the softball game was a small Caesar salad and a roll. He considered going back inside the convenience store and buying something else to eat, but a roller dog or a rewarmed slice of pizza sounded like a bad idea. Getting food poisoning would truly be the icing on this shit cake.

According to his phone, fifteen miles remained before he reached the Green & Gold Motel. Fifteen agonizing miles, thanks to the giant semitruck that pulled out ahead of him, forcing him to stay within the speed limit.

When his phone rang again, he braced himself. Knowing his luck, Jeeves was going to tell him the worst hotel in Green Bay had suddenly filled up. "Yes. Hello?"

"Brody? It's April's brother, Ollie."

"And Mags," another voice chimed in.

His hands tightened on the steering wheel. At least he wasn't anywhere near Ollie. The guy was probably aching to give him a beatdown on behalf of the entire Beckett family. He spoke quickly. "Hey, Ollie. I'm sorry I lied to you. It's not something I normally do, but—"

"But you did it for April." Ollie didn't sound mad. Not even a little.

"It's not cool you lied to us," Mags said. "But we get it. Do you know what Drianna told me the first time I had dinner with the Becketts?"

"That she could kick your ass in a race?" Brody asked.

Mags laughed. "That came later. She told me the Sam Jameson story. Like, it was literally the first thing I learned about April. The Becketts are a tough crowd."

"No lie," Ollie said. "I guarantee if April had showed up here without Chris—especially after bragging about him for five months—Drianna would have been ruthless. Avery, too."

"Thanks for understanding. To be fair, April and I were going to tell you the truth, but we wanted to wait until after the wedding. We didn't want to steal any attention away from you."

"Well, you sure as hell did tonight," Ollie said. "Not you—but Chris. Not a fan."

What? "But he fits in perfectly with your family. The guy's an actual runner, not a faker like me." His stomach growled. With his free hand, he unwrapped the other Hershey bar and took a bite. "And don't forget his grand gesture."

"That was impressive at first," Mags said. "Until I thought about it. If he truly loved April, why'd he wait until the last minute? Why didn't he give her some warning?"

"Besides, man, I told you before—April's wild about you," Ollie said. "And you admitted you were in love with her."

"Wait—you did?" Mags's voice was breathless. "How could you let her go?"

Brody swallowed the chocolate in a big lump, then wished he still had some soda to wash it down. He coughed and cleared his throat. "She...she didn't want me. You saw what happened."

"Because Chris blindsided her. And the Becketts weren't much better with the way they swooned over him," Mags said. "You need to get her back."

"I'm not sure if she still wants me."

The app announced he had reached his destination. Which didn't bode well since the Green & Gold looked like the type of run-down, creepy-ass roadside motel he'd only seen in horror movies. A large sign advertised *Cheapest Room's in GB*. Above it, a neon Vacancy sign blinked erratically.

"I should go," he said. "I need to check in to my hotel."

"You're not flying home tonight?" Ollie asked.

"Tomorrow morning. I think. I'm not sure what flights are available."

Did he want to leave a day early? Not if he could help it. More than anything, he wanted to talk to April and win her back. But he might have missed his chance. "I don't know what else to do. Even if I could work things out with April, I'm sure everyone in your family hates me."

"Who cares what they think?" Mags said. "It's *our* wedding. And we want you there as April's date."

"Yeah, man. You can't let Chris win," Ollie said.

"Thanks. I'll let you know. And thanks for the support."

If nothing else, Ollie and Mags were on his side. Brody had genuinely enjoyed meeting them, and he liked the way they treated April.

He pulled up to the front office, making sure to lock the car behind him. The tiny space reeked of cigarette smoke. Piped-in music assaulted his ears with an instrumental version of "Sweet Caroline." Behind the grimy counter sat an old guy with a bushy gray beard, reading a copy of *Sports Illustrated*. Dominating the back wall was an enormous Green Bay Packers calendar, with Sunday's date circled in red.

"Excuse me?" Brody said. "My travel agent made a reservation for me. The name's Brody Blackwood."

"Hang on." Graybeard set down his magazine, stood up, and shuffled over to the computer. After squinting at the screen for a minute, he thumped it with his fist.

"Everything okay?" Brody asked.

"Screen's blank. Might be on the fritz. Don't suppose you know anything about computers?"

Brody forced himself to speak calmly as he asked the most obnoxious IT question known to man. "Did you try rebooting it? You know—turning it off and on again?"

"Might work. Won't hurt to try, right?"

"Right." Brody tried not to drum his fingers on the desk as the computer booted up at a glacial pace.

"Welp." Graybeard scratched his head. "Computer's working, but we've got another problem."

"No rooms?" Brody didn't know whether to be annoyed or relieved.

"Plenty of rooms. But we don't take American Express. Cash only."

"That's fine." He still had a lot of cash since he'd been putting most of his expenses on the company credit card. "How much is it?"

As soon as he asked, a sinking feeling crept over him.

Graybeard confirmed his fears. "Per hour? Or for the whole night?"

Sweet Jesus. "The whole night."

"With tax, that'll be seventy bucks. We have to charge extra because it's a Packers weekend."

"Right. Go Packers." Brody brought out his wallet and gave him the money.

In return, Graybeard handed him a key attached to a dark

green disk, bearing a giant letter G. "That's a custom-made Packers key chain. You lose it, and it'll cost you ten bucks. Check out's at eleven."

"Great. Thanks."

"You have a good night, now." Graybeard went back to his chair and picked up his magazine.

"Good night." Brody beat a quick retreat. Since his motel room was the furthest one from the office, he drove his car over and parked in front of the door. He grabbed his phone and backpack from the passenger seat, then retrieved his suitcase from the trunk. The breeze swirled up the detritus around his feet and sent an empty beer bottle rolling onto the asphalt. He leaned against the battered door of the motel room and took a deep breath.

You don't have to stay here. You could go back to April.

Nope. I don't need her.

She could have Chris, and he'd move on, start a new life in Napa, and block this whole experience from his memory.

Who was he kidding?

Running away wouldn't solve his problems. Even if he left Temecula behind, he'd still be the same guy, plagued with doubts and self-esteem issues. And he'd always wonder if he'd given up too easily.

With Taylor, he'd tried like hell to win her back, and it hadn't worked. But he hadn't even fought for April. If he'd stood up for himself and told her he loved her, he might have had a chance with her. Instead, he'd taken the coward's way out and conceded to Chris.

Even if it led to more humiliation, he needed to lay his heart on the line. He could start by calling April.

Bracing himself, he brought up her number, but his call went straight to voicemail.

He tried again. Voicemail. This time, he left a message.

"Hey, April. It's Brody. Sorry I left so abruptly. And that I didn't explain the situation with Taylor. I'm not going back to her. The only woman I want is you. I realize this thing between us is kind of new, and that I'm no substitute for Chris, but I'm in love with you, and I...hope you feel the same way about me. I'm at the Green & Gold Motel in Green Bay, and I won't leave until I hear from you. So...can you call me back?"

Pathetic, to be sure. But worth it if April took his words to heart.

He waited, hoping she'd see the voicemail notification, listen to his message, and return his call immediately.

Five minutes passed, then ten. Nothing.

Was she ignoring him? Blocking him?

Or was she too busy with Chris to pick up the phone?

CHAPTER 33

*A*pril clutched the receiver of the landline tightly as she waited for Ginger to answer the phone. For all she knew, her cousin could still be at dinner or having a drink at the bar.

But she answered after three rings. "Hello?"

"*Ginger*. It's April."

"About time. Were you able to find Brody?"

"He's gone. I don't know what to do. I was going to call him from the phone here, but I can't remember his number. I feel like such an idiot."

Ginger snorted. "Who memorizes phone numbers? The only one I know is my mom's because I use her as my emergency contact." She paused. "So…now what?"

"I'm guessing he might be headed for the airport. If I go there, I could try to stop him before his flight leaves."

A weak plan, at best. But she couldn't think of any other options.

"This isn't the '90s. You can't just follow him up to the gate. Besides, how are you going to get to the airport? Didn't he take your rental car?"

"*Shit*. What am I going to do? Chris probably rented a car, but I can't just take it. What if I got pulled over? I could get arrested." If that happened, the fallout would be a hundred times worse than the Sam Jameson incident.

"Calm down," Ginger said. " You don't need to steal a car—not when you have me at your disposal. I can drive you there."

"Are you serious? It's an hour away. An hour and a half, maybe."

"It's only nine o'clock. On a *Friday*. And I'm already in my pj's. Making a frantic run to the airport sounds a lot more appealing than spending the next three hours watching *Law & Order* reruns with my parents. Give me ten minutes and I'll meet you in the main parking lot."

"Thanks. I owe you, big-time."

"No problem, Cinderella. Let's go catch that prince."

After April hung up the phone, she glanced at the bathroom door. Knowing Chris's propensity for lengthy showers, he wouldn't be done for another ten or fifteen minutes. If she was being practical, she'd wait for him to finish so she could kick him out properly. But at this point, she couldn't waste any more time. If he wanted the bed tonight, he could have it. All she cared about was getting Brody back.

Not that she had any idea what she'd do when she got to the airport. Or if he'd even be there. At this hour, he might not be able to book a flight back to San Diego until tomorrow morning. If that was the case, he'd probably check into a hotel somewhere near the airport. Finding him would be nearly impossible.

But she had to try.

Telling herself she needed to be prepared for every possible scenario, she grabbed her backpack and shoved in a change of clothes. Her toiletries bag and makeup pouch still sat on top of the dresser where she'd left them when she'd gotten ready for the rehearsal. She threw them in the pack, along with the last bottle of wine and the remaining snacks from the fridge.

Before she left, she grabbed the pad on the nightstand and scrawled a quick note.

Chris,
Bed's all yours. I've made other arrangements. But I want you out of here by tomorrow morning. And don't come back!
April

Hoisting her backpack over one shoulder, she left the cottage, shutting the door softly behind her. The bracing wind made her shiver, her legs prickling with goose bumps. Her dress and heels were hardly practical for a late-night rescue mission, but she didn't want to waste time by going back and changing.

As she approached the parking lot, a noisy group emerged from the restaurant, laughing and talking. She turned away, hoping it wasn't anyone from her family. The last thing she needed was a confrontation with her sisters. Upon sighting Ginger, she kept her head down and hustled over to meet her.

Ginger leaned against a beige sedan, wearing a Hello Kitty hoodie, a knit cap, and polka-dot pajama pants. She unlocked the car. "Green Bay airport, here we come. We can listen to *Another Roadside Murder* on the way. I'm a couple of episodes behind, and I need to catch up."

What was it with these true-crime podcasts? Was April the only one who found them disturbing? Still, if Ginger was willing to volunteer her services as chauffeur, then she wasn't about to object. "Sounds great."

Ginger set her phone on the center console. "Before I start the podcast, you need to fill me in. Was Chris mad you were leaving him to go after Brody?"

April buckled her seat belt. Unlike Brody's rental, which was already littered with water bottles and candy wrappers, this vehicle was pristine, still giving off a heady new-car smell. She set her backpack on the floor in front of her.

"I...I didn't tell him I was leaving," she said.

"What? Why not?"

She recounted the conversation she'd had with Chris at the cottage, even though it pained her to admit he'd only shown up for a race. At times she cringed, afraid to imagine what her cousin thought of her. How could anyone respect her when she'd put up with Chris for so long?

"I know I was a total loser around Chris," she said. "But I was just so flattered he wanted to be with me."

"You don't have to explain," Ginger said. "There's nothing wrong with booty calls. Or friends with benefits. But only if it's mutual on both sides. Chris's behavior wasn't okay, but Brody seems like he actually cares about you."

"I think he does. That's why I don't want to lose him."

"I get it. But this airport scheme doesn't sound too solid. Most people check in and go through security right away, even if they have a long wait."

April sighed. "I know. And I'm not even sure if he's there. What are the odds of him finding an available flight to San Diego at this hour?"

"Good point. That airport didn't seem like a bustling hub of transportation. So, maybe he found a place to stay overnight?" Ginger frowned. "If that's the case, I have *no* idea how we're going to find him. Are you sure you can't remember his number?"

"Nope." Once again, April was struck by how stupid she felt, not knowing her best friend's phone number. Especially since she and Brody usually texted multiple times a day.

"Anyone else who might have it?" Ginger asked. "Like someone in your family?"

The realization struck her like a lightning bolt. "*Ollie.* I gave it to Ollie because he asked for it before his pub crawl." She groaned. "But I don't know his number either."

"Check my contacts. I think I have it."

April scarcely dared to breathe as she grabbed Ginger's phone and scrolled through her list of contacts. When she saw Ollie's number, she almost cried in relief.

She sent her brother a quick text. *It's April but I'm using Ginger's phone because mine died. Do you have Brody's phone number? I can explain later but I need to reach him ASAP!!!*

Her brother replied immediately, sending the number, followed by a message. *Go get him, sis.*

Thank God. Even though she'd messed up Ollie's rehearsal dinner, he was coming through for her when she needed him. "It worked!"

"Great. So, call Brody." When April hesitated, Ginger pointed at the phone. "What are you waiting for?"

"A heaping dose of courage?" At Ginger's salty expression, April pushed past her fear and called Brody. Though she still didn't know exactly how he felt about her, she couldn't back down now.

As she waited for him to answer, she was so skittish she could barely hold on to the phone.

His response was tinged with caution. "Umm...hello? Who's calling?"

"Brody?" She couldn't keep the waver out of her voice. "It's April. I'm calling from Ginger's phone."

"April?" He sounded hopeful. Like he was *glad* she'd called. "Did you get my voicemail?"

He'd left her a voicemail? Maybe she still had a chance.

"I...no. Sorry. My phone died right after you left the restaurant. And then I had to deal with my family. And Chris. And..." *Enough excuses.* "But I'm done letting them boss me around. I'm coming to get you. Because I don't want you to leave."

"Where are you?"

Hell if she knew. "Maybe fifteen or twenty minutes south of

the resort? Ginger's driving me to the Green Bay airport so I can stop you from boarding that plane."

His warm chuckle spilled over the phone. "Beckett, you watch too many rom-coms. You realize you'd never be allowed past the security checkpoint, right?"

She gave a shaky laugh. "I'm willing to do whatever it takes, even if I have to bluff my way into the TSA line."

"No need to. I didn't go to the airport. I'm staying in Green Bay. At a place called the Green & Gold Motel. I'll text you the address. Fair warning, it's not a Hilton. Not even close."

A powerful wave of relief coursed over her, so intense it almost left her light-headed. There was still so much she wanted to say but not while Ginger was seated next to her. "Can we talk when I get there? Because there's...um...stuff I want to tell you."

"I'll be right here. Waiting."

Seconds after she hung up, his text arrived. She turned to Ginger. "He's staying at the Green & Gold Motel, room 108."

"Perfect. Can you put the address into my phone? I'll drop you off there, and then he can drive you back in the morning."

April twisted her hands together. "In theory, that sounds great. But...I still don't know what's going on with his ex. What if he's planning to go back to her?"

"I doubt it. But you won't know unless you ask. And you need to be honest about how you feel. If you're in love with him, then tell him."

"Do you think I'm jumping the gun with the whole 'love' thing? We've only been...you know...*together* for two days."

"Yeah, but he's like your work husband. You *always* talk about him. You've spent more time with him than any of the guys you've dated since you moved to Temecula, including Mr. D-Bag."

April mulled over Ginger's words. Sure, the sex was new, but she'd been crushing on Brody for two solid years. And they shared a deep connection that went beyond casual friendship.

"Before you start obsessing over Brody, can you cue up the next podcast?" Ginger asked. "It sounds nice and gruesome."

Nice and gruesome weren't words April usually used in the same sentence, but she obliged. Despite her initial trepidation, she got so caught up in the grisly murder case that she barely noticed the miles passing. But she paused the podcast when the sign for the Green & Gold Motel came into view.

As Ginger pulled into the lot, her mouth dropped open. "What the fuck?"

There had to be a mistake. The shabby, run-down motel looked like the ideal setting for the story they'd just been listening to. But Brody's rental car was parked in front of door number 108.

Ginger pulled in beside his car. "I thought Brody was rich. Doesn't his family *own* Blackwood Cellars? Why's he staying here?"

April groaned as the realization hit her. "This is what Chris was talking about. He couldn't find a room either—not in Green Bay or Door County. This place must have been the only one available."

Ginger glanced around the lot. "It's shady as hell."

The motel might have been sketchy, but it wasn't as terrifying as taking the next step. "I'm kind of scared."

"No kidding. This dump has crime scene written all over it."

"Not about that. What if Brody doesn't feel the same way I do?"

Ginger sighed. "I don't know. But he obviously wants to talk to you, or he wouldn't have told you where he's staying. Don't you work in the same department? No matter what you decide, you should talk things over before you go back to work on Monday, otherwise it will be awkward as fuck."

"*Oh God.* Work." With everything that had happened in the last few hours, April hadn't thought about work. Her voice rose to a shaky pitch. "What if Brody decides that he's had enough and takes that job in Napa?"

"What job in Napa?" Ginger let out her breath. "Scratch that. Don't tell me. Not when Brody's waiting for you on the other side of that door. If you don't want him to move to Napa, then *tell him*. Got it?"

April gnawed on her lower lip. Could she really be that brave? Only one way to find out.

"Okay. Right. I can do this." She pulled down the passenger-side mirror and checked her reflection. Grabbing her brush and a lipstick out of her backpack, she tamed her windblown hair and touched up her lips. "I'm ready."

"Let's go." Ginger unbuckled her seat belt.

April grabbed her backpack, and the two of them ventured out of the car. After staring at Brody's door for a full minute, she forced herself to knock. Softly at first, and then with more force. "Brody? It's April."

When he answered, her whole body sagged in relief. He looked exhausted and rumpled, having swapped out his crisp button-down and khakis for a faded Einstein t-shirt and baggy sweats. His light brown hair was so disheveled she had to resist the urge to smooth it down.

He offered them a faint smile. "Hi, April. Hi, Ginger. I'm glad you made it. Sorry this place is so…"

"Creepy?" Ginger said. "Please tell me it's not as bad on the inside."

He laughed. "Actually, it's worse." He ran his hand through his messy hair. "Thanks for bringing April. I appreciate it."

"No problem. But I don't plan on sticking around Hotel Hell any longer than I need to." She checked her phone. "I have twenty-five minutes left on this podcast, so I'm locking myself in the car and finishing it. When I'm done, I'll text you and see if you've worked things out. If not, I can take April back to the resort with me."

April leaned over and hugged her. "Thanks, Ginger."

"You got it. And if by chance you hear frantic honking, that means my life is in imminent danger, and I need backup." She walked back to her car, unlocked it, and settled in.

Brody fixed his gaze on April. "Want to come in and talk?"

Never had such a simple question filled her with so much hope.

CHAPTER 34

$\mathcal{H}$olding the door open, Brody gestured for April to come in. She looked as beautiful as he'd ever seen her, still wearing the burgundy dress from dinner, her chestnut-brown hair falling to her shoulders in soft waves. Heart pounding, he waited as she took a few tentative steps into the motel room. The fact that she'd shown up meant everything. Especially since she hadn't even gotten his message.

Once she was inside, he locked the door and set the dead bolt. As her gaze swept around the room, he wished they were somewhere less sleazy. The queen bed sported an ugly plaid comforter that no doubt hosted an armada of germs. A flimsy nightstand stood beside it, containing a box of generic tissues and a lamp with a burned-out bulb. In the corner was a small table with two matching chairs; the upholstery on one was patched with duct tape. Everything in the room was shabby and threadbare, save for the shiny clock above the bed, bearing the Green Bay Packers logo.

"Do you want to sit down?" he asked.

"It's okay. I'll stand." She shrugged off her backpack and set it on the floor. When she faced him again, her posture was rigid, her hands clenched tight.

He wanted to take her in his arms and tell her he'd already forgiven her, but he needed to let her have her say.

She smoothed her hands on her dress. "I'm so sorry about what happened at dinner. I had no idea Chris was going to show up. I didn't invite him, and I certainly didn't want him there. He's a complete and utter dick."

Brody tried to keep his expression neutral, even as a small smile threatened to break through. He let her continue.

"I was so overwhelmed I didn't know how to react. And when he said he loved me, I was caught off guard. It didn't help that everyone in my family adored his grand gesture. Chris knows how to play to a crowd." Her eyes welled up with tears. "When you left, I should have told him how I felt. And I should have gone after you right away."

His heart melted for her. Even if she'd given Chris too much leeway, he could understand her reaction. He'd had a hard enough time turning down Taylor over the phone. He had no idea how he would have handled things if she'd shown up and made a grand gesture of her own.

He grabbed the box of tissues from the nightstand and held it out to April.

"Thanks." She pulled out a few and dabbed her eyes. "After you left, I was going to text you and tell you to come back, but Drianna took my phone. When I tried to grab it, I spilled water all over it."

"Shit. Is it dead?"

"I'm not sure. I turned it off so I wouldn't make it worse. But I can deal with it when I get home. The thing is, I should have walked out right away. Maybe then I could have stopped you from leaving. But my mom got mad at me for disrupting Ollie's rehearsal dinner, and I backed down." She sniffed. "I let my family walk all over me. I'm so fucking spineless."

"It's okay," he said softly.

She crumpled the tissues into a ball. "It's not. You deserved so much better. But...truthfully? I was kind of afraid you didn't want me anymore."

Her uncertainty gouged a hole in his heart. "What do you mean?"

"I...thought you might have left because of Taylor. Like, now that you didn't have to help me out, you could go back to her without feeling guilty." She paused. "We had a great time together, but I'm still not sure how you feel about me. Before this week, you said you'd never think of me romantically because I wasn't your type."

"What?" He stared at her, baffled by her confession. "I never told you that."

"You didn't have to. Taylor did it for you."

"She said that?"

"It was true, wasn't it?" she asked.

"Not exactly. Taylor hated that you and I were so close. When she asked if there was something going on between us, I said I didn't think of you that way because we were just friends. Which was true at the time. But I never said you weren't my type. I don't have a type."

April gnawed on her lip. "You sort of do. And most of them have been way hotter than me. Especially Taylor. That's why I was afraid you'd decided to go back to her."

"But you were driving to the airport anyway?" The depth of her feelings filled him with love. She'd made herself vulnerable in the hopes of winning him back. *This*—not Chris's stunt—was a true grand gesture.

She offered him a small smile. "You're worth it."

"So are you. If you ever recover your phone, you'll find a lengthy message from me, apologizing for leaving and telling you I wanted you back."

"Really?" Her eyes shone with happiness.

"Absolutely. You're not the only one who messed up. I'm sorry about Taylor and those photos. I should have explained everything right away."

The ancient air conditioner on the wall kicked into gear, startling them with a loud, thrumming noise. April backed away from it, rubbing her hands along her arms.

"You sure you don't want to sit down?" He went over to the bed and pulled off the nasty-looking comforter, tossing it across the room. Underneath, the sheets appeared to be clean. He motioned for her to sit next to him. She did but put a little space between them.

He was ashamed it had taken him this long to share the truth with her. "About Taylor...when she called me this morning, she wanted to complain about Pierce. You knew that already. But she also asked me to call her back. I figured I'd do it when you were at Ollie's rehearsal because I didn't want you to feel bad."

Her shoulders slumped down. She looked away. "I wish you'd told me."

"I do, too. Especially since she called me right before you left. And...you were right. She asked if we could start over." At the sight of April tearing up again, he continued quickly. "I said no. I didn't give her any details, but I told her I'd moved on."

"What about those pictures she sent?" April's voice carried a sharp edge, warning him he wasn't off the hook.

"After you left for the rehearsal with Mags, I felt guilty because I hadn't been honest with Taylor. I called her back and told her the truth. I said the real reason I didn't want to get back together was because I was in love with you."

April finally met his eyes. "You told her that?"

He scooted closer and took her hand. "I did. And she was kind of...snarky about it."

"Let me guess. She said you'd lowered your standards by settling for me?"

He cringed at the accuracy of her guess. "Something like that.

Those pictures she sent? That was her way of showing me what I was missing." He put his arm around her shoulder. "I'm really sorry. I never meant to hurt you."

She leaned against him. "Did you mean what you said? That you're in love with me?"

"One hundred percent. After all the time we've spent together, I was half in love with you already but too dense to realize it. I love being with you. You're sweet and sexy and just as nerdy as I am. When we're together, I feel like I can finally be myself."

Saying the words gave him a glorious, lighter-than-air feeling. Like he could do or be anything, as long as he had this woman by his side.

"I feel the same way. I mean, I've had a crush on you since the week I met you, but this is much better. I've never fallen in love with someone who accepts me exactly the way I am." She hesitated, then kept going. "I have no right to tell you what to do with your life, but I hope you don't move to Napa."

Though he'd already made up his mind, he loved knowing that she wanted him to stay. "I'm not leaving. I told Marc I wasn't taking the job when he called me on Thursday morning. After..."

She grinned at him. "After one night together? You were *that* confident in your bedroom skills?"

"I'd like to think so." He laughed. "It wasn't just that. When we talked on Monday night, you made me think about what I wanted. And it sure as hell isn't a management position in Napa."

"You think your parents will be okay with that?"

After his phone call with Marc, he wasn't as worried about their opinions. "I think so. What matters is that I'm okay with it. I like where I'm at."

At some point he might consider pursuing his dream of video game design, but, for now, he was perfectly happy to keep working in Temecula, with April by his side.

"Good." She put her hand on his thigh and let it travel a little further, until she was tugging on the waistband of his sweats. She gave him a naughty smile. "Should I text Ginger and let her know I'm staying?"

"We don't have to stay here. If we leave now, we can be at the cottage before midnight."

"Didn't you pay for the night already? Or is this the kind of place that only rents by the hour?"

"I paid for the whole night, Beckett. But I'd rather go back to the cottage. Wouldn't you?" He glanced around the room, noticing a stain on the carpet that looked suspiciously like blood. One of the walls was missing a large chunk of plaster. "This place is a total mood killer."

April pulled her hand away and gnawed on her lip again. "This thing is—I kind of gave Chris the cottage for the night."

"What? Why?"

"I felt sorry for him. When I told him he had to leave, he begged me to let him stay. He said there weren't any other rooms available—not in Door County or anywhere else in the area."

Brody nodded. "That's why I'm here. Believe me, I tried to find something nicer."

"I almost told Chris to go sleep in his car, but then he admitted he was competing in this huge race tomorrow and needed to get a good night's sleep." She rolled her eyes. "That's partly the reason he came here in the first place. That true love stuff was bullshit."

What an ass. "Why am I not surprised?"

"I know, right? I should have kicked him out, but once I got Ginger on board with my airport plan, I didn't want to waste any more time dealing with him. I wanted to go after you right away. All I cared about was getting you back."

For once, Brody pitied Chris. The bastard might have stolen their king bed, but he didn't have the privilege of sharing it with April.

"I'm so glad you came," he said. "But you don't have to spend the night here just to prove your love. If you want to go back with Ginger, I'll totally understand."

She grabbed his shirt until his face was inches from her. "You don't want me, Blackwood?"

He kissed the tip of her nose. "Of course I want you. In a hundred different ways. But this place is skeevy as hell."

She laughed. "Yeah, it's the worst. Was it really the only hotel left in Green Bay?"

"The only one. Number forty-eight on TripAdvisor. Out of a possible forty-eight choices."

"Yikes. But I'm still going to tell Ginger she can go. I'd rather be here with you than anywhere else." She grinned. "That okay?"

"Very much okay."

CHAPTER 35

Brody went outside with April to update Ginger. She set down her phone and lowered the window. "Status report?"

April placed her arm around his waist. "It's all good. I'm staying here for the night."

"You're not going to get much sleep." Ginger pointed to an oversize truck parked two doors down. "A bunch of guys pulled up, carrying a couple cases of Bud. Something tells me they'll be noisy neighbors."

"We won't need much sleep," April said. "But thanks for the warning. And thanks for bringing me here."

"Happy to oblige, especially since you chose wisely, young Padawan." She grinned at Brody. "That's a *Star Wars* reference, by the way."

He laughed. "Got it. Thanks for helping us out. Drive safely, okay?"

After flashing them a thumbs-up, Ginger peeled away from the parking lot.

Once they were back in his motel room, Brody locked and bolted the door. For extra measure, he propped one of the chairs under the door handle. As he took in their crappy surroundings —the battered furniture, the stained carpet, the musty smell— regret surged through him. He couldn't think of a worse place for makeup sex.

"Sorry this isn't more romantic."

"Are you kidding? We're in love, we're alone, and we banished our exes. This is romantic as hell." April grabbed her backpack and set it on the bed. "See if there are cups in the bathroom. And maybe a towel to eat on?"

Trust her to put things in perspective. He found two plastic cups, still wrapped in plastic, and brought them out, along with a hand towel.

April pulled a bottle of merlot out of her backpack, along with a container of spicy beer cheddar spread, a bag of pretzels, and a small box containing their last piece of cherry-chocolate fudge. She set them on the towel but cursed when she checked the wine bottle. "Damn. I forgot a corkscrew."

"Got you covered." Brody went to his suitcase and rooted around the zippered compartment until he found one. "As a Blackwood, I always have a corkscrew at the ready." He uncorked the bottle and poured them each a cup of wine.

April kicked off her heels and leaned against the headboard. "This is perfect. I barely ate any dinner."

"Same. I'm starving." Though he would have preferred a more substantial meal, at least April had thought to bring food. And the merlot went surprisingly well with the cheese spread and the pretzels.

His phone rang, startling them both. He set his cup on the nightstand.

April gave him a fierce glare. "If that's Taylor, I'm telling her to fuck off."

"It's not. Hang on." He answered the call. "Yes?"

"Mr. Blackwood, sir?"

Jeeves. "Hey. Thanks for booking the hotel. I appreciate it."

"You're quite welcome. I realize the hour is late, but I wished to let you know a more suitable flight opened up. There is one space available on a plane leaving for San Diego at one thirty tomorrow afternoon. It only makes one stop along the way. Would you like me to book it?'

"Thanks, but I'm going to stick with my original flight on Sunday."

"Very good, sir. Is there any other way I could be of assistance?"

Brody was starting to like this guy. Forget Travelzoo—he was using Jeeves from now on. "Can you find me a luxury hotel in the San Diego area and book me a weekend there? Price is no limit." He glanced at April. "Any preference?" When she shook her head, he added, "Try for the second weekend in November."

That way they'd have something to look forward to before the holidays set in.

"Excellent, sir. Would you like me to call you back with the available choices? Or should I wait until morning?"

"Morning's better. Thanks."

After he ended the call, April gave him a shy smile. "You didn't have to do that."

Clearly, he did, because she was glowing with happiness. "It'll make up for tonight."

Since there was nowhere to store the wine, they finished the bottle, toasting everything they could think of. Great sex. Door County. Pirate hats. Kayaks. And sex again, because why not? He'd never been more at ease with anyone than with April, drinking wine in the world's crappiest motel. By the time they'd drained the last few drops of merlot, he was so tipsy he no longer cared about their surroundings. He set the wine bottle, the cups, and the leftover food on the side table.

He turned back to April. "So...you want to watch TV, or..."

From the sultry smile she gave him, he didn't think TV was on the agenda. She stood up beside the bed and unzipped her dress.

She let it drop to the floor, revealing a black lace bra and matching panties.

His groin tightened at the sight of her. "You were wearing that? Underneath that dress?"

She cocked her hip. "Is there a problem?"

He stared at her unabashedly, practically drooling at the sight of her luscious curves like a wolf from one of those old-school Warner Brothers cartoons. How was it that he'd spent two years hanging out with her—hell, he'd spent the night on her couch multiple times—and never realized how sexy she was?

"Brody? You okay?"

He was at her side immediately, his pulse pounding. She was all but naked, the lacy bra barely covering her full breasts. He smoothed his hands along her back and cupped her butt, pressing her body against his. The desire coursing through him eclipsed everything. He was so far gone that he would have taken her on the worn carpet if that was the only option. He kissed the sensitive skin beneath her ear, inhaling her familiar scent. "You smell so good," he murmured. "Rosemary and mint."

"My shampoo." She tipped her head back, sighing as his lips trailed along the curve of her neck. When she unclipped her bra and tossed it aside, he lowered his head and ran his tongue across one nipple, sucking on it until she groaned in pleasure. She twisted her hands in his hair. "Oh, yes, Brody. Yes."

He eased her onto the bed and gazed down at her in awe. She looked so enticing, her face flushed with desire, her silken hair splayed around the pillows. How had he gotten so lucky?

APRIL PROPPED herself up on her elbows, letting Brody take a good, long look. The mix of admiration and lust in his eyes flooded her with warmth. A throbbing ache built inside her, so intense she had to press her thighs together. "Brody? I don't want you to take this the wrong way, but…"

He was halfway to taking his shirt off but pulled it back on. A concerned look crossed his face. "What? Is this location not doing it for you?"

"It's fine." She licked her lips. "But I can't wait any longer. I want you inside of me. Now." She shimmied out of her panties and flung them across the room. Giving him a coy look, she leaned back and stretched out on the bed. "I'm not being too demanding, am I?"

The grin on his face told her everything she needed to know. He went over to his suitcase and pulled out the box of condoms.

"I notice you took our supplies with you," she said.

"Good thing, right?"

She crooked one finger and motioned him over. As he undressed, she watched him unashamedly, her desire growing by the second. She beckoned him closer and sheathed him with the condom, but only after she'd stroked him and teased him with her tongue. He groaned in response. "You're killing me, April."

"Good." She lay back down. "I don't want you to hold anything back."

He set his glasses on the nightstand and climbed onto the bed, positioning himself above her. She ran her hands along his chest, glorying in the firm, muscular feel of him. He met her eyes, seeking her consent. Her breath caught in anticipation. "Yes. *Please.*"

Parting her legs with his knee, he slipped himself inside her, nice and easy. When his body molded against hers, she clutched onto his shoulders, feeling more connected to him than she'd ever been. She angled her hips, wanting him deeper inside her. This wasn't the time for slow, gentle lovemaking. She wanted it hard and fast and a little bit rough.

At his first thrust, the bedsprings let out an unholy squeak. He stopped. "What the hell?"

"Ignore it." She grabbed his butt. "Don't stop, Brody. It feels so good."

He started up again, but the squeaking increased in volume. The bed sounded like it might give way and send them crashing to the floor.

She erupted in giggles. "I'm sorry. I know it's not funny, but I can't help it."

But he was laughing, too. He touched his forehead to hers. "You think they can hear us in the next room?"

"I don't know. But we can't stop now." She smoothed her hands along his back and met his lips for a hungry, passionate kiss. His tongue twisted against hers, tasting of red wine and chocolate. She threaded her hands through his thick hair as his lips brushed the hollow of her throat. It didn't matter that they were stuck in a sketchy motel, making love on the world's noisiest bed. She wanted Brody more than she'd ever wanted anyone.

"You sure this is okay?" he asked. "What if I break the bed?"

"Then we sneak out of here, drive like hell, and spend the night in the nearest Walmart parking lot. Under no circumstances are we paying for this piece-of-shit bed."

"Beckett, I like the way you think."

She smacked his butt playfully. "Come on, Blackwood. Let's put this bed to the test."

With a laugh, he started up again, his rhythm quickening, despite the noisy bed. April wrapped her legs around him and clung on tight. As she came close to the precipice, she tuned everything else out, focusing on the feel of him deep inside of her. He sucked on her nipples again, his rough stubble grazing her skin, and she moaned in response. As he teased the sensitive buds with his teeth, the sensation sent her careening over the edge. Her cries mingled with his as they reached their peak at the same time. He collapsed on top of her, breathing heavily. She let out a long breath as her heartbeat resumed its normal pace.

A hard pounding shook the wall behind them. A man's voice carried clearly. "Shut the fuck up!"

April froze, too petrified to move. "Oh, shit. We're going to die."

"Shhh. Maybe if we're quiet, he won't break into our room and kill us."

The pounding in her heart started up again. "Sorry," she whispered. "I didn't mean to be that loud."

His lips brushed her forehead. "You can't help yourself around me, can you?"

They waited in silence as the minutes ticked by. When no further pounding ensued, Brody rolled off her and lay on his back. "Holy shit. That was terrifying."

She rested her head on his chest. "We should probably wait until we're back at the cottage to try *that* again."

"Agreed." He wove his fingers through her hair. "Tomorrow night, I'll make it up to you."

A wave of exhaustion washed over her. Now that her adrenaline had worn off, she could barely keep her eyes open.

"The wedding's not until two, right?" he asked. "So we can sleep in?"

They could. She wouldn't be needed for photos until one. But she didn't want to show up without explaining things first. Her family needed to hear the whole story.

She sat up and reached for the digital clock on the nightstand. "I'm setting the alarm for seven. I want to get back by nine." When Brody groaned, she gave him a mock glare. "This is important. There's a family breakfast at the lodge tomorrow morning and I need to be there."

"We could stop for breakfast along the way. Then we could sleep in."

"I know, but I need to apologize to them for lying and tell them exactly how I feel about you. I don't want them giving you a hard time because you're not Chris."

"Are you sure? Your sisters will be ruthless. Especially Drizella."

"I'm not letting her bully me. Not anymore."

"C'mere, you." When she lay back down, he drew her close, nuzzling her hair with his lips. "I'll be at your side, no matter what. But it's not going to be easy."

For once, she didn't mind. She was done taking the path of least resistance.

It was time she stood up for herself.

CHAPTER 36

*W*hen the alarm went off with a shrill beep, April
struggled to open her eyes. Last night's wine had
left her groggy, and she hadn't slept well. At some point in the
middle of the night, a loud confrontation in the parking lot had
woken her and Brody. They lay together, tense with fear, until
the yelling subsided. After that, she had disturbing dreams.
Whether they were caused by her surroundings or the impending
showdown with her family, she couldn't say. Either way, she was
hardly at her best.

She patted the sheets beside her, surprised to find them
empty. Stumbling out of bed, she checked the bathroom. Also
empty. Had Brody been insane enough to go for an early
morning run? If so, she needed to jump in the shower before he
got back. She grabbed her toiletries bag and spare clothes out of
her backpack, grateful she'd thought to bring them along.

The shower gave off a feeble spray, lukewarm at best. As she
was rinsing out her hair, the hot water kicked in, nearly scalding
her. She shrieked and turned it off. Shivering, she reached for a
towel and winced as the rough material made contact with her
skin.

When she emerged, dressed in jeans and a flannel, Brody sat at the tiny table, drinking from a cardboard to-go cup. "Morning. I brought you a double-shot latte for the road."

"Thank you." She sat down next to him, sighing at the tantalizing aroma of coffee. The first sip was a sweet slice of heaven. "How did you wake up before me?"

"After that screaming match in the parking lot, I figured we'd need coffee to get through the drive. I set my phone alarm for six, grabbed a shower, and found a coffeehouse nearby."

"You are truly the best boyfriend ever." She bit her lip, as her chronic insecurity reared its ugly head. "Can I call you that?"

"Definitely. I like the way it sounds."

"Is this going to be okay with work? You and me, together?"

"I don't see why not. As long as we behave ourselves while we're on the clock." He wagged his finger at her. "No sexy texts. Not until after hours."

She rolled her eyes. "I think I can control myself."

"Good." He grinned. "Because once work ends for the day, Captain Blackwood comes out to play."

She shivered in anticipation. No matter how anxious she felt right now, she and Brody had a lot to look forward to.

"We should get on the road soon," he said. "I don't want you to miss breakfast with your family."

She set down her coffee, her hands shaky. "I'm nervous." The thought of Drianna's reaction made her nauseous.

He placed his hand over hers. "You don't have to do this."

"I do." She took a deep breath. "I hope everyone isn't furious at me."

He rubbed his forehead. "I forgot to tell you. Ollie and Mags called me last night when I was driving here. They told me they were on our side. And they want me at the wedding."

Hope bloomed inside of her. Trust Ollie to come through when she needed it. No wonder he'd given her Brody's number without question.

She took a few more sips of coffee, then set it aside so she could get ready. Packing took all of five minutes, including a final sweep in the bathroom, where the tap was still dripping. No matter how hard they'd tried, they hadn't been able to shut it off completely. The leaky faucet was probably to blame for the rust-colored stain at the bottom of the sink.

Following Brody, she grabbed her backpack and coffee and went out to the car. Despite last night's altercation in the parking lot, their rental car appeared untouched. She got in, brushing a couple of Hershey bar wrappers off the seat. She wasn't surprised to see an empty can of Dr. Pepper on the floor beside her feet. Typical Brody. She leaned back in her seat and sipped her coffee as he punched in the address for the North Bay Resort.

THEY REACHED the lodge with fifteen minutes to spare. As they hustled along the trail toward their cottage, April tensed up. Since Chris was probably mid-race, she didn't expect to see him, but he might have left his stuff behind. She exhaled in relief as she opened the door. He'd cleared everything out, including the bouquet of roses and the tasteless black negligee. On the bed was her note with a reply scrawled underneath.

Thanks for the bed. Call me if you want to hook up when we get back.

Ugh. She crumpled up the note and threw it into the fireplace. At least he'd had the courtesy not to leave any of his crap.

Once they dropped off their bags, they walked to the lodge. As Mags predicted, the weather was made-to-order for a fall wedding. Sunny and warm, with a clear blue sky and a slight breeze off the lake.

Inside the Bay Breeze, a substantial breakfast buffet took up most of the bar. Customers filled their plates from a long row of chafing dishes, and a separate table held a bountiful assortment of pastries. When Brody lingered next to the pastry display, she tugged on his hand to keep him moving. She spotted her family at a large table by the window. Only her immediate family were in attendance—her parents, her sisters, and Ollie—and their empty plates suggested they hadn't yet hit the buffet.

As she approached the table, everyone looked her way. Her heart beat erratically, making her wish she hadn't downed an entire double-shot latte.

"What is *he* doing here?" Drianna said. "Where's Chris?"

"April, what's going on?" her mom asked.

Her mouth went dry. The scorn on her sisters' faces made her want to curl up into a little ball. But Brody squeezed her hand, and Ollie winked at her. Somehow, she found the courage to keep talking. "I need all of you to listen. Please."

When Drianna opened her mouth to interrupt, April held up her hand. "Wait until I'm done." She swallowed back her fear and forced herself to speak up. She wanted to sound like an adult, not a child.

"First of all, I'm sorry I lied. No matter what the circumstances, I behaved terribly."

"I'll say," Drianna muttered.

April ignored her and focused on her parents. Their approval meant more to her than anyone else's. "I'm not trying to make excuses, but you need to understand what I went through. By bringing Chris to the wedding, I figured I could finally show you I was capable of having a real boyfriend. Not just a hot cover model from a stock photography site." When Ollie laughed, she flashed him a quick smile. "But—like I said last night—Chris bailed right before our trip. Around that time, I realized he hadn't been treating me right. For most of our relationship, he took advantage of me, and I let him."

"But he seemed so nice," her mom said.

"He talks a good game, and he's an amazing athlete, but..."

April wanted to explain that he'd kept her around for quick, no-strings sex, but she couldn't admit that in front of her parents. "He criticized me constantly, for my eating habits and my weight. And he made me feel like I should be grateful he wanted to spend time with me."

A waitress approached their table, carrying a coffee pot. "Did you still want to do the buffet? We have menus if you'd prefer to order."

April's mom shook her head. "We'll get to it in a moment, thanks." She turned to April after the waitress left. "If Chris treated you that way, why did you put up with him for so long?"

She twisted her hands together, ashamed of what she was about to admit. "I didn't want to be alone. I also wanted to show you I could sustain a real relationship. But breaking up with him was the right move. I deserve to be treated better."

When her parents nodded, the tension eased from her shoulders. "With Chris gone, I found myself dateless, with no way to prove he existed. But if I didn't bring him, I was afraid you'd think I was pulling another Sam Jameson, and you'd spend all week teasing me about it."

"We wouldn't have been *that* bad," Avery said.

Ollie shook his head. "Sure, you would. Even before we got here, you and Dree were making bets about whether Chris was real. If April hadn't brought him, it would have been open season, no matter what excuse she gave."

"Exactly," April said. "When I told Brody about my problem, he offered to help me out. He could have come as my friend, but he agreed to pose as Chris because he knew how much it meant to me. He was willing to do whatever it took to keep up the ruse, including running in a 10K." She beamed at him.

Avery stared at Brody. "You did that for April? Why?"

"Because she's one of the best friends I've ever had." His voice carried an unwavering confidence. "Three months ago, I went through a terrible breakup. April was there for me, whenever I needed her. I wanted to help her out, even if I had to pretend to be someone else."

"Oh my God." Avery placed her hand over her heart. "That's so romantic."

April grinned. "I know, right? Brody came through for me. That's why I fell in love with him." Saying the words out loud gave her an additional boost of courage. Especially when her brother gave her a thumbs-up from across the table.

Her mom rubbed her forehead, as though she was trying to make sense of her daughter's words. "But you let him leave last night. I don't understand."

"I was overwhelmed by Chris's grand gesture. When he appeared out of nowhere and declared his love for me, I let him steamroll over my feelings. By the time I saw through his bullshit, I almost lost Brody."

Her dad gave a shake of his head. "Sounds like Chris should have stayed home. Or at least let you know he was planning to show up. What was he thinking?"

"Honestly? He didn't come here for me," April said. "He only showed up so he could compete in the Fall 50. Something he told me *after* we left dinner." She crossed her arms. "He needed a place to crash because there was nowhere else available."

Avery smacked her fist into her palm. "What a prick. And to think he spouted all that bullshit about being in love with you."

"No kidding," Ollie said. "The guy was so over-the-top. Mags thought he was going to propose."

"None of it was true," April said. "He did it to impress all of you."

She let the words sink in. She wanted her family to understand she wasn't the only one Chris had manipulated.

"I feel terrible," her mom said. "I'm usually a better judge of character." She smiled at Brody. "I'm sorry we misjudged you. I hope you're planning on staying for the wedding."

"I'd like that," he said. "Especially if I don't have to pretend to be Chris."

With her parents on board, April was tempted to let things lie. She didn't want to make everyone uncomfortable. But when Brody squeezed her hand again, she found the strength to keep going.

"Thanks. But there's something else I need to say. I wouldn't have gone to all this trouble if you weren't always on my case. Every time I come home, it's the same thing—you criticize me for being single or for not having a high-powered career. You tease me about things that happened years ago, making it hard for me to move on. I shouldn't have lied, but I didn't want to spend the entire week trying to prove Chris existed. I admit I sometimes make stupid mistakes, but that doesn't mean you should treat me like I'm a little kid."

Her mom sighed. "Oh, honey. I'm sorry we made you feel that way. But you're our baby. And we worry so much about you."

"Can you blame us?" her dad said. "We almost lost you once."

April fought back tears. "I know, but that was twelve years ago. I'm perfectly healthy."

Her dad nodded. "But we still worry about your future. What if you get laid off?"

"We don't want you to end up jobless, with no prospects in sight," her mom added. "Or still single when you're thirty."

Her mother was obviously a product of a different time. "There's nothing wrong with being single at thirty. Or any age. And my job is stable. I might not make as much as Dree or Avery, but I like what I do. And I'm good at it."

"She is," Brody said. "And I'm not saying this because I'm in love with her. She really did head up the design team for our company's app. We're lucky to have her."

April leaned against him, loving him more than ever.

"I'm sorry, sweetie." Her mom sniffed and wiped her eyes. "I'll try not to nag so much. But I'm a mom, so worrying is my default."

"We're incredibly proud of you," her dad added. "We always have been."

April dabbed at her eyes with a tissue. As hard as it was to speak up for herself, she was glad she'd had the guts to do it.

Drianna's voice rang out. "Are you kidding me? April spent five days lying to us. And now you're apologizing to *her*?"

Clearly, this wasn't over.

CHAPTER 37

Of course Drianna would object.

Brody wanted to speak up in April's defense, but he restrained himself. He knew better than to get between two sisters.

April stalked over to Drianna's chair and stared her down. "What's wrong with you?"

Drianna stood to face her. "With me? You're the one who lied to us for an entire week."

Her strident voice carried across the crowded restaurant, causing other guests to look their way. Mrs. Beckett scowled. "That's enough. I won't have you two causing a scene again. The rehearsal dinner was bad enough."

"Sorry, Mom," April said. But neither she nor Drianna sat down.

"I don't know what your problem is or why you keep cutting me down, but I'm sick of it," April said. "I'm sick of you telling everyone the Sam Jameson story and trying to humiliate me. I'm sick of your snide remarks about my job. And I'm sick of the way you belittle me—like making fun of me for needing a bigger life jacket when we were kayaking."

Yes. Brody could not have been prouder. Maybe it had taken April years to get to this point, but for once she wasn't letting Drianna intimidate her.

"Will you get over the kayak incident?" Drianna said. "You want to know why everyone treats you like a baby? Because you act like one. Instead of being such a coward, you should have told us the truth about Chris."

"And have you make fun of me for an entire week?" April said. "Do you know how much that would have sucked?"

"You're so sensitive. You need to grow up. Maybe then we'd treat you like an adult."

Brody clenched his fists, trying to contain the rage building up inside him. He couldn't imagine talking to his brother this way. Or anyone else in his family. If no one spoke up for April, he was going to defend her, regardless of what the Becketts thought.

But Ollie beat him to it. "God, Dree, stop being such a bitch. April's right. You never let up. Even Mags noticed it. No one gives a shit about that stupid Sam Jameson story, but you always bring it up."

Their mom nodded. "Enough's enough, Drianna. You need to stop bullying your sister."

"You always favor her!" Drianna yelled. "It's so unfair."

Their waitress scurried over. "Um…did you want any more coffee? Or anything else? Are you still planning on the buffet?"

"I'm so sorry," Mr. Beckett said. "We'll go in a few minutes. And we'll keep it down." He glared at Drianna.

She matched her father's glare with a murderous look of her own. "You want to know why I'm sick of April? Because you worry about her constantly. No one ever asks me how *I'm* doing. Or if I have any problems. If I bring them up, you act like they're unimportant. I'm not the oldest. Not the boy. And not the baby. Just good old Drianna, the forgotten middle kid, barely worthy of your attention."

"We don't worry about you because we don't need to," Mr.

Beckett said. "You have a great job and a wonderful husband. What problems are you talking about?"

Drianna slammed her fist on the table, rattling the coffee cups. "This is what I mean. For weeks, I've been trying to tell you about Gary. The guy at work who keeps sabotaging me." When Avery started to speak, Drianna held up her hand. "Let me finish. On Thursday, in the middle of our Monopoly game, I found out he's been shortlisted for the managerial position I wanted. He's only been there for eleven months, and he's never busted his ass the way I have. But he keeps making me look bad. At first, it was just annoying, but now it's impacting my whole career. So, no, I'm not being paranoid."

"I'm sorry, Drianna," April whispered, but her sister silenced her with a scowl.

"I'm not done. Not only has work turned into a toxic sludge pit, but Ian's been no help at all. He never listens to me. Do you notice how he's not here? How he's *never* here?"

"Come on, Dree," Avery said. "You know how much Ian and Hunter love golf. It's not about you."

"It *is* about me. We've been arguing nonstop since we got here."

Brody recalled Ian's comments when they warmed up for the 10K. Something about being unsatisfied. Drianna had also reacted in anger when April asked her why Ian wasn't joining the family softball game. But Brody had never suggested April check in on her sister to see if she was all right, because Drianna gave off such a hostile vibe.

"Ian's barely been around these last few months. And ever since we got here, he's been sending a lot of late-night texts," Drianna said. "This morning, I almost checked his phone when he was in the bathroom, but I chickened out. I couldn't handle more bad news."

April placed her hand on Drianna's shoulder. "I didn't know things were that bad."

Drianna let out her breath. "It's not your fault. Not entirely. But this shit has been happening for years. Ever since you got sick."

"Oh, when you wanted April to die?" Ollie said.

April gasped. Her hand flew to her mouth.

"You didn't know about that?" Avery said. "I thought Ollie told you."

April shook her head. "Dree barely spoke to me when I got back from the hospital, but I didn't think it was about me. I figured she was upset about her breakup with Bill."

Brody's heart went out to her. By now, he assumed someone in the family would have told her about Drianna's thoughtless remarks.

Drianna scowled at her brother. "I didn't say I wanted April to die, dickhead. I...I said Mom and Dad would still be okay if she didn't make it, because they had three other kids."

"You hated me that much?" April's eyes welled up with tears again.

Brody tightened his grip on her hand, wishing he could console her. But that had to come from Drianna.

"No," Drianna muttered. "I was just a bratty, selfish sixteen-year-old. But I was failing chemistry and fighting with Bill, and I wanted someone to pay attention to me, for once. I didn't mean what I said. But Mom grounded me anyway. When Bill found out I couldn't go to prom, he dumped me for someone else. My whole junior year went downhill from there."

"So, you spent the next ten years blaming me?" April said.

Drianna put her hands up in surrender. "It wasn't just about you. I felt like I didn't matter. Like I *never* matter. And it hasn't gotten much better."

Mrs. Beckett shook her head. "I never meant to turn you against your sister. It was such a stressful time. Of course you matter. I'm sorry if we made you feel like we don't care about you. Your problems are just as important as April's."

"We can do better," Mr. Beckett said. "The next time you need our support, we'll listen."

"Okay, thanks." Drianna sniffed and wiped her eyes. "And I'm sorry, shrimp," she said to April. "I don't hate you. I never have."

When April didn't reply right away, Brody tensed up. Given what she'd been through, she had every right to stay mad at Drianna. But this was a family wedding. If she didn't call a truce, at least temporarily, her parents might be upset.

April let out her breath. "Okay. But no more backhanded comments. All right?"

A hush settled over the table. Brody noticed their waitress hovering in the background. "Um…we should probably hit the buffet before they kick us out of here."

Mr. Beckett stood up. "Let's go. If we need to, we can continue this conversation after we've filled our plates."

"No, thanks," Drianna said. "I've emoted enough for one meal."

As the Becketts walked over to the buffet, Brody hung back so he could talk to April alone. "You okay?"

"I think so. I'm glad I stood up for myself, but it wasn't easy hearing that stuff from Drianna. I don't think she's going to become sweet and caring overnight, but it might be nice if my parents focused on her for a change." She kissed his cheek. "Thanks for being here."

"Anytime." He motioned her forward. "You first. Save some bacon for me."

The heavily laden buffet offered numerous choices—eggs Benedict, thick strips of bacon, scrambled eggs with sausage, waffles, breakfast potatoes, fresh fruit, and a wide assortment of pastries. Brody loaded up his plate, snagged a glass of grapefruit juice, and followed the others back to the table. For once, he didn't order any coffee. As soon as breakfast ended, he planned to crash in the cottage for a pre-wedding nap.

They were a few minutes into eating when Mags showed up. She leaned down and kissed Ollie.

Avery waved her fork at her brother. "You're not supposed to see the bride on her wedding day."

"Be serious," Mags said. "We woke up together. I just finished breakfast with my family and wanted to join you."

"Second breakfasts, am I right?" Brody said. When no one except April laughed at his joke, he cringed inwardly. Maybe the Becketts weren't ready for his full arsenal of nerdiness.

Mags beamed at him. "Brody! You're back. I'm so glad. I want you to know I was solidly Team Brody the whole time."

"You make him sound like a character from a teen romance novel," Avery said. "Like Team Edward versus Team Jacob."

Drianna laughed. "I was totally Team Edward. Sexy vampires for the win."

"Not me," Mags said, perching on Ollie's chair. "Team Jacob all the way. What's not to love about a hot werewolf?"

"Yeah, the wolf pack was great," Ollie added. "Better than a bunch of dumb vampires who sparkled in the sunlight."

Drianna shook her spoon at him. "Those vampires lived thousands of years. They could do *anything*."

Brody smiled. If April's family could nerd out over a series of vampire novels, maybe he'd fit right in.

CHAPTER 38

*A*fter breakfast, April walked back to the cottage with Brody. Now that her adrenaline had worn off, she was flat-out exhausted. Over the last twenty-four hours, her emotions had been through the wringer. The confrontation with Drianna had been the final straw, nearly pushing her over the edge. If she didn't rest up, she'd never make it through the wedding.

As they reached the porch, Brody tugged on her hand, bringing her to face him. His brow creased with concern. "You sure you're okay?"

"I was mulling over everything Drianna said. It sucks thinking she was angry at me for such a long time."

He stroked her cheek. "You realize it wasn't your fault, right?"

"I know. I'm too wiped to think rationally. Right now, I just need some sleep." She managed a weak smile. "Thanks for being so supportive. If there's anything I can do in return, just name it."

She took the key out of her purse and unlocked the cottage door. The huge bed looked so inviting. For the first time since she arrived in Door County, all she wanted to do was sleep.

Brody kicked off his shoes and plopped down on the bed. He yawned. "Okay if I join you? I'm worn-out."

April sat next to him and gave him a stern look. "No shenanigans, got it?" She undid her jeans and tossed them on the floor. When he raised his eyebrows, she laughed. "What? I can't sleep with my jeans on. It's too uncomfortable."

"Fine," he grumbled. "I'll behave. But if you can go pantsless, then I can, too." He shucked off his jeans and gave her a warning look. "No grabbing my butt. No matter how much you want to."

She was tempted to grab it, just to tease him, but she restrained herself. Right now, she had to make sleep her priority.

He took off his glasses and lay down beside her. "I thought of something I want. In return for being Chris."

Honestly, he was shameless. "No sex. Not until tonight."

He rolled over so he was facing her. "Not that. Something else. But it's a big favor."

"You spent six days with my family, pretending to be a different guy. You ran a 10K and played shortstop in the Beckett Family Softball Challenge. It can't be much bigger than that."

"It's about Thanksgiving."

April tried to hide her discomfort. She hadn't been planning on having this discussion yet, because the thought of Thanksgiving filled her with guilt. "This is going to sound awful, but I'm not sure about Thanksgiving."

The hurt in his eyes was evident. "Sorry. Too soon?"

She placed her hand on his shoulder. "It's not about you. If I was going home for Thanksgiving, I'd bring you in a heartbeat. But I was thinking of staying in Temecula for the holiday, and I haven't broached it with my family. After this week is over, I need a little break from them."

"I get it. I was actually hoping you'd spend Thanksgiving with me at our family's lodge at Big Bear Lake."

Relief flooded through her. "That would be perfect. Is your whole family going to be there?"

"Yeah, they're driving down from Napa the day before. Marc's wife, Gabi, is in charge, and she's already got this twenty-step plan leading up to the big meal. I'd like to bring you as my plus-one. Then you could meet my parents."

She gave him a wry smile. "Are you forgetting I met your dad when he flew in for our big app presentation?"

"But you weren't my girlfriend then. I want to show my parents I've moved past Taylor. And that I've found someone I care about—who feels the same way."

Her heart swelled with affection. "I'd be happy to come. Any chance I could bring a couple of pies to show off my baking prowess?"

"I was counting on it." He placed a gentle kiss on her lips. "Now let's get some sleep."

He turned and lay on his side, facing the window. April snuggled against him, placing her arm around his waist. As she closed her eyes, the tension ebbed from her body.

Yesterday's nightmare was in the past. Brody was here. And all was as it should be.

BRODY WOKE to the chime of his phone alarm. He silenced it, then rolled over and nudged April. She made no move to get up but instead nestled even closer. "Is it time already?"

"You said you wanted an extra half hour to shower and do your hair."

"I suppose I should since that shower in the Green & Gold was so pitiful." She placed a soft kiss against his throat. "Though I'd rather stay in bed with you. I'm glad we have one night left."

"Same." He cupped his hand around her butt. "You still up for our James Bond fantasy?"

She looked up at him, a wicked grin in her eyes. "Definitely.

This is going to be perfect because you'll be dressed in a suit, just like Bond. I might have to tie your wrists to the bed."

His dick immediately sprang to attention. He'd done the same to her when he was Captain Blackwood, and the sex had been incredible. Who knew they both shared a secret passion for role-play?

"Don't go easy on me," he said.

She laughed. "Oh, I don't intend to."

He couldn't wait.

She sat up and stretched. "I'd better get ready. I'd invite you to join me in the shower, but I can't risk being late."

He watched as she hopped out of bed, gathered up her clothes, and strutted off to the bathroom. Even if he had to deal with a little delayed gratification, tonight's shenanigans would be worth it.

He lay back down and closed his eyes, feeling more content than he'd ever imagined. Tomorrow, he'd be heading back to Temecula with April. Now that they were together, he'd have her by his side, to love and tease and share life's little joys. He'd have his job and all its challenges. Even if he never opted for a management role, he was damn good at what he did and proud of what he'd accomplished so far.

For once in his life, he didn't feel inadequate.

He felt worthy.

CHAPTER 39

By the time April finished primping—hair curled, makeup done, legs smooth as silk—she felt radiant. She preened in front of the mirror, delighting in the way her purple, off-the-shoulder dress flattered her curves. The woman in the reflection looked gorgeous and confident, which was exactly how she felt.

When she emerged from the bathroom, Brody was sitting up in bed with his laptop. He let out a whistle. "You look stunning."

She twirled for him, glowing with pleasure. "Thanks. The shower's all yours." With fifteen minutes to spare before photos, she went outside to sit on the porch. Turning her face to the sky, she basked in the sunlight.

"Look at that satisfied smile." Ginger hopped onto the porch to join her. She wore a short crimson dress with long flared sleeves; around her neck were three necklaces made of multicolored glass beads. "Someone got laid last night."

April grinned at her. "Maybe. But the bed was noisier than a carnival ride. Then some creep pounded on the wall and yelled at us. We're lucky we made it out of the Green & Gold alive." She still couldn't believe they'd survived the night in that motel. "How was the drive back?"

Ginger sat beside her and stretched out her legs, showing off red platform heels. "Easy. But my parents were waiting up for me. Like they were worried I'd get into trouble driving to Green Bay and back."

April snorted. "Good thing they didn't know you risked your life at the Green & Gold."

"Yeah, that place was hideous." Ginger shaded her eyes against the sun. "What time did you get back this morning?"

"Believe it or not, we got here by nine and joined the family for breakfast. They're solidly Team Brody now."

"They weren't mad that he'd been lying to them for five days?"

"I think they felt embarrassed about the way they fawned over Chris. Especially when I told them what a prick he was. Not only that, but I stood up for myself and told them to stop nagging me about my job." She held out her hand for a high-five, and Ginger smacked it.

Though she didn't know if her parents would ever stop regarding her as the baby of the family, she was proud she hadn't backed down. Having Brody at her side had given her the courage to speak up.

"Nice going," Ginger said. "How did Her Dreadfulness react?"

"Get this—she had a full-on meltdown because no one ever pays attention to her. Apparently, her life is a giant shit show, and we were all oblivious."

"Damn. I wish I'd been there."

"It was rough. I kind of felt sorry for her."

Ginger raised her eyebrows. "You think she'll turn into an actual, caring human being?"

"Hard to say. She's been stewing about this stuff for years. But even if she's twenty percent less hostile, that would be a huge improvement." She'd like to believe Drianna could change, but her sister had spent twelve years resenting her. That wasn't something anyone could overcome in a few days.

"Did you figure out what to do about your phone?" Ginger asked.

"Brody said he could probably fix it once we get back. Dating a tech nerd has its advantages."

"Are you two officially dating now?"

April laughed. The concept of dating sounded oddly formal, given that she'd been hanging out with Brody for two years. She couldn't imagine much would change between them, except an added level of intimacy. And a lot of amazing sex.

"We were kind of doing that already," she said. "He's always been my go-to movie buddy."

"I wouldn't call action movies romantic."

"Sure they are. Few things top going to the opening night of a Marvel movie and sharing a jumbo-size popcorn with extra butter." The thought of it made her mouth water. Brody never skimped on the butter.

Ginger nudged her. "You're such a nerd." Her phone chirped, and she peeked at it. "Ten minutes until pictures."

"Let's go," April said. "For once in my life, I might be on time."

AFTER THE CHAOS of the rehearsal dinner, April worried something else might go awry. Like Chris showing up, mid-ceremony, with more roses and another declaration of love. But he didn't return, and the wedding proceeded without a hiccup. During the ceremony, April stayed dry-eyed until Ollie lovingly recited his vows. Listening to her brother speak with such devotion made her tear up with happiness. Brody, being the sweetheart he was, handed her a cloth handkerchief.

After the ceremony, the wedding party moved into the lodge's ballroom. As she and Brody heaped their plates at the delicious buffet, she was glad she could enjoy the meal without judgment. By the time the dancing portion of the evening began, she'd loosened up. At Mags's suggestion, she'd ordered a Wisconsin cocktail known as a brandy old-fashioned and quickly followed it up with another.

When the DJ cued up "Unchained Melody," Brody led her onto the floor for a slow dance. She leaned into him, inhaling his delicious aftershave. Cedar and eucalyptus—two scents that she would forever associate with the man she loved. Around her, other couples swayed to the music. Mags looked resplendent in Ollie's arms, every inch the happy bride.

As she watched her brother and his new wife, April wondered if she'd be carrying on the family tradition in two years. Up until now, she hadn't imagined loving anyone enough to consider marriage. But Brody was different. She could easily envision a future with him. And she suspected he felt the same way.

He leaned down, his lips nuzzling her ear. "Thanks for inviting me to the wedding. This week has been unbelievable."

"Are you kidding?" She laughed softly. "I put you through hell."

"Yeah, but it was one hundred percent worth it."

"Even your stay at the Green & Gold?"

"Especially our stay at the Green & Gold. It's not often you get to have mind-blowing sex and almost end up the subject of a true-crime podcast."

The music switched over to "Your Song," and April leaned her head on Brody's chest, grateful for another slow jam. She glanced around the room, taking note of the couples. Avery and Hunter. Ollie and Mags. Her parents. But Drianna and Ian hadn't joined in. They sat at their table, staring off into the distance, like they'd rather be anywhere else. April made a mental note to check up on Drianna in a few weeks to see if she needed any support.

"I forgot to tell you," Brody said. "When you were taking photos with your family, Jeeves called back."

"Jeeves? You have an English butler now?"

Brody laughed. "He's the travel agent who booked the Green & Gold for me. He found us a romantic hotel for our weekend getaway. It's called the Rancho Valencia Resort." He pulled her closer. "And get this. Every suite has its own fireplace."

More fireplace sex. She couldn't imagine anything more romantic. "Sounds perfect."

When the song ended, Brody tugged on her hand, leading her over to the dessert table, which was laden with caramel apples, pieces of pumpkin cheesecake, and two towers of cupcakes.

"Umm...Brody? We already *had* dessert," she said. They'd both enjoyed slices of Mags and Ollie's fall-themed wedding cake—a delicious spice cake with a hazelnut buttercream frosting.

"Second desserts, am I right?" He grinned. "Come on. You know I can't resist a good cupcake."

"Oh, really? I had no idea." Laughing, she grabbed two red velvet cupcakes from the top tier and handed one to Brody. They strolled over to a quiet corner of the ballroom, away from the dancing.

April watched as he took a bite. "What do you think?"

"Nice. Decent flavor. But it doesn't hold a candle to yours."

A rush of happiness enveloped her. "You're just trying to sweet-talk me into bed."

"Given that the cottage only has one bed, I don't have to try that hard. But I'm being honest. Your cupcakes are still the best I've ever tasted." He took another bite. "Which means you're going to have to make the desserts for *our* wedding."

Even if his words had been tossed off casually, they made her heart swell with love. "*Our* wedding? I thought you hated weddings."

"Just rehearsal dinners," he said. "Those are a nightmare. But weddings? I'm all in."

～

Thank you for reading *Red Velvet*!
I hope you enjoyed April and Brody's story.
If you did, please consider leaving a review wherever you
purchased this book.
Thanks! Your support is much appreciated!

Website and Newsletter Sign-up:
www.carlalunabooks.com

∿

Books in the Blackwood Cellars Series
Blue Hawaiian (Book One)
Red Velvet (Book Two)
White Wedding (Book Three)

∿

Stay tuned for the next book in the Blackwood Cellars series,
White Wedding, a holiday-themed second chance romance
featuring Victoria Blackwood, coming November 16, 2021.

Keep reading for a sneak peek of *White Wedding!*

(*Twenty-Two Days until the Wedding)*

VICTORIA BLACKWOOD FACED down her father, waiting for him to make the first move.

Brian Blackwood hadn't told her why he'd summoned her into his office at ten thirty on a Friday morning. He'd merely sent her a text, assuming she had nothing else on her calendar.

Which couldn't be further from the truth. With Christmas less than a month away, her plate was full, dealing with holiday banquets, parties, and weddings. As one of the event coordinators for the Blackwood Cellars Estate, much of the legwork fell to her. Especially since her boss, Lindsay, was on maternity leave until mid-January.

Smart woman.

Victoria loathed her father's office. The space was dark, stifling, and aggressively male. A shrine to his achievements as the CEO of Blackwood Cellars, her family's wine empire based in the Temecula Valley. Stuffed animal heads were mounted on the wall above rows of framed awards. A glass case displayed trophies from numerous wine competitions. On the sideboard, a decanter tray held crystal glasses and bottles of premium liqueurs. For his *important* guests.

When her father lit up a cigar, she recoiled at the strong smell. Setting aside all pleasantries, she addressed him directly. "Why am I here?"

He leaned back in his chair. "I spoke to Ben today. He told me the caterer quit."

Though almost two months had passed since Ben Macalister had left her for Missy, Victoria still flinched at the sound of her ex's name. But she kept her cool façade in place.

"He didn't need to call you. His assistant got in touch with me yesterday." She allowed herself a satisfied smile, grateful her father hadn't blindsided her. "It's handled."

"Why did it happen in the first place? What did you do?"

"Me? Why do you assume this was my fault?" The unfairness of his words rankled her.

"Ben thinks you're trying to sabotage his wedding."

She wanted to leap off her chair in a rage, but she stared into her father's piercing blue eyes without blinking. "May I remind you that I *never* wanted to coordinate my ex's wedding in the first place? You forced me into it."

"I didn't have a choice. Lindsay's on leave until January fifteenth."

"You could have asked June. She loves doing weddings." As Lindsay's assistant, June had worked on dozens of weddings. More to the point, she adored them. For a woman who'd been divorced twice, she was surprisingly optimistic about the institution of marriage.

"I didn't think she was capable of taking the lead on such a significant event. Besides, you'd already planned so much of Ben's wedding before he switched things up. It made more sense to keep it in your hands."

Switched things up. Is that how they were describing it now?

She clenched her fists, digging her nails deep into her palms. Her father could justify his decision all he wanted, but that didn't make it any less vindictive.

"When Ben made the request, I begged you to turn it down. But you didn't listen. And though I've hated every minute of it, I've given Ben and Missy the same level of service I'd show any other couple. So you've got no business accusing me of sabotage."

If anything, she'd been extra gracious, even when Missy acted like a raging Bridezilla.

When her father didn't respond, she continued. "Do you want to know why the caterer quit? Heather said in all her years at Blue Willow Catering, she's never dealt with someone like Missy. And, trust me, she's handled plenty of demanding brides. But Missy had already changed the menu five times. Then, last week, she brought two of Heather's assistants to tears. She behaved terribly, and Heather called her on it. I don't blame her for quitting."

And I'd quit, too, if I could.

That day couldn't come soon enough. But first, she had to repay her debt to her father.

She owed him thousands. Tens of thousands. All because she'd screwed up and he'd bailed her out. But he'd promised to wipe the slate clean if she coordinated this wedding.

On days like today, she wondered if the stress was worth it.

He shook his head, as if to express his sympathy. "You could show Missy a little more compassion."

"Are you serious?"

"Ben told me she's having a rough time of it with the pregnancy."

She couldn't keep her voice in check any longer. "I don't care. If it wasn't for her, I'd be the one getting married. She didn't just steal my fiancé, she stole my whole damn wedding."

The irony continued to smack her in the face each and every

day. Before Missy had stepped in, Victoria was engaged to Ben and in the midst of planning her own wedding.

She'd first met him at a charity ball, where he'd won her over with his polished charm. When he proposed a year later, she accepted without hesitation. As the the oldest son of Senator Frank Macalister, he easily met her father's approval. Not only was her father in favor of the match, he told Victoria if she married Ben, she'd earn her Get-Out-Of-Debt-Free card.

But six months before their wedding, Ben cheated on her with Missy Cavendish, an old flame who'd moved back into town. Though he apologized and promised to mend his ways, Victoria only took him back after her father pressured her into it. A terrible mistake, since Ben broke off their engagement three months later and confessed he was still in love with Missy. And since she was pregnant, they needed to get married as soon as possible.

Finding a venue to host their two-hundred-person extravaganza was no easy feat, given that Missy wanted an elaborate, Christmas-themed wedding. So, Ben—being the dick he was—asked if he and his new bride-to-be could use the same date, the same venue, the same *everything* that he and Victoria had originally planned for *their* Christmas wedding.

Victoria wanted nothing to do with it. He wasn't getting married on her home turf. And she wasn't lifting a finger to help him. But instead of supporting his only daughter, her father kissed up to Senator Macalister's son and said, "Of course you can have your wedding here. Victoria will be happy to arrange it."

There was no coming back from that.

A flicker of remorse crossed her father's face. Like he was sorry he'd put her in such an excruciating position. But the moment passed. He set down his cigar in a glass ashtray. "Have you lined up any other caterers?"

"Actually, I have." She glanced at the antique grandfather clock beside his desk, bought at auction, worth thousands. Pretentious as hell. "I should get going because I have an interview in a few minutes."

And if I spend another second talking to you, I'm going to throw that stinking cigar in the trash.

"That was quick," he said. "I'm surprised you got anyone with the holiday season in full swing."

"It wasn't easy." After her conversation with Heather, Victoria had gone through her roster of backup caterers, to no avail. She'd almost bottomed out when she got a yes.

"Who are you interviewing?"

"Martin Sanchez. From Tres Hermanos."

"The Mexican place in Escondido? You think Ben's family will approve? You can't just serve tacos and call it a day."

She gritted her teeth. "Tres Hermanos is one of the best Mexican restaurants in San Diego County. I've heard nothing but good things about their catering company."

She'd already called a couple of their clients, who'd given rave reviews.

Her father grunted. "Wouldn't be my first choice. Or my second. But I guess you're out of options, aren't you?"

"I guess so. If you'll excuse me, I'll be on my way. I don't want to be late." She stood and left her father's office.

One day, she'd be free. Then she could work for whomever she damn well pleased. Date whomever she wanted. Take back her life.

But today was not that day.

RAFAEL SANCHEZ CHECKED the boardroom for a thermostat. One he could adjust, preferably ten degrees lower, because he'd worked up a sweat. The room was far too oppressive with its massive cherrywood table, dark leather chairs, and heavy, crimson drapes. Along one wall, a series of black-and-white photos depicted the early days of Blackwood Cellars, back when it was just a humble winery in the Temecula Valley rather than a multimillion-dollar company.

He wiped his forehead and wished, for the tenth time, that one of his older brothers—either Martin or Tony—was here instead of him. Both of them had far more experience managing high-end catering gigs than he did. Though he'd joined them on dozens of jobs, he'd never overseen an event of this magnitude.

But there weren't any other options. Both his brothers were unavailable.

"You can do it," Martin had said. "Turn on that lady-killer charm and you'll win over Victoria Blackwood."

"But not too much charm," Tony said. "Keep it professional."

"And keep it in your pants," Martin added.

His brothers needed to stop with the lady-killer shit. Sure, Rafael had gone through a wild phase when he was younger, but he was over that now. If he wanted to prove himself to his brothers, this was his chance. Win Victoria Blackwood over. Secure the contract. And deliver an amazing wedding banquet, Sanchez-style.

"If you can pull this off, the word of mouth would be fabulous," Martin said. "Got it?"

He did. Blackwood Cellars was known for their high-profile events, but they'd never called on Tres Hermanos before. Getting in good with them could be huge.

On the table was a pitcher of ice water and a few glasses. He poured himself a glass and cleared his throat. All he had to do at this meeting was show Victoria his menus and convince her to bring her clients to Tres Hermanos for a tasting. Once they tried the food, they'd be hooked.

As the door handle turned, he plastered a bright smile on his face, fully prepared to wow Ms. Blackwood with his charm and his brother's creative menus.

But as soon as she walked in, all his goals flew out the window.

Because the last time he'd seen her?

She'd been naked.

And she sure as hell hadn't called herself Victoria Blackwood.

~

Want to read more of Victoria and Rafael's story?
White Wedding releases on November 16, 2021

ACKNOWLEDGMENTS

Writing may be a solitary endeavor, but it takes a village to support a writer. As always, I'm incredibly grateful for all the encouragement I've received on this journey.

First of all, I want to thank my readers. Much of the joy in creating a fictional world comes from sharing it with other people. Whether you started the Blackwood Cellars series with *Blue Hawaiian* or are discovering the books now, thank you for spending time with my characters.

Thanks so much to the professionals who made *Red Velvet* the best it could be: Bailey McGinn, for her delightful cover design; Serena Clarke at Free Bird Editing for her copy-edits; and Sandra Dee at One Love Editing for her proofreading. I'm also thankful to Carly Dhein for her valuable insights on the field of Graphic Design.

I'm grateful for my long-standing writing group (the FITWIGs): Lolly Rzezotarski, Jennifer Motl, Lisa Minneti, Rufina Garay, Shlomo Levin, Steve Srok, and Virginia Small. Thanks, also, to all those writers who read earlier drafts of *Red Velvet* and gave me valuable feedback: Stephanie Quinn, Jennifer Rupp,

Michelle McCraw, Kailee Saunders, Jennifer Motl, Lorelei Scott, Gail Werner, and Susan Keillor.

Thanks to the invaluable writer friends who went the extra mile with their feedback, advice, humor, and guidance: Liz Lincoln Steiner, Liz Czukas, Amy Reichert, and my longtime critique partner, Tricia Quinnies.

Through all the steps on my journey, my wonderful family (Mike, Tasmine, and James) offered their love, support, and enthusiasm. My husband, Mike, went the extra mile by driving me around the Door County Peninsula so I could take photographs, indulge my love of jam at the country markets, and get all the details right. I've always loved visiting Door County, but it has now become our go-to spot when we need a weekend getaway. I hope *Red Velvet* was able to provide you with a fun fall escape to one of my favorite parts of Wisconsin.

ABOUT THE AUTHOR

Carla Luna writes contemporary romance with a dollop of humor and a pinch of spice. A former archaeologist, she still dreams of traveling to far-off places and channels that wanderlust into the settings of her stories.

When she's not writing, she works in a spice emporium where she gets paid to discuss food and share her favorite recipes. Her passions include Broadway musicals, baking, whimsical office supplies, and pop culture podcasts. Though she has roots in Los Angeles and Victoria, B.C., she currently resides in Wisconsin with her family and her spoiled Siberian cat.

For sneak peeks, giveaways, and recipes from the Blackwood Cellars books, sign up for Carla's newsletter.
www.carlalunabooks.com

CPSIA information can be obtained
at www.ICGtesting.com
Printed in the USA
LVHW052207111021
700186LV00030B/1610

9 781736 866139